SHADOW TOWN

RICHARD LAMBERT

EVERYTHING WITH WORDS

Published in the UK by Everything with Words Limited
Fifth Floor, 30–31 Furnival Street, London EC4A 1JQ

www.everythingwithwords.com

Text copyright © Richard Lambert 2021
Cover © Holly Ovenden 2021

Printed and bound in Great Britain by
CPI Group (UK) Ltd, Croydon CRO 4YY

A CIP catalogue record for this book is available
from the British Library.

ISBN   978–1–911427–22–3

For Dad

I could be bounded in a nutshell and count myself a king of infinite space – were it not that I have bad dreams.
                              – William Shakespeare, Hamlet

Contents

Shadow

Steady drifts of rain blew in from the sea against roof tiles and window panes, rainwater trickled inside drainpipes and from somewhere in the sleeping city came the howl of a dog. The dog was crying to be let in. The shadow stopped and listened. Unlike the dog, the shadow had no desire to be let in, no desire for a dry place, no desire for sleep. And the city did well to sleep. Or pretend to sleep. Because the shadow was full of hate.

The shadow kept the semblance of a human being. It stopped at a new noise – a rumble. Above, in one of the houses, someone snored. The shadow rose easily through the air. It moved along the sides of the houses, peering in at each upper window that was not curtained or shuttered. Dark room after dark room until – there. The snorer.

On a great bed of white sheets, on his back, lay a large man. His chest swelled as he inhaled and his snore was so loud it buzzed the panes of glass. The man exhaled and his chest sank. A moment of silence then his chest inflated once more and his snore buzzed the glass. At the hinge of the window was a gap where a draft entered the house, and here the shadow slipped inside. The man's eyelids flickered. Dull brass gleamed on a mantelpiece. The shadow approached.

The shadow bowed, and as the man inhaled with one of those gigantic snores, the shadow shrank until it was as thin as a thread and slid up a nostril. The man snorted as if a gnat had got up his nose, and rolled over.

The man was dreaming of his childhood. When he was little, on Friday afternoons after school, he would come home to the smell of pretzels, fresh out of the oven and sprinkled with crystals of sugar. His mouth used to water. His mother would bring the warm pretzels to him at the kitchen table. He would swing his legs, happy. He lifted a pretzel, smelled its delicious aroma, took a bite. It was the tastiest pretzel he'd ever eaten. Then, in his dream, in one moment, sweet pastry turned foul, fresh bread turned mouldy and his mother began to cry. The man felt such a jolt of something nasty, something that hated him and his mother – it was like plunging into a bath of hate – that he sat bolt upright in bed, wide awake. He knew something hateful had got inside him. He leapt out of bed. Still the feeling didn't leave so the man began running round the room, as if he could run away from the feeling.

The shadow left his body. It flowed under the door. It crossed the hallway to a room that smelled of sour breath, where an old woman dreamed, and it fell on her. It leaked into her dream with such hatred that when she woke the next morning she was weighed down as if her body was heavier than a sack of compost. Her low mood did not leave her for three days. The shadow didn't wait around to see that mood pass. It left the old woman and floated downstairs to the

2

kitchen where, snoozing by the fire, it found a cook happily dreaming that she was flying like an angel. That is, until the shadow brought a cliff into her dream and the cook flew into it with a splat. The cook woke with a shock, convinced that all her bones were broken. She began weeping. The shadow popped out of the house via a keyhole.

If it could have, it would have slammed the door and put a curse on the place.

It made its way through the city. It didn't sense the rain blown in from the sea or the coldness of the air. In the sheds beyond the marketplace, the animals in their pens stirred nervously. Rain drummed on the high tin roof. The animals sensed the shadow. The pigs grunted and the cows bumped against each other. The shadow flew above them. The pigs squealed. The shadow reared, grew larger, seemed to fill the whole space of the windy sheds, and the pigs screamed and the cows bellowed and all the creatures rattled the galvanised metal rails of their fences the way prisoners condemned to death rattle the bars of their cell doors on the night of their execution. But the shadow did not enter the animals' bodies. It passed through the sheds and out the other side and floated on towards the harbour.

There, it climbed the rocks that rose towards the castle and by a pool the last tide had left, it sat. In the harbour water near the rocks stood a heron, waiting to spear a fish. The heron was completely still. It either did not notice or did not mind the shadow. All that moved were the multiple rings

3

opening on the water from each drop of rain and the waves lapping against the rocks. The shadow seemed almost to cross one leg over the other. It waited. What did the shadow wait for? For its food, like the heron? Perhaps. Or perhaps it did not know why it waited. Perhaps it only knew what it wanted when the thing it wanted arrived.

The rain drifted in from the sea. The shadow turned and scanned the city from the long hill on one side that sloped steeply down through a jumble of tenements and houses to the municipal buildings and warehouses, then across the river and up the hill on the other side to the castle that towered over the harbour. Not a light shone anywhere. Not in any window, not from any streetlamp. Nowhere.

Except above. Right above the shadow a light shone at the end of the castle. Like a challenge.

Seeing that light, emotion stained the shadow, made its substance thicker, as if it was about to shudder into a physical body. Startled, the heron took flight. The shadow shot upwards like a firework, but a dark firework.

Through the rain-spotted window, at a desk, by firelight and the glow of a table-lamp, in a low-ceilinged room so pokey it was more like a ship's cabin than an ordinary room, sat a tall, thin man with black hair. His back was to the window and he was working at papers. The shadow gulped and a deeper darkness spread through it as if it had swallowed a whole tub of ink. The ink of the deepest inkwell, the deepest ink-mine (if ink could be mined), the deepest ocean of the blackest ink that wrote the blackest messages of hate. The shadow leapt at the window. It didn't even try to find a gap.

Glass shattered. The wooden muntins that held each individual window pane splintered. The shadow hurtled across the room, bringing with it the sweeping rain, sending the flames in the fire roaring and flapping in fear. It skidded to a halt by the door. Now it turned and expanded, like a balloon filling with air, only it was not air it filled with, but black vengeance. In the firelight, the man's eyes widened, as if with terror. The grey in the man's black hair caught the light. And now the shadow shrank, condensing all its hatred and vengeance until its emotions were contained in something the size of an arrow-head. It aimed itself at the man's heart. It would shoot itself through that heart faster than an arrow, faster than a crossbow bolt, faster than a bullet. Then, at the very moment it was about to hurl itself, something about the man stopped it. His eyes twinkled. The shadow could not believe it. The man's eyes twinkled and the brackets of a smile twitched at the ends of his cruel mouth. The shadow hesitated. Then it understood – this was a trap.

The door was thrown open and stark lights flooded in, hurting the shadow's eyes. A net of light was flung and when it touched the shadow, the shadow felt searing pain. If it could have screamed, it would have done. It made no sound. Figures moved beams of light that stabbed its eyes, and the net of light was drawn tighter and tighter as the men bellowed, shouting instructions, and their boots thudded on

5

the floorboards of the cramped, cabin-like room. The shadow thrashed. The shadow strained upwards, the men pulled the net, and for a moment the battle between shadow and men hung in the balance. Then one man lost his footing and the shadow was released with tremendous force. It catapulted upwards. A man's skull knocked against the ceiling and made a noise like a bowling ball hitting a skittle. Another man's body thudded into a wall. He grunted and fell like a sack of rocks.

The shadow zipped out of the window.

'Catch it!'

The shadow flew. It glanced backwards, saw lights take off from the roof of the castle and come after it. The lights drew nearer quickly. There were several flying figures, and beneath them they carried nets of painful light.

The shadow faced ahead and, as if taking a deep breath, gathered all its being into its head with the rest of its shape tapering behind it like a tail, and fired itself across the night.

When the shadow looked back several miles later, the figures were still there. But they were lagging. And each time the shadow checked, they were further behind. Except for one figure. Though it grew smaller, it did not give up. Five minutes passed, ten, fifteen, and still that one figure with a net of light pursued the shadow. At last the shadow grew tired. It had been flying for half an hour and the figure behind kept its steady pace, and now the shadow lost its speed, and its pursuer neared. By this time the shadow had reached the mountains and the great forests there, and still the figure came on steadily, like a wolf hunting a wounded deer.

The shadow descended to the forest.

It moved through the forest. The shadow was travelling slowly now, drifting from side to side with tiredness, almost crying in desperation to escape, but each time it checked behind, the figure with the net of light was there. Growing nearer. They slalomed between the trees. The figure behind was almost upon the shadow. The shadow put on a final burst of speed, weaving between trunks, and when it looked behind, the figure had gone. The shadow slowed, then floated over ferns and bracken. The forest was silent. The shadow was safe. Air rushed and the figure – a teenage boy with blond hair – dropped like a hawk, his net of light opening. The shadow wrenched itself sideways. It fell through ferns and bracken. It would have crashed into the damp ground. It could actually smell the damp ground – wet bark, pine needles, and soil. But, to the shadow's surprise, it did not touch the ground.

It fell through the ground.

There was a hole there.

*

The shadow fell into another world. It knew that it was in another world because the air was warm and dirty and not clear like the air of the mountain and the shadow was not beneath the ground but falling upwards, which was

7

impossible. It fell upwards through the air, into the sky. By the time it managed to slow itself and hover, it was high above the land of this other world and it was looking down on a city, a metropolis so large it dwarfed the city the shadow knew. The shadow had never seen so many lights. Roadways of light in a vast, endless web, large rectangles of brightly lit grass where people ran around chasing a ball, towers of glass taller than the tallest towers of the castle in the shadow's home city, and in the distance a broad snaking river, crossed by lamp-lit bridges, and beside the river a great wheel of light as tall as the castle in the shadow's city, with people in glass bubbles on the wheel. There was the sound of an earthquake in the sky, the shadow turned, and bearing down upon it was an iron bird the size of a ship. The shadow jumped just in time and the flying-earthquake-bird-ship sailed past, and through its portholes the shadow glimpsed lots of people before the thing left in its wake filthy fumes stinking worse than farts. The shadow coughed several small shadows, and shuddered in disgust.

It moved away, avoiding more of the iron flying machines, and seeing no sign of its pursuer – the young blond man with the burning net of light – it descended.

It searched for an uninhabited place to stop and rest. But the city was endless. Finally the shadow could go no further and it drifted with the warm air along a street of houses. The streetlamps were on but each house was dark, their curtains closed, except for one room which was lit up and the window *open. And the shadow would have passed on beyond this room, too, it was so tired, except that a boy's voice came from the window, uttering a word the shadow recognised. 'Balthasar.' That was the word. So the shadow sank to the small front garden only big enough for a few bushes and a patch of grass, and here it came to rest, under that window on a warm night – it was summer here – and lay down on the ground under a bush and fell asleep.*

CHAPTER 1

Bad Dreams

Toby woke from a bad dream. He couldn't remember it but he wondered if his parents had been arguing in the night and their argument had somehow entered his sleep. If they had been arguing, they were quiet this morning. He could only hear the distant wash of rush-hour traffic. He scrambled out of bed and tore back the curtains to dispel the lingering feeling of the dream. Warm sunlight streamed in.

Toby liked his room. He knew it was a young sort of room for a boy of thirteen and some of his classmates would have made fun of him if they saw it but no one at school was going to see it, that was for sure. The curtains had pictures of boats and so did his duvet and pillowcase. Propped on a bookshelf was a model yacht, white with blue trim, which he used to sail at a boating pond on the other side of town until his dad stopped taking him, and beside it a money box in the shape of a red fire engine. The floor was strewn with plastic construction pieces, not from superhero or science-fiction sets but less popular ones, and he was in the middle of making an aqueduct. It ran from a castle he'd designed to the bookshelves stacked with his old toy-boxes, board games and, above them, his books. He had no computer games; they did not interest him. Most of his books had broken or missing spines, they had been read so often; they were about cars, aeroplanes, boats, engines, and DIY. There were also books with shiny unbroken spines. These were the fantasy novels his dad kept giving him, which he couldn't get into. *The Lion, the Witch and the Wardrobe* was the only one he had finished.

Toby sat at his desk where he'd cleared a space for the model aeroplane he'd been working on until late the previous night. It was his first model aircraft. He'd bought the kit after his dad suggested he try making one. It was an early biplane, a Bristol Boxkite, and it looked like its name – a box-shaped kite with a pair of wheels underneath. Its tail had another, smaller box at the end of it. He touched a join. The glue was dry. With whooshing noises he flew the aeroplane towards the landing, sending cardboard planets on his hanging mobile bobbing into orbit, elbowing the door wide so his leather tool-belt that hung on the back swung away then bumped back, and steered the Boxkite on towards the stairs.

The windows at the half-landing gave a view of the garden. The beech tree at the end was already going gold and yellow and dropping its beech mast on the lawn. On the next floor he passed his parents' small bedroom and his dad's big study and on the ground floor went through the living room to the dining room and down the stairs to the basement kitchen. The tall, narrow house was built on a slope, so the back was lower than the front, the basement kitchen opening onto the back garden. Toby liked the kitchen being half under the ground; it made home feel like a burrow – squished-in and cosy. The house had belonged to his grandparents and he could still vaguely remember them, not their faces, more their shapes, Grandad smelling of cigarette smoke and Grandma having much softer skin than his parents' or his own.

'Look, Dad!' said Toby, landing the Boxkite on the kitchen table. 'I finished it last night.'

His dad, his hair on end, his shirt collar up on one side and tucked under his jumper on the other, tapped at his laptop.

'What's that, love?' said Mum, making sandwiches.

'A Bristol Boxkite,' said Toby, opening the throttle and roaring it off its landing strip.

'Go away, Toby,' his dad murmured.

13

The Boxkite cut its engine, glided down and the brakes screeched softly.

'You finished it last night?' Mum prompted, putting sandwiches in lunchboxes.

Toby grunted.

'Well, I think it's wonderful.'

'I don't care what you think, I want Dad to like it.'

His mum frowned, hurt. Toby felt unhappy but didn't know why. He stood beside her. He felt the dark shape of the bad dream – a sort of smoke – somewhere inside him. He didn't know what to do about it. Mum started filling flasks.

'I don't need two,' he said quietly.

'One's mine.'

'But aren't you going to work?'

'She's going to that stupid protest afterwards,' said Dad, sitting back and crossing his arms.

Mum was in an environmental action group – she went on marches and campaigned against deforestation, pollution, the sea full of microplastics, the loss of the earth's creatures and plants and trees – she said it hurt her physically, the thought of all that loss.

'It's not stupid, David,' she said, wounded. 'It's important.'

'You're better off putting your energy into your thesis.'

Mum stood very still.

14

'Look, Dad!' said Toby, taking the opportunity to roar the Boxkite past him.

'Not now, Toby!'

'Is it as good as yours?' Toby said, pushing on regardless. 'Dad? Dad?'

'Hmm?' His dad was pulling at his lip, reading what he'd written.

'You said you made model aeroplanes when you were my age. You told me to make one.'

Dad looked up. 'No I didn't.'

'Yes you did,' insisted Toby. 'You said, "Why don't you make a model aeroplane or something? That's what we did when we were your age and got bored." That's the exact words you said.'

For several seconds Dad gazed at Toby. Then, as if he had a genuine interest in the answer to the question, he said, 'Are you deliberately being stupid, Toby?' and he emphasised 'stupid' with a sneer.

'David!' exclaimed Toby's mum.

Toby blushed. He hated his biplane now, and its jaunty plastic pilot with his stupid goggles.

The bathroom was off the kitchen, partly under the front yard, and its door opened and a large middle-aged woman appeared in a voluminous white kimono stitched with flowers, her hair hidden beneath a towel-turban. She proceeded regally through the kitchen, nodded at Toby's mum, at Toby, and finally and curtly at Toby's dad.

'Morning, Mrs Papadopoulos,' said Toby.

'Morning, Theodora,' said Mum.

'Mrs P,' said Dad as their lodger climbed the stairs. Toby stifled a snigger. Mrs Papadopoulos glared at Dad.

'David,' hissed Mum after she'd gone. 'I wish you wouldn't call her that.'

'It sounds rude,' said Toby, laughing.

'Exactly, Tobes,' said Dad, and winked.

Toby laughed, happy again.

'Right, I have work to do,' said Dad, shutting his laptop and standing up.

'I'll see you when I get back from school, then, Dad?'

'No. I'm going to the ministry this afternoon.'

'But I'm going on this protest,' said Mum. 'Somebody needs to be here when Toby gets home.'

'He's old enough to look after himself. Aren't you, Tobes?'

'Maybe I could come to the ministry with you?'

'No,' said Dad, going upstairs. 'Besides, Mrs P will be here.'

'Don't call her that,' said Mum. 'Anyway, that's not the point. You should be here for him.'

Disappearing from sight, Dad said, 'Don't get arrested, Helen.'

There was a quiet. Mum was looking towards the patio doors, holding her packed lunch. The only thing outside was the great beech tree. He felt the lurking bad dream. 'You're not going to get arrested are you, Mum?'

'Hmm?' said Mum, turning from the window. 'No, Toby, I won't get arrested.'

'Oh! Dad didn't finish his coffee. I'll make him a new one.'

'You'll be late for school.'

'Nah. Plenty of time.'

*

Taking the cup of coffee upstairs proved a more difficult job than Toby expected. He had filled the cup to the brim and had to go up three flights with several turns. At the half-landing, light flickered on the wall through the leaves of the beech tree. One good thing – the sunlight banished the bad dream. He went on without spilling a drop, entering his dad's study where he began the riskiest moment of his journey, lowering the cup to the desk. He spilled it and a big splatter of coffee hit the spread papers.

'Oh for – !' yelled his dad. 'Toby!'

'Sorry, Dad.'

'Are you deliberately being stupid? Why'd you fill it to the top?'

'I was trying to –'

'Go away!'

Toby stared at the brown liquid sitting on the surface

of the paper, some seeping in. 'That's not your novel, is it, Dad?'

His dad was searching for something to mop the spill.

Toby's dad was a writer who specialised in curses and put-downs, which he supplied to TV and radio programmes. He also wrote sarcastic newspaper articles, and recently he'd become a speechwriter for the government. Toby liked telling people about his dad working for the government. And he liked visiting his dad at the government ministry. He noticed how all the other workers admired his dad, called him 'Mr Porter', told him how great he was. What his dad was really interested in, though, was his novel. He was always working on it. He worked on it in the early mornings, evenings, and weekends; every spare minute lately, and he didn't have time to take Toby to the boating pond the way he used to. Or anywhere else. He had been working on the novel for as long as Toby could remember. Mum said he'd been working on it since before Toby was born. It took up an entire bookshelf and every day a little more was added. Toby wondered if it was the longest book in the history of books. Much of it was printed on variously coloured paper but most was handwritten – on regular paper, and on sheets that had been crumpled and binned before being rescued, on old envelopes, and even, Toby once noticed with a mixture of annoyance and pride, in one of Toby's old exercise books. The novel was set in a world named Balthasar and it was supposed to be a fairy tale but Dad couldn't bring himself to give it a fairy-tale ending. As far as Toby could see, Dad couldn't bring himself to give it any ending at all.

Toby's chest tightened as he stared at the coffee seeping into the paper. He had ruined his dad's life's work. 'That's not *The Kingdom above the Sea* is it, Dad?'

'Are you still here?'

*

Actually there was another reason why Toby had wanted to bring his dad a cup of coffee, beyond trying to please him. It meant he could delay getting ready for school. Toby hated school. It wasn't so much the schoolwork, which he sometimes liked and generally didn't mind, or the teachers, whom he generally liked and sometimes didn't mind – it was his classmates. They loathed Toby.

As he left the house, the feeling of the bad dream returned, and he felt its weight physically across his shoulders. It seemed to follow him down Arnold Street like a heavy cloud until a light sensation climbed the back of his neck and tickled over his scalp, transforming into a feeling of being observed. It was such a strong feeling that Toby glanced behind him but there were only the usual morning shadows of the trees.

The nearer Toby came to school, the slower he walked,

regularly stopping to inspect something that caught his eye. At the entrance to the park, he stopped to investigate new roadworks. Red-and-white barriers surrounded a trench. A sign required that PEDESTRIANS GO ROUND. Toby peered into the trench.

It was deep, there were no pipes or cables, and only one workman. He had white hair and silvery stubble and was staring into space, the end of a roll-up cigarette sticking out of the corner of his mouth. Gradually he became aware of Toby. 'All right, Chief?'

'That's deep,' said Toby. 'What's it for?'

'Mending.'

'Mending what?'

'Never you mind. Aren't you going to be late for school?'

Toby took a deep breath, sighed loudly and walked on, kicking tiny stones along the pavement and annoying several people coming the other way, who had to avoid him.

*

School was as bad as he expected it to be. It was as if the bad dream (which he still could not remember, though he tried) had followed him right into the building. Late for registration, he received a warning that next time it happened his parents would be contacted. In the first lesson, one of his classmates gave the wrong answer to an

20

easy question and Toby, seeing an opportunity for what he considered an excellent joke, said, 'Are you deliberately being stupid?' which made several people tell him to shut up. After morning break, while waiting for the teacher to arrive, Toby told the people sitting round him how his dad had a meeting with a government minister that afternoon. When no one showed any interest, Toby added that his dad was friends with the Prime Minister (this wasn't true). Toby was always going on about his dad. After the lesson, as they were filing out, one of the big boys thumped him on the arm.

'What was that for?' said Toby.

'Shut up, you self-important little –'

Toby was pulled away by the flow of his classmates so didn't hear the final word but he could guess what it was.

After break their science homework was returned. He'd enjoyed doing it and was confident of a good mark. But when he opened his exercise book the page was littered with thick red crosses in felt-tip. His shoulders slumped. The lesson started while he was still reading the comments. He'd misunderstood the problem that had been set. The teacher asked him a question and because he'd been reading the homework comments he didn't have a clue to the answer.

'Focus, Mr Porter! Focus!'

In the last lesson before lunch, the English teacher

was in a grouchy mood (perhaps she'd had a bad dream like him). Others in the class had noticed too and were deliberately trying to wind her up.

'If I hear another word out of you lot, I'll keep you back five minutes. Then you'll be at the back of the lunch queue and there'll only be pizza crusts left. Which are as hard as volcanic rock.' She said this with a smile of vengeful satisfaction.

The class fell silent. But only until Toby spotted the ideal moment to improve his popularity by making a joke: 'It's all right, Miss, the lunches here are awful whatever time you turn up. You go right ahead. My mum made me a packed lunch.'

'Right, you lot! I'm keeping you in.'

There was a collective groan. After the lesson, Toby pretended he couldn't feel hatred directed at him like lasers.

Toby didn't have any friends so he wandered the playground during lunch break, smiling as if he was quite happy on his own. Actually, he longed for a friend, but whenever he tried to make one it seemed to go wrong. He kept rubbing the back of his neck, feeling someone was watching him or even following him but when he looked round, there was no one there. Except there was. A girl from his class was smiling at him. Toby couldn't work out why. She wasn't one of the people who were usually mean to him so it wasn't a trick. He tried smiling back.

She blushed and broke into a grin. Toby felt giddy and his thoughts turned cloudy. He'd experienced this before. He would get a feeling for someone, like a cloud or a deep sea, and he didn't know what it was. And he didn't know what words to say that would fit with this feeling. When he tried to use some words they came out wrong. This happened now. He went over to her. She had a straight fringe above her eyebrows and without thinking he said, 'God, that's a weird haircut', and the expression on the girl's face dropped like a curtain. Her eyes filming with tears, she strode away.

And that was his school day.

*

'Hello, Mrs P,' called Toby, then remembered she didn't like being called that and changed the word so it came out sounding like *Pee-apadopoulos*. Toby had always had problems with their lodger's name. When she first arrived, years ago when he was small, he had heard it as *Hippopotamus*. It had taken him months to realise it was not.

She was an opera singer and had a house back in Greece but kept her room at Arnold Street even though she spent a lot of time touring and recording in other countries. London was the best place to be for her work, she said. It was a hub for other places. Toby had grown to love the woman, and liked to listen to her sing. But that afternoon, her attic room was silent. Toby went to his own room where he was confronted by the Bristol Boxkite. It was a stupid idea, building a model aeroplane. The pilot was still jolly about something, hunched over his controls like he was going on a great adventure. Toby pressed the end of the wing with his forefinger so the biplane tilted off its wheels. He increased the pressure through his forefinger. Something crumpled and cables broke and the top wing slumped, like the wing of an injured bird.

'Well, that was pointless,' said a voice.

Toby turned. Mrs Papadopoulos stood on the stairs with a glass of water.

A feeling surged through Toby. He couldn't have named it but it overcame him and he began to cry. Not just to cry, but to sob. Mrs Papadopoulos came in and Toby hung his head so she wouldn't see his tears. Her perfume smelled of lily of the valley. He felt her fingers comb through his hair until her hand cupped the top of his skull.

'It must be a difficult business, I think, being a young man,' she said. 'Why don't you go and make yourself a hot drink and have a biscuit. Alfred's in the kitchen.'

'Is he?'

'Don't worry about the aeroplane. You'll fix it. You're good at fixing things.'

Toby nodded, not daring to look up in case he'd cry again.

She was right, he decided as he went downstairs. He was good at fixing things. He had once attempted to fit a pane of glass that had popped out of the window in Mrs Papadopoulos's room. He couldn't do it and Mum had to get a handyman because she was too clumsy to do it herself while Dad was scared of heights and didn't want to lean out of the window. Toby observed the handyman carefully, who showed Toby how to warm the putty in his palms then knead it along the edge of the glass, and together they refitted the pane.

In the kitchen, Toby sat beside Alfred on the back step. Alfred had a round face with sickly yellow eyes. He had a notch between his sickly eyes like he was continually considering deep matters. He also had bags under them as if he'd been considering these matters until the early hours. He had long, soft white fur and he was the fattest, laziest cat in Arnold Street, possibly London. Possibly the world. He belonged to Mrs Papadopoulos and was Toby's best friend.

With Alfred, it didn't matter what Toby said, it wasn't going to be wrong. And if Toby didn't want to speak, Alfred didn't mind. Toby didn't want to speak that afternoon so for a while they sat together in the warm September sun, listening to Mrs Papadopoulos. She had her window open (the one with the pane that Toby and the handyman had fixed) and her singing was very clear and very lovely. Toby didn't understand the words; they were in a different language. Down the long garden, at the end, Toby could see people in the block of flats at the back. There was something odd about that as usually he couldn't see them. There was something odd about the garden, too. It felt emptier, barer. It brought back the feeling from the bad dream of the previous night. A sort of desolation. There was a fine blond dust everywhere. On the grass, on the plants, on the patio paving stones, even drifting in the air.

Alfred sensed something odd too because he kept turning his head and staring at a spot in the air above the lawn.

'What is it?'

Alfred rose stiffly and padded over the grass until he was right beneath it. Mum said he needed to diet. Dad hated him and took every opportunity to shoot at him with a water pistol. Now Alfred regarded a spot in the air. Toby wondered if he could see a subtle shade hovering there but he wasn't sure.

'What do you think it is, Alfred?'

Alfred peered but after a time he gave up and returned to Toby, and Toby lost interest in the shadow too and told Alfred about his bad dream and how everything had gone wrong since then. How Dad thought he was stupid for making an aeroplane. How Dad got cross when

Toby spilled the coffee. How bad school was. Alfred listened, and Toby told him – for the umpteenth time – about the novel that Dad had been working on for all of Toby's life; about cruel kings and queens, and people with supernatural powers, only Toby inserted into it the tale of a boy named Toby and his white cat Alfred, who had to escape the forces of evil and rescue the people of Balthasar from tyranny.

And the shadow drifted in the air above the garden as if it was listening too.

*

Dad came home.

'Where's your mum?'

'Climate protest.'

'Shouldn't she be back by now?'

'Don't be stupid, Dad. Protests aren't timetabled.'

'What have we got to eat?' His dad went to the fridge, looked inside then swung it shut, only to discover that Alfred had snuck up behind the door while it was open.

'Agh!' cried Dad, jumping. Toby laughed. Dad lunged at Alfred, who shot into the garden.

When Mum hadn't returned by seven, Toby texted her. Dad cooked beans on toast for them, and afterwards Toby phoned his mum. She didn't answer. He kept trying and by nine, he was worried. His dad had the television on. The news was showing footage of the protest. Some

27

protestors had pushed against the police and the police had struck them with their batons and plastic shields. People had blood on their faces. His dad thought the protestors got what they deserved. Toby thought his mum might have been hurt and made his dad phone the local hospitals. There was no news of Helen Porter. Then it was past Toby's bedtime but he couldn't go to bed without knowing if Mum was all right. He lay on the sofa in front of riot footage, eyelids flickering, head nodding, and half-dreamed Mum being trampled by police horses so he sat up, forcing his eyes wide. He opened the sash window for some air to wake himself up. The night was cool. The flats behind were all lit up. That was when Toby realised what was different about the garden, and he was so surprised he said out loud, 'But the beech tree has gone.'

'Hmm?' said his dad.

'The beech tree in the back garden has gone.'

'They came and cut it down.'

'Who did?'

'Tree surgeons. While you were at school.'

'They can't do that, can they?'

'We asked them to. It had a disease. It had to be cut down.'

'But that was our tree,' said Toby.

His eyes gummy with sleep, Toby stuck his head out to see exactly what had happened. The beech tree was gone. It had left a physical emptiness in the space it used to occupy. All that remained was a blond, freshly cut tree-stump. The lawn was sprinkled with that strange pale dust he'd noticed earlier. And there was a dark spot in the air half-way between him and the lawn. The place that Alfred had noticed earlier. Toby could definitely see it now. It was weird. It was as if the air was thicker there. It had a physical density. The spot blocked what lay beyond it. Toby moved his head from side to side, to see if he was mistaken, but he wasn't. If he moved his head enough, he could cause the patch to hang between him and the beech-tree stump so that the stump was completely blotted out.

It moved.

The shape was about five metres from Toby, and it moved towards him. It moved with steady slowness. There was something about this steadiness, this slowness, that Toby didn't like. The blot had the quality of a fast slug. Toby took a step back from the window. The tar-coloured shadow kept travelling towards him. Toby had no doubt when it reached the window it would come in, close around him, enter him. It would thicken inside him with its alien darkness. It was now less than two metres from the window. Its substance seemed the consistency of treacle. Up and down Toby's skin ran a prickling sensation and he stepped forward quickly and slammed down the sash window.

'Don't bang the windows!' yelled Dad.

Toby flicked the catch and backed away.

Dad's mobile rang.

The big panes of the sash window reflected Toby and, behind him, his dad with his computer open on his lap, talking on the phone, running one hand through his thin, wild hair. Beyond the glass was the darkness of the garden, the lights from the flats opposite. No floating blot. No shadow.

'Toby,' said Dad.

Toby waited.

'Toby,' said Dad.

'What?' whispered Toby, unable to move.

'Your mum's been arrested.'

CHAPTER 2

On Margate Sands

When Toby's mum came home in the morning, Toby jumped up and hugged her then stepped back and studied her carefully. He had seen the protestors on the news – their faces hideous with shouting, scruffy and shoving, screaming when they were carried away by the police. It seemed impossible for Mum to be one of them. Mum was her usual placid self. She wore the white shirt and brown shoes she always did for her part-time work at the GP's reception, with jeans and a light summer jacket. She put down her small red rucksack and, while she stood dazed, Toby searched inside for criminal evidence. He found her work skirt, her empty lunchbox, a bottle of water, an apple, and a flask. Her brown, straight shoulder-length hair was a bit messy and she seemed distracted, but that was all that was different.

Mum was hungry so they went downstairs and Dad, who had gone to collect her from the police station, clattered angrily, preparing food. Mum sat at the kitchen table, put her head in her hands and massaged her temples.

'Have you got a headache?' said Toby.

'A slight one, yes.'

Toby raced to fetch a painkiller then poured her a glass of water. While she drank, he eyed her wrist for handcuff marks – there weren't any. Although, she did have bright red palms, as if she'd been scrubbing her hands.

'What happened, then, Mum?'

'In a minute, Toby.'

Toby sat. Alfred slinked round Mum's leg then jumped into Toby's lap and together they waited for the story of her arrest. Toby had never known her to raise her voice, let alone get into an argument with anyone, except with Dad, and even then she didn't get angry; she just seemed to be in pain when the arguments happened and they usually ended up with her crying. How could she have got into trouble with the police?

'What happened, Mum?'

'Shh. After I've had some food.'

So, after boiled eggs and toast, with her small, criminal hands wrapped around a mug of jasmine tea, Mum told them the tale of her arrest.

The protest was in the City of London. It was a march that had not been authorised by the police, so she was already in trouble before she began. The march was against the companies based in the City, ones that damaged the planet through emissions and the dumping of waste, and also against the banks that lent money to these companies. The march wound its way between steel and glass towers. At one point, several protestors broke away and glued themselves to the big glass doors of a bank, and Mum joined them.

'Oh, for God's sake!' interrupted Dad.

Mum had put glue on the palms of both hands and fixed herself to the main door. No one could get in or out without Mum shuffling forward or backward. The march moved on, and soon the only people remaining were the handful of protestors stuck to the glass, and a security guard, who was very nice, Mum said – he took the bottle of water from her rucksack and held it to Mum's mouth when she was thirsty.

'His son's very good at piano, apparently,' said Mum. 'Grade Seven.'

'We're not interested in the security guard's son,' snapped Dad.

'Well, I was, David.'

'Were any press there?' said Dad.

'There was a TV cameraman and reporter. And someone from the papers.'

'You didn't give your details did you?'

'Tell us about the arrest, Mum!'

What happened was that a specialist police team arrived with some soapy water and chemicals and spent a couple of hours unsticking the protestors from the glass. They had to do it very slowly so they didn't pull the skin off the protestors' palms.

'And they arrested you?' said Toby.

'Um, well, er, no.'

This group of specialist police had been drafted in from Wales to help with the spate of climate protests taking place across London, as the London police couldn't cope. By the time they had unstuck everyone it was near the end of their shift and they didn't want to spend time arresting people and taking them to the police station. They had tickets for *Les Mis* and didn't want to be late, so they let her go with a warning.

'Oh,' said Toby, vaguely disappointed, as he was starting to like the idea of Mum as an outlaw.

'Well, how did you get arrested, then?' said Dad.

'I went up the road and stuck myself to another bank.'

'You did it again? Who'd you think you are, Greta Thunberg?'

Toby couldn't believe that this quietly spoken, even-tempered woman was so determined. It was amazing really. He looked at her with admiration.

The Met police were not as forgiving as the nice Welsh police. After they'd unstuck her (roughly), they were only too pleased to arrest her. Put in a police van, she was driven to a police station where she was locked in a cell for the night. In the morning they brought her out, told her the date she had to be in court, and released her.

Toby's heart gave a terrified thud. 'You're going to prison?'

'No.'

'She might,' said Dad.

'They'll fine me.'

'You don't know that, Helen.'

'Can't you be a bit more supportive?'

'You've got a TV reporter and newspaper journalist watching you break the law and I've just started this new job with the government. Were you deliberately being stupid?'

Mum slumped in her chair the way Toby had slumped in his when he'd got the bad mark in Science.

'David,' she breathed.

'Oh, I'm sorry, Princess,' said Dad. 'But did you stop to think what your arrest might mean for the rest of us?'

Toby gnawed his lip. He thought it was pretty great getting arrested by the police for doing something you believed in, even if it was against the law, but he didn't think now was the moment to make his view known.

Mum rose and went over to the patio doors and stared out at the pale, dewy morning.

'It'll be all right, Dad,' said Toby.

'What do you know about the laws of the land?' snapped Dad.

Alfred, who had sat patiently in Toby's lap during Mum's story, now got onto all fours as if he was personally affronted by Dad's tone, but it turned out he was just stretching. He dropped onto the kitchen floor and went over to Mum.

'It can't go on like this, David,' she said.

'What's that?' said Dad, eyeing the white cat then glancing around, possibly for his water pistol.

'We can't go on like this. I can't take it any more.'

'Well, in that case you shouldn't –'

But he didn't finish the sentence because Mum let out a cry of dismay, opened the patio door and stepped outside.

'The beech tree,' she said. 'The beech tree is gone.'

'It got cut down,' said Toby.

'But we didn't agree –'

'Yes we did,' said Dad.

'No, we didn't.'

Mum walked across the lawn through the dew and the fine dust that Toby realised now was sawdust. Mum stood at the blond stump, and Toby and Alfred joined her. The presence of the tree seemed to remain, like a ghost, rising thickly and strongly into the air and spreading over them all.

'That tree has been here since I was a baby,' said Mum.

'Sorry, Mum,' said Toby, not knowing what to do. He gave her arm a squeeze and she and Toby and Alfred looked up at all that emptiness.

*

The bad dream came again that night. He didn't want it to. It seemed to get hold of him physically and throw him around. He was trying to wake up but he was so tired he couldn't. He stayed in an in-between state, as if he had been drugged by his own tiredness. The dream: running through a mountain forest along dusty, pine-needled paths then falling from a great height which morphed into descending a stone staircase in a city. And someone at the bottom of this staircase – or was it a well? – was asking for help. When he finally did wake, he was so hot he had to throw back his duvet. His T-shirt was soaking. He pulled it off and scrambled out of bed, the thickness of the dream still on him. He stood in the middle of his bedroom, swaying. He didn't want to be in the bed, near his sleep. Because there was a bad dream there. The shadow caused it. That dark, treacly blot.

There was a warm strip of light beneath his bedroom door, which comforted him. He went onto the landing.

He could hear the murmur of voices downstairs. He wanted to go down and see his parents but he didn't want to show Dad his fear. He shivered in the cold that came now his sweat had cooled, and from his chest of drawers searched out an old velveteen pyjama top that was too small for him. He wanted his mum to come up and sing to him like she used to do when he was small. She liked musicals, and he liked it when she sang. She couldn't sing as well as Mrs Papadopoulos but she had a nice voice. Songs from *The Wizard of Oz* and *Annie*. 'Tomorrow' and 'Over the Rainbow' and 'We're Off to See the Wizard.' He went down to the half-landing. And now he could hear them in their room. They were arguing. And Mum was crying.

*

Toby went to Margate with his dad that weekend. One of Mum's old friends from university was coming to stay and Dad couldn't stand her so he booked a weekend at a hotel. Toby was surprised his dad was taking him as on the few occasions his dad had gone away for work, he had not let Toby join him, even when Toby begged. Toby was also pleased because he hadn't felt comfortable in the house since the bad dreams. Although Toby hadn't seen the shadow since it had floated towards the window, and in spite of the fact he had managed to convince himself that the shadow was the result of some unknown optical effect, he felt uncomfortable when he was on his own in the house. He woke uneasily each morning, certain there was another presence somewhere nearby.

Margate was cliffs declining to a sweep of sandy bay and the only things Toby wanted to do were paddle in the sea and visit a steam railway which was a drive away. But the beach was being lashed by a horizontal rain so fierce even the beach donkeys had decided to remain indoors, and the steam railway was shut for repairs.

Toby's dad had booked a twin room in a dilapidated hotel and when they found their door, Toby's dad went straight to the desk by the window, took out his laptop and set to work.

'I thought we were going out,' said Toby.

'What does that look like?' said his dad, pointing.

'The sky?'

'No.'

'The sea, then?'

'No. Rain.'

'No, it's not, it's sky and some seagulls being blown about.'

'And rain.'

Toby sighed and sat down heavily on his bed. The springs creaked.

'Shh!' hissed Dad. 'I'm trying to write.'

'Are you writing your novel, Dad?'

Dad didn't answer.

'Mrs Papadopoulos says you should finish your novel, then you'd be happier.'

His dad stopped tapping, raised his head and stared straight out the window as if he'd just been hit by the most astounding idea in the history of ideas.

'Did you have a new idea about Balthasar, Dad?'

Slowly, Dad turned in his chair. 'Well, you can tell Mrs P that she'd better stick to opera singing or I'll stick her opinions up her *aria*.'

'Oh, all right then, be like that, I don't care. What are we going to do?'

'I'm going to write,' said Dad, turning back to his screen. 'You can go out and explore the hotel or something.'

'Or something,' muttered Toby to himself. 'Come on, Dad,' he wheedled, 'Let's go out.'

'Go away, Toby!'

'She's right,' Toby said, standing up and raising his voice to the level his dad used, 'you are a difficult person.'

His dad seemed to see Toby for the first time. 'Sit down, Toby,' he said, pointing at the bed.

Toby sat, bobbing several times on the ancient, bouncy springs, a little scared because he knew he was going to get told off.

'Listen,' his dad said, 'I was going to tell you later but, well, this is as good a time as any. Your mum and I are getting a divorce.'

His dad had one arm along the back of his chair.

Behind him were acres and acres of rainy sky and seabirds hanging in the heavens then diving, showing off insane acrobatics to one another. They reminded Toby of kids on a skateboard park.

'So until the house is sold,' his dad was saying, 'you and your mum are moving out.'

'What?' said Toby.

His dad frowned in frustration, then repeated the sentence he'd just said, word for word.

'Why can't I stay with you in the house?'

'Because you're going with your mum.'

'But I want to stay with you.'

'Well, you can't. We've discussed it and you're going with your mum.'

'Well, that's not fair, is it?'

'Life isn't fair, Toby.'

'You didn't even ask me.'

His dad sighed a long-suffering sigh, shook his head as if saying to some invisible observer, *See what I have to deal with?* and gently, as if speaking to a total fool, said, 'Well that's the way it is, Tobes.'

Toby, as the seagulls cartwheeled and zoomed behind his dad's head, said, 'What will happen to Alfred?'

'Well, he'll go with Mrs Papadopoulos. He sure as sh – ... He's not living with me.'

'Oh.'

There was a silence.

'All right?' said his dad.

Toby stared at the threadbare carpet's swirls.

'All right?'

In the gloom of the room, Toby couldn't see his dad's face properly against the sky. Finally his dad faced his computer and tapped at the keys.

Toby sat there a while. Then he stood up. 'I'm going out for a bit.'

'Hmm?' his dad said, tapping.

'I'm going out for a bit.'

'Oh, all right, Tobes. D'you want some money?'

'No.'

'Here, take some money.' His dad fetched his wallet from his jacket and took out a ten-pound note. 'Go and play on the amusements.'

Toby took the money and went out, crushing the banknote in his fist.

He wandered the hallways for a while, circled a damp-stained ballroom, poked around a conference room of stacked chairs, and in a lounge opened all the drawers. They contained table mats and candles. Then he went down to the lobby and through the revolving door. Instantly the wind turned his jacket into a billowing parachute on his back and the rain soaked him. He walked down from the cliff and plodded the great expanse of Margate Sands.

The shadow, he decided, had come into his life and brought catastrophe.

Toby avoided the amusement park (its sign shouted in huge letters DREAMLAND as if amusement was brilliant) and escaped the rain in a large seafront shelter, not wanting to sit down because his soaking jeans were shrunk so tight on his legs it was unpleasant to bend his knees.

'All right, Chief,' said a voice, and Toby turned to see an old man in overalls, with white hair and unshaved cheeks, with a crooked roll-up cigarette in the corner of his mouth.

Beyond the man stood a small enclosure of tall wire fencing with concrete blocks at the base, to which canvas sheets were tied so that whatever was being done behind them was entirely hidden.

'What are you fixing?' said Toby, nodding at the wire fence.

'The universe,' said the old man, and winked.

It took Toby a long time to realise what the man meant by this, perhaps half a minute. In the meantime, he stared at him blankly, then finally it hit him, and he understood that he was trying to be funny. Toby had had enough of people being sarcastic, so he walked out of the seafront shelter into the furious wind and as he passed the old workman, shouted at him, 'Shut up, you idiot!'

CHAPTER 3

Angel Lane

On the morning that Toby and his mum left home for the final time, Toby went up to Mrs Papadopoulos's room to say goodbye. He didn't notice, and neither did she, the shadow that slid behind him up the stairs and hovered on the ceiling. Alfred did, and sat frowning at it.

Mrs Papadopoulos had tears in her eyes and sang 'Tomorrow' into Toby's ear while hugging him.

'Look after your mum,' she said.

Toby, his throat swelling, nodded and picked up Alfred, burying his face in the cat's long, soft fur. 'Bye, Alfred,' he whispered, and managed not to cry. Going downstairs, he didn't notice the shadow drift after him, nor Alfred trot after the shadow.

Toby's dad sat at his desk working on Balthasar. Toby hesitated in the doorway. Behind him on the landing the shadow didn't stop but descended the next flight of stairs, followed by Alfred.

'Don't hang about, Tobes,' said Dad. 'Your mum wants to make tracks.'

Toby couldn't bring himself to enter the room and hug his dad and he couldn't bring himself to leave either.

'Listen, Tobes,' his dad said, swivelling away in his ship captain's chair and peering out at what was a baking hot September day. 'The sooner you understand that things don't work out for the best in this world, the better.'

Toby waited for his dad to say something more. He waited for him to come over and hug him. But his dad sighed and spun back to his screen. Toby took a step into the room, planning to ask if he could stay in Arnold Street until the house was sold, but just as he was about to speak his dad sucked in breath, sat up straight and said, 'Right, Tobes, don't hang about. Your mum wants to leave.'

As Toby crossed the landing, he traced his finger along the linen chest. It had a scar. It had been made accidentally by a chisel from his tool-belt two years earlier, and a beam of the hot morning sun made the scar glow.

Outside, he gazed up at his dad's window. He couldn't see Dad. He hoped he would be okay in the house with the shadow. He was so intent on his dad's window, he didn't notice the shadow sail out the front door, down the path and slip into the open boot of the car where it disappeared among boxes. And he didn't notice Alfred either. The cat trotted after the shadow and sat on the pavement peering up into the open boot.

Alfred was a cat of great curiosity and fond of travel. He often visited other countries on his cat passport with Mrs Papadopoulos, most regularly Greece. For international flights he travelled in a comfy pet carrier but on journeys around London he nestled in Mrs Papadopoulos's roomy leather shoulder bag, poking his head out to see what was happening. He had even been known to squirrel himself into Toby's rucksack to be discovered only on arrival at school. If Toby had not been so preoccupied with leaving home, he would have checked that Alfred was safely locked in the house, but he was preoccupied so he didn't check, and didn't see Alfred gracefully jump into the boot after the shadow and wriggle into Toby's duvet.

*

Summer had returned with a vengeance. They whooshed along the motorway past fields of stubble, bleached grass and exhausted-looking trees with the sun fierce on the windscreen. The indicator ticked and they whooshed up the slip road.

'Oh,' said his mum after a few minutes, her eyes flicking between her mobile phone on the dashboard and the road. She pushed at buttons.

'Careful, Mum.'

'It's ... packed up ...' Slowing, she squinted ahead. The car behind honked. 'I – um – I don't recognise this.'

'Best find somewhere to stop.'

She pulled in at the side of the road.

'You can't stop here, Mum.'

The driver behind overtook, horn blaring.

Toby checked his phone but – brilliant, there was no signal. Another horn sounded and a dark shape overtook them, then another. A lorry driver wound down his window and shouted.

Mum buzzed open her window. 'Eff off!' she shouted.

Toby stared. She had never lost her temper before. Ever.

There was a sign up ahead on a side-road. Toby jumped out and ran.

'Toby!' his mum screamed in panic.

Toby reached the sign. It read:

ANGEL LANE
unadopted

As he turned to run back, he noticed at the end of the dusty lane some workmen. They were digging a trench with pickaxes and spades, and one was putting up some red-and-white barriers around the trench. He was older and had white hair and a cigarette dangled from his lips.

Toby could see the smoke squirming upwards. Surely not. It couldn't be. Not the workman he'd seen before, in London and Margate.

'Toby!' his mum called, standing by the car.

Toby ran back and they got in.

'Please don't run off like that, Toby.'

'I went to see where we are. Angel Lane. Put the hazard lights on, Mum. We can't stop here.'

'I thought you were running away.'

'Mum, I'm thirteen, where am I going to go? Have you got the map?'

'I – um – er …'

'You put it in your bag.'

She dug and found it, but seemed unable to work it out. He took it from her.

'Okay,' said Toby. 'We go up here.'

Another horn sounded beside them. Mum was staring into space.

'Mum!'

His mum's chin wrinkled and he saw she was going to cry. In a quieter voice he said, 'It's all right, Mum. We're nearly there. You got us here.'

It took her a moment to understand what he'd said. Then she gave a sob and he grabbed her hand. She had bluish-green circles of tiredness under her eyes.

'You got us here,' he repeated kindly.

Now she really was going to cry.

'Don't cry, Mum! Not now! We're nearly there.'

She laughed, then hunted out soggy tissues from her bag and blew her nose. Toby glanced down Angel Lane as they passed, deciding that either working on road repairs attracted white-haired old smokers or something strange was going on.

*

While Toby and his mum took either end of a large container box and carried it up the stairs to their new flat, the shadow slipped out of the boot. After a moment, Alfred jumped after it and followed as the shadow disappeared round the side of the flats by the communal bins.

Their new flat was gloomy. The hallway light didn't work and the other bulbs had no lampshades and gave off a dismal glow. Even the savagely bright sun seemed unable to penetrate. The mustard-coloured furniture didn't help. Or the brown carpets. And the smell added to the gloomy feel of the place – stale except in the kitchen where the staleness was mixed with a claggy odour of mould.

Toby's room was at the back. The carpet there was bright green and made of stiff fibres, a dead fly lay on the windowsill, and the brown theme from the rest of the flat continued in the curtains, which were coffee coloured. He hadn't been sure whether to bring all his things with him because he'd still be going back until they sold the house (it seemed unbelievable to him that it would be sold) so he had just taken essential items. Now, though, in this empty room with the brown curtains and green carpet, he wished he'd brought everything. Most of all, he wished he'd brought Alfred. After all, the cat spent as much time with Toby as he did with Mrs Papadopoulos.

Toby surveyed the gardens of dried grass and withered shrubs, and the identical houses differentiated only by conservatories, their glass blinding where the sun reflected. A gang of seagulls rose from a roof. Their cries were piercing. There was something so desolate about the noise that he felt the urge to phone his dad to tell him he couldn't stay here.

The seagulls were going crazy. They were shrieking and diving then rising and flapping. Now they were swirling in a vortex around one of their gang. They seemed to be attacking it. Toby watched as their victim whirled black wings to shield itself. It was the wrong colour for a gull. The birds suddenly scattered like pieces of shrapnel from an explosion. Some were coming directly for his window.

Screeching, in a storm of feathers, the gulls veered left and right and Toby faced the creature they had been attacking. It was hurtling towards him and it wasn't a bird, it was the shadow, the blot, that treacly substance. In a vaguely human shape, limbs sprawling, moving with the velocity of a rocket-propelled grenade, it targeted Toby. He ducked.

Green fibres centimetres from his nose. Awaiting the smash. Teeth gritted. Straining muscles against impact.

Nothing.

After some seconds, Toby unclenched his jaw and unknotted his muscles. He got up. Acres of gardens and conservatories and identical houses. And no shadow.

*

Toby sat on his bed with his back against the wall, his eyes flicking between window and door. They flicked to his phone. It took him a while to locate the number, he was so jumpy.

'Dad,' said Toby, and didn't wait for a response: 'Can I come home?'

There was a crackle like paper being scrunched.

'Dad?'

His dad sighed. In a tone mixing finality, forbearance and sarcasm, he said, 'No, Toby.'

'I saw the – I have to come home.'

'No, you don't. You just think you do.'

'But I – Please, Dad, it's weird here.'

'Everywhere's weird, Toby. The world is weird.'

'I hate it here. I hate it.'

'We can talk about it when you visit, all right?'

'But that's a fortnight away!'

'Tobes, I've got to finish this speech so I'll speak to you soon, all right?'

'What's it about?' Toby blurted. 'Maybe I can help.'

Toby watched the window, saw no gulls or flying shadows.

'See you soon, Tobes. Don't fret.'

The line died. Toby crept to the door and stood listening. Then he risked it and opened the door wide. He checked each room.

He was glad when his mum got back. He heated tinned spaghetti and put on some toast and asked her about her day while she made a salad. Then the pair sat, Mum exhausted, Toby watching for the shadow.

*

Toby woke to the remnants of a hideous dream – the blackened walls of a castle.

The sky was cloudless and the lawns were even more parched than the day before. Violently, angrily, Toby dressed. He didn't see how the shadow could have followed him. He didn't see how it could even exist, but he believed the evidence of his eyes. Mum had made him a packed lunch – cheese sandwiches, a packet of crisps, an apple, and a carton of juice. He stowed his thin outdoors jacket in his rucksack, made sure he had his mobile, and was ready.

His mum gave him a lift as it was his first day. As they approached the school, they began to see burgundy sweatshirts all funnelling towards the gates. They hadn't had time to buy his new school uniform so he was wearing the black jumper and tie from his old school and, feeling exposed in the wrong clothes, and dreading what he would encounter in the new school, he slid lower in his seat. Mum pulled up behind other cars. Buses were moving away.

'You'll do great,' his mum said.

'I want to go home,' he whispered, lifting his rucksack from the seat well. He didn't move to get out.

'What is it?' she said, turning off the engine. 'What's wrong?'

'Why can't you just love him? Why'd you have to get a divorce?'

'Let's talk about this later, love. You have to get to school and I have to get to work.'

'But it's not fair.'

'I know,' said Mum sadly.

'So, why, then?'

'I couldn't do it.'

'Why?'

'I just couldn't.'

'What sort of answer's that? If I gave that answer to any question in school, I'd get zero. Are you deliberately being stupid?'

'Toby, don't speak to me like that.'

'But why do you have to leave and get a divorce?'

'I don't love your dad any more.'

'Why?'

'There's no why. Sometimes things simply are.'

'Things have reasons. Always.'

Mum sighed, then said, 'It's complicated.'

'No. It's not. It's simple. Tell me. You just won't tell me.'

'He's changed.'

'Changed how?'

'Oh, Toby, I don't know.'

'Yes, you do.'

'Oh, all right. I suppose ... when I first met him he was ... He had ideals. Optimism. He's been disappointed in life. He's got very ... bitter. And it just stopped working between us.'

'It's that stupid novel about Balthasar, isn't it?'

'It's nothing to do with –'

'He's got bitter about that, hasn't he? Because he hasn't finished it. That's what Mrs Papadopoulos thinks.'

'That's a symptom of his bitterness, I suppose. It's not all of the reason.'

'We could help him finish it,' Toby persisted, no longer listening to his mum but envisaging himself and his mum sitting beside Dad while he finished his novel the way his mum used to sit with Toby while he finished his homework.

'It doesn't work like that, Toby.'

'How does it work, then?'

She shook her head.

'How does it work?' he said again.

A kid brushed against the wing mirror.

'Toby, you'll be late for school.'

'You're not telling me.'

'The marriage between your dad and me is finished.'

'Why don't I have a say?'

'Because you don't. I'm sorry.'

'But it's not right. It's not fair. I didn't want to leave home. I didn't want to come here. This is your fault.'

'It's no one's fault.'

'Yes, it is someone's fault. It's your fault. And I don't care if you've moved here. You'll go to prison for that stupid climate protest and then what'll happen to me?'

'I'm not going to prison.'

'Yes, you are.'

'No, I'm not. I told you. My lawyer says I'll either get a fine or community service.'

'I want to go home,' Toby whined. 'I want to go back to Arnold Street. To Alfred and Dad and Mrs Papadopoulos and the garden and my bedroom.'

'I'm sorry, Toby,' she said, putting up her hand to stroke his hair.

He banged her hand away.

'Oh,' she said, pulling back in pain.

'It's your fault, all of it!' It was only after he said this that he saw the blood, bold scarlet on her right hand. 'Mum,' he gasped. He'd caught her with his fingernail. He reached out to take her hand. She blocked him with her arm, leaning away. She was frowning crossly and had pursed her lips.

Horrified at what he'd done, at his mum's response to what he'd done, Toby leapt out of the car, threw shut the door and, trembling, walked into his new school. After a minute, his mum drove away.

A short while later the shadow arrived at the school gates. And a short while after that, Alfred arrived. The pair waited patiently for the school day to finish.

*

After school, Toby was confronted by the sight of crowds milling at the bus stops. He didn't want to be near strangers a moment longer. He thought he could remember the way back to the new flat so he set off on foot. He didn't notice the shadow fall into step behind him, or Alfred behind the shadow. These three straggled through the streets of the new town until Toby stopped, lost. He wandered on beneath a beating sun, having no

56

desire to go back to the flat anyway, where he would have to speak to his mum after their row. Then he came to a place he recognised. Angel Lane.

On either side of the dusty lane stood wire fences with grassy waste ground behind. A sign read: 'For Development'. At the end of the lane, beyond the workmen's red-and-white barriers and trench, stood another wire fence and beyond that the ground shelved down to what looked like a railway cutting. Toby could see the overhead electric cables and an embankment on the far side. The workmen had finished for the day and Toby considered investigating their trench then decided he had better get back to the flat in case his mum began to worry. It was hot so he took off his jumper, tied it round his waist, and continued along the main road and his whole future would have been different if he hadn't caught sight of a white shape out of the corner of his eye. He turned to see a fat cat with long white fur strolling towards the trench.

'Alfred?'

The cat did not respond. Alfred was intent on the shadow that had already slinked into the trench. Arriving at the edge, Alfred sat and gazed down.

'Alfred!' called Toby, and hurried up the lane. When Alfred jumped down into the trench, Toby ran. He didn't see how it could be Alfred but he was sure it was.

From where Toby stood behind the barrier, the trench

looked empty. It appeared to form the entrance to a tunnel.

'Alfred!' called Toby, crouching down and peering into the dark.

He could not see the end of the tunnel but it had to be a short one because Angel Lane only extended a few more metres. The lane stopped at the wire fence. Beyond the fence was the steep slope of the railway cutting down to the train line. So the tunnel must emerge – Toby supposed – on that steep slope. It was a distance of about five or six metres between the entrance to the tunnel and the slope.

Angel Lane was empty and silent. Toby ducked under the barrier and dropped into the sandy trench. Squatting, he could see a short way into the subterranean passage but not the end.

'Alfred?'

He crawled in. The ground was dry and grainy beneath his palms.

'Alfred!' he called. The walls extinguished his voice. He had the sudden thought that it was a bad idea to be crawling into a tunnel. What if he got trapped? What if the tunnel collapsed? No one knew he was here. He would die.

It had become completely dark. Soon he should be coming up against the slope of the railway cutting but instead the tunnel went on. A draft of warm, almost hot air touched his face. His palm slapped mud. That was strange. Perhaps the trench was to fix a water leak. Perhaps he should reverse in case he muddied his uniform but the thought of Alfred being in some kind of danger spurred him on. Toby smelled woodsmoke. It got in his throat and made him cough. Then through the darkness came a soft roaring sound. 'Alfred!' he called and was cheered because he could hear from the way his voice echoed that the tunnel opened out ahead. He couldn't understand, though, why he couldn't see daylight.

The soft roaring grew louder and it was accompanied by a fierce crackle, and Toby thought it must be a train coming along the railway line and that in a moment he would emerge on the slope. Then something hot touched his face. He brushed it away. The roaring and crackling continued. It wasn't a train. There was a pattering now, too, that sounded like rain. But it couldn't be rain because it was a bright, sunny day. It must be the water-pipe leak. Then a burning object, a black leaf edged with orange light, floated down the tunnel towards him. It hissed into his hair and Toby smelled burning and had to pat quickly at his head to put out the flame. Toby knew he should turn back, he wanted to turn back, but Alfred needed him and he crawled on, quickly, to get the rescue over with. Then he came out of the tunnel.

Toby was not where he should be. He was on a slope, yes, but it was not the slope of the railway cutting. Nor was it sunny; in fact, it was not even daytime. It was night and it was raining and it was hot – not as hot as a summer afternoon but as hot as if he had just stepped into an oven. It was also windy and smoky and he was on a steep mountainside in a forest. All this was impossible. Yet this is where he was. Toby's senses proved it. But worse than all of this were the flames. The trees of the forest were on fire. Behind the trees, even taller than the trees, was a wall of fire – from left to right this fire-wall ran, as far as the eye could see. The roaring crackling sound was the burning forest, and Toby was no longer in Angel Lane, but in the middle of a fire-storm.

CHAPTER 4

Fire Season

Flames surged into the night sky. They turned the trees closest to Toby into black silhouettes. Taller than any of the trees or the flames were towers of grey and black smoke that rolled endlessly upward. In the other direction, all around the mountainside, the sky was a jelly-red. The noise was terrifying – the roar of the wind, the roar of flames, and a crackle of branches. Sometimes whole trees ignited – even the greatest, oldest oaks and beeches, a hundred years old, lost their lives like this, in a moment. Then there were the frequent, deep thuds as huge limbs fell and trunks toppled. And amongst it all, the pattering rain.

The heat was so intense that Toby lifted his arm to shield his face but it did little good; the heat was in the very air that touched his skin, that he drew painfully into his lungs, and the wind was blowing so hard he had to set his feet wide and crouch to keep steady against it, and it wasn't coming from a single direction but from everywhere, circling him constantly and shoving him like a bully. And he was being stung. At first he thought it was the rain, which was still, somehow, falling in spite of the fire, then he realised it was embers. They were flying around him like wasps and stinging his exposed neck, hands and face.

The ground was black mud with pools of low flame and fallen branches still alight, like burning veins in a black marble floor, and in all that motion and chaos, he could not see his friend.

'Alfred!' he shouted. 'Alfred!'

It was no good; his voice would not carry above the noise of the fire and wind. He had to escape, to get back into the tunnel, and he probably would have done except at that moment he spotted Alfred. He was blithely trotting downhill.

'Alfred!'

Toby raced after the cat, hurdling the fallen, smoking branches.

'Alfred, come back, you idiot!'

His white school shirt was soon riddled with holes from the embers, as if an army of hungry moths had attacked it. The embers burned his skin. He dug inside his rucksack and, crouched on a patch of steaming mud, tugged out his jacket and pulled it on. Alfred was further away, trotting on in that haughty, Alfred way of his, as if he didn't mind – or didn't notice – that there was a forest fire burning all around him.

Alfred vanished into a wave of smoke. Toby plunged after him. The wall of fire lay behind them now and the smoke was hot and he coughed, and again he had to stop. He took his school jumper from round his waist, tied it round his mouth like a scarf, and went on. The smoke thinned and in a hollow was Alfred. He was creeping forward as if stalking prey. Toby didn't call out but ran lightly down, threw himself at the cat, and missed. Alfred trotted over the lip of the hollow and out of sight. Toby charged after him, surprising Alfred, whom he scooped up. Then Toby kept going. The slope was too steep for him to stop.

At the bottom stood three figures. Beyond them was a cliff edge, from which billowed brown and orange smoke like steam off a pot. The three figures were standing alarmingly close to the edge.

'Help!' Toby yelled, seeing that his momentum was going to carry him over the precipice.

His legs tangled as he twisted to slow down, and he fell. He landed with a thump, still cradling Alfred. He found himself before the toe-caps of a pair of leather boots and the hem of a long leather coat. A yard beyond these boots lay the gulf of smoke. Toby splashed to his knees and, slipping about in mud, not wanting to let go of Alfred, got to his feet. Alfred squirmed.

Above the leather boots, the skirts of the long coat narrowed to the waist. Further up, at the throat, the collar was fixed by a round metal clasp decorated with the emblem of a swan. The man who wore the coat was tall and thin and had a very white face. He had a high forehead rising to black hair with some grey, swept back with rain, and he had a thin-lipped mouth and dead eyes.

To the man's right, at the very edge of the precipice, stood a teenage boy with rain sparkling hair. He looked slightly older than Toby, sixteen or so. He had no jacket and his shirt was clinging to his chest which was sticking out because his arms were being pinned back by the third figure, a man with a shaved head wearing a long cagoule. The cagoule was also fixed at the throat by a round clasp with the swan emblem.

The teenage boy had a strange expression in his eyes. Toby thought he knew what the expression meant because he had made that same face whenever he was trapped in the changing room at school by the big boys who laughed at his unathletic body. The boy was widening his eyes at Toby as if pleading secretly with him, then he mouthed the word 'Help'.

Toby looked between the boy and the tall man with the thin cruel mouth. The dead eyes twinkled into life and the man turned from Toby, the skirts of his leather coat twirling wide. He took a step towards the teenage boy and punched him in the stomach. The boy's expression changed. He continued to gaze towards Toby then the focus went. The tall thin man turned back to Toby. His eyes still twinkled.

'I have to get home,' said Toby, backing away and holding Alfred even more tightly. 'My mum will be worried.'

The teenage boy crumpled in the arms of the man who held him. Smoothly, with no more difficulty than letting go of a glass of water from a hand, the man relaxed his grip and stepped away and the teenage boy's body flopped over the edge of the cliff.

Toby stared at the empty space where the boy had been. There was nothing there. He looked between the shaven-headed man and the tall thin one with the cruel mouth and twinkling eyes. The tall thin one held something in his hand, the hand that had punched the boy. It was a knife, and it was dark with blood. He hadn't punched the boy; he had stabbed him. Toby turned to run. A palm thumped his shoulder and he half collapsed under its weight. He wriggled but fingers dug in hard, pried under his collar bone. His whole shoulder felt as if it was going to implode. Another hand came round in front of him and a slippery thumb-heel pressed Toby's throat. Toby clutched Alfred. Alfred mewled and fought to escape. Something blurred at the corner of Toby's vision – the bloody tip of the knife. Close to his ear, a voice said, 'I'm going to slit your silly little throat.'

The hot wind flapped the man's long coat against Toby's side. The man's thumb began to slide along Toby's throat and Toby knew that at the end of that thumb was the blade. In less time than it takes to pour a carton of milk onto a bowl of cereal his throat would be opened and his blood would flow away.

Staring up the smoky hillside, Toby had a vague impression of bloodshot eyes belonging to an animal the colour of mist. It was coming for him. Then he saw what it was. The shadow. But this time it did not stop as it had at the window in Arnold Street, or veer away as it had at the window of the new flat, it kept on coming, driven by a muscular hatred. It leapt. It went right through Toby. Or, more accurately, it scraped through the top of his skull, aiming at the man with the knife.

When the shadow touched him, pain splintered through his head and jagged down his spinal cord. He writhed, trying to get it out of him. It was filling his body, heart, lungs, kidneys, bladder. A scream louder than a fire-alarm bell ripped through him. He passed out.

He found himself lying in the mud. Alfred crouched in front of him, watching with frightened eyes. The tall thin man was on his knees, staring blindly, his rain-slick skin white as bone, then he vomited in a splatter onto the mud and tipped forwards and landed face-first in his own sick. The second man tottered back and forth along the cliff edge. As Toby watched, this shaven-headed man put his left foot over the gulf, threw both hands into the air and was gone, lost in the smoke of the chasm.

Toby got to his feet, opened his rucksack, and Alfred, as if he had finally realised how dangerous his situation actually was, jumped inside. Then Toby ran.

It was hard work, going uphill on the mud. He fell several times. Eventually he was at the hollow, and beyond that he dived into the rolling wall of brown, hot smoke. Each breath he drew burned his chest. He coughed and choked. He couldn't stop or he would suffocate. Then he was through. But the fire had crept down the mountainside and it was still moving, coming towards him through the forest, devouring the trees. Even if he could locate the tunnel – and he wasn't sure he could – it was further up, beyond the fire-line, and it was impossible to get through. Toby hurried away, not back toward the killer with the knife, but along the side of the mountain.

A shape shot past him, a dark blur. As it hurtled he saw it was a terrified deer, bounding in a long swerving arc. The fire seemed to follow it. Toby sped up. Bangs and cracks pursued him as trees burst into flame. Several more deer flew past him, eyes white and wide, mouths hanging open in terror. A hedgehog hurried downhill, its thorny prickles aflame. The forest was dying. Toby was watching it die. He gave up all concern about meeting the killer with the knife, and raced downhill.

A thirteen-year-old boy is no match for a forest fire when the fire gets up to storm-force. The fire ran faster than Toby. It shot tendrils of flame across the wet earth and fired embers after all the creatures of the mountainside, including Toby. Toby crossed patches of flame, smelled the burning rubber of his soles, slapped at singed hair, then he smelled burning plastic, and felt heat across his back and realised his jacket was alight. He tore it off.

The shadow appeared then, at his side. He changed direction to escape it. He was still racing downhill, but on a different line. The shadow no longer had an animal form, it seemed almost a human figure, a darkness. Then, as Toby began to outpace it, it shifted shape again and fell forwards onto all fours and galloped towards him like a black dog. The thunder of its paws travelled through the ground, even above the noise of the fire. A clump of bushes was over to his side. Toby changed the angle of his run towards the bushes and as he heard a roar behind him – he was not sure if it was the wind, the fire, or the shadow – he charged through the undergrowth and ran into emptiness.

He fell for some seconds, branches whipping his face as he plummeted, fir-tree needles flicking across his eyes, fir-tree limbs punching his body but slowing his fall. He hit the ground with an *oomf* as all breath exited his chest.

When Toby came round after losing consciousness, he realised he had passed out only for a moment because above him he could see the faint orange of the clouds of smoke at the top of the tree, illuminating the path he'd torn through its still-swaying branches. He was lying on a soft cushion of fir-tree needles at the foot of a rocky cliff and his rucksack was trying to crawl away from him. Toby hooked a strap with his fingers. The rucksack miaowed.

For a while Toby lay on his back, looking upwards through the creaking tree. Embers were drifting down but mainly getting caught in the upper branches. He could see the flames of the fire-wall, flickering at the edge of the clifftop. Soon an ember or a flame would take hold and the fir tree would start to burn. He had to go immediately.

But of the shadow – thank goodness – there was no sign.

He rolled over, feeling great pain across his body, and got to his feet. In the dim light he checked on Alfred, who looked filthy with mud but otherwise fine. Leaving a small gap for air at the top of the rucksack, Toby put his arms through its straps so it rested against his front – he didn't want Alfred sneaking out to explore. His mobile had no signal. It had reset its clock too so he couldn't even tell what time it was. He checked himself for any injuries.

His white school shirt had become a polka-dot top of burn-holes, he had thrown away his jacket, his trousers had a tear and the soles of his shoes had melted so badly he could feel the fir-tree needles through his socks. He had cuts all over his body from the tree branches, and hot embers had burned his skin. His hair was singed. His lungs hurt from the smoke. He found his flask of water, and drank. He wanted to drain the flask but poured some into the lid-cup and held it for Alfred. Alfred declined but Toby was patient and finally the cat consented to a little water. Toby finished the rest. Then he hurried downhill.

CHAPTER 5

Widgeon

Toby had to get away from the fire and the killer with the knife and if that wasn't enough to worry about there was the shadow too, who seemed to be the cause of all his recent troubles. He knew if he kept heading downhill he would come eventually to the end of the forest. To streetlights, houses, people. He knew deep down that in fact he had stepped into another world but he refused to admit this to himself. He had not travelled between worlds and he was not in *The Lion, the Witch and the Wardrobe* for goodness' sake – or that is what he told himself. Everything can be explained. If a thing can't be explained that is only because it isn't yet understood. That there was a forest mountainside in the new town could be explained: it was a large country park. That it

71

was night could be explained: it wasn't really night but smoke blocking the sun. That the tunnel had led to a mountain not a railway cutting, however, could not be explained. But it would be explained if he kept thinking about it.

But there was one thing that could not be explained, that Toby had been unable to explain since it had first appeared and which he knew he would never be able to explain – the shadow. He had seen it in Arnold Street and at the new flat and now he had touched it. To be precise, it had touched him. For the briefest of moments, it had gone inside him and he felt its hate and ... something else.

Toby pushed what could not be explained down inside himself. The unexplained didn't disappear, it lurked somewhere within and made him physically uncomfortable.

Now Toby came to a part of the forest where the fire had already passed. The rain had stopped and the sky glowed a ghastly orange, and daylight was coming through. The earth was muddy, squelching underfoot, and so warm that steam hung over the ground like mist. And from the mist rose figures. Not people but trees – blackened, dead. And twisted branches reached like the arms of injured people begging for help. Toby had to step over some of them. It was like crossing a vast battlefield. The air stank of burned wood, and something else. Toby wasn't sure what it was. Alfred, deep in the rucksack, seemed to smell it, too, because he began mewling. Then Toby saw an inert lump, charred by flames. And Toby realised what the smell was – roasted meat.

The forest was silent. There was no rustle of leaves, no creak of branches. No birdsong either, because the birds were dead. He kept coming across them, small blackened shapes, some the size of a fist, some the size of a cat. Birds that had been unable to flee in time or who had been overwhelmed by smoke. The light continued to come up. There were more animals lying dead – badgers, foxes, hares, an entire herd of deer including stags with great horns, and then some strange-looking creature with six legs which Toby decided was actually two animals who had died together. Alfred was going crazy inside the rucksack and Toby tried to calm him, murmuring, 'It's all right, it's all right – you're safe.' But it wasn't all right, and Toby wasn't safe, and Alfred wasn't safe either.

The light was coming up fast now, and it wasn't because the smoke in the sky was clearing but because the low sun – a blood-orange haze – had risen above the mountain. It was dawn. The sun grew higher as Toby descended but it was impossible for it to be morning because that would mean he had passed an afternoon, evening and night in the forest. Yet it seemed less than an hour. Perhaps he had passed out for longer than he realised.

73

If it was morning then his mum would be seriously worried but he couldn't call her. His phone still had no signal.

Through the burned skeleton of the forest, in the distance, life gleamed – grass. Toby ran towards it, and as he came closer, the air grew clearer, and now he could hear birdsong, and he came out of the burned forest onto a broad, scruffy mountain meadow. There were bits of blue in the sky between the smoky clouds and Toby took great gulps of air. He had never been so relieved to see the sky and to breathe fresh air. He took off his rucksack and dropped onto the earth and smelled the wet long grass.

Beyond a stream stood a small wooden house with a thatched roof, and on the roof sat dozens, perhaps hundreds of birds, furiously cheeping. Before the house lay a large neat lawn with plants in the borders and beside the house a leafless, rust-brown tree, its branches stretched over the thatch like an outspread hand. Fixed to the broad trunk was a large wheel – like a hamster-wheel but made of wood – and some of the tree's exposed roots hung down the bank into the stream.

Someone screamed.

The birds rose into the air and swept across the meadow and Toby dropped to the ground and lay flat. The scream was not one of shock or fear but of pain, and it came from the house. Nothing moved. The windows were dark. There were pot plants on the verandah, and a fence on the left-hand side around a vegetable patch. On the right side was a lawn-roller near the big tree. With a rushing sound the birds returned to the thatched roof where they began to chortle and chatter and from behind the house, dogs yapped and howled hungrily.

Then, subtly, something changed. Toby wasn't sure what. The air grew a little dull, and it felt like it was going to rain, although it didn't. But it wasn't that which had changed. After a few seconds he saw what it was. Or rather, who it was. Because in the shadows under the tree stood a girl. She was sixteen maybe. About the age of the teenage boy killed on the mountain. Her arms were at her sides, held awkwardly, self-consciously, the way people hold themselves when they are on stage in assembly. Although, unlike someone on stage at school, she wasn't gazing into the distance but at Toby.

Toby's heart gave a thump. She had seen him. He scrambled into the forest, swinging his rucksack lightly to his shoulder, which is when he realised Alfred was no longer in it.

'Alfred!' he hissed, turning frantic circles.

Alfred was on the far bank of the stream.

'Alfred!' hissed Toby, coming to the edge of the trees. 'You stupid cat!'

The girl knelt and stroked him, and Alfred miaowed a thank-you. She picked him up. Then, as Toby watched, the girl – who wore a dark ragged dress and had bare feet – sat down on the rusted lawn-roller. Still stroking Alfred, she gazed at Toby as if she was intrigued by what he might do. Alfred's eyelids closed and he purred contentedly, like a tiny outboard motor.

Toby didn't know what to do. She seemed strange, only faintly there, perhaps because of the shadows or the odd rain-light. But she didn't seem dangerous, not capable of causing someone to scream. And her attention on him didn't seem mean. Also, Alfred wasn't scared of her. Alfred knew a thing or two about people. Toby decided that whatever the scream was, this girl was no danger. He walked across the grass to the bank of the stream.

'Give me my cat back,' he called, then broke into a coughing fit, his throat and lungs were so irritated by smoke. Finally, his eyes wet with tears, he could breathe again.

She put Alfred down and the cat mooched about, sniffing.

'Have you got a phone?' Toby croaked. 'I need to phone the police.'

The girl looked blankly at him.

'I have to get home.'

Toby climbed down the bank's steep side and leapt across the water, nearly falling backwards but clinging on to the grass then scrambling up.

'Listen,' he said, 'I need to use your –'

The girl had gone. Toby couldn't see her anywhere. Going over to Alfred, he said, 'We've got to get home, you stupid cat.'

Alfred purred and jumped into the open rucksack. The tree was covered in rivets. Toby touched the trunk. It seemed to be made of metal. He knocked on it with his knuckle and it clanged hollowly.

He approached the verandah. After a moment, he stepped up and peeked in a window. There was no sign of the girl but a plate was on the table with some bread beside a half-full mug. A door stood open to a far room where Toby could hear her clumping heavily about. He knocked. The clumping stopped and there was a silence. The birds chirped on the roof.

'Hello?' called Toby. 'I really need to use your phone. It's an emergency.'

Footsteps boomed on the bare floorboards and Toby stepped back for the door to open. Above it was a coat of arms showing a white swan with a collar and chain of gold.

Toby's legs turned heavy and a pounding started in his ears. It was the same symbol as the killer wore.

The door opened and there stood a man. He was broad and stocky with a wild brown curly beard that went right down his throat and merged into a kind of fur on his chest. He wore a once-white apron with bloody stains. His blue eyes contrasted with the red of the blood and they were fixed on Toby. Toby stepped backwards, fell off the verandah, and a hunting dog shot out and onto the grass. The dog blocked any retreat and barked and snapped at Toby's rucksack. Realising the dog had smelled Alfred, Toby jumped to his feet and held the rucksack high in the air, out of reach.

The man bellowed something but Toby wasn't listening – he could not take his eyes from the dog.

'Beeswax!' the man roared. 'Down!'

At once the dog lay flat and whined.

The man bellowed again, the words merging together, and it took a moment for Toby to decipher them. It sounded like, *Wheredyoucomefrom?*

'London, originally,' said Toby, eyeing the bloodstains on the man's apron.

The man bellowed something Toby couldn't decipher then marched angrily inside. Toby tried to sneak away but the dog growled, lips rising to show big incisors. The man stormed back out.

'Drink!' he said, shoving an earthenware jar at Toby.

Toby drank. The earthenware jar was heavy and the water cold. He kept his eyes on the man and when he lowered the jar the man grabbed Toby's chin in his bloody fingers and turned Toby's head sharply from side to side then marched back into the house. The dog lay with its head on the grass, ears flat, not daring to move. Toby thought it was best not to move either. The man returned with a small pot, grabbed the earthenware jar out of Toby's hand and, dangling from a finger what had taken most of Toby's strength to lift, grabbed Toby's shoulder and crashed him down on the verandah. He sat down beside Toby. His face was inches away. His teeth were dirty and some were missing. His breath smelled meaty. His eyes were ice-blue. First he wiped his hands on the rain-wet grass, then he poured water over them, washing off the blood. He dried his hands on a non-bloodied edge of his apron, scooped in the pot, grabbed Toby's hand and dabbed something on a burn. The ointment cooled the burning sensation. The man got to his feet and put the pot on the verandah.

'Do the rest of your burns. I've things to do. It's feeding time. You can have some if there's any left.'

Beeswax jumped up and trotted inside after the man.

Peering into the house, Toby could see the bearded man moving around in what must be a back yard, from which came the yelps and barks of perhaps a dozen dogs. Toby washed his hands and face which, he discovered, were covered in soot and grime. He took Alfred from his rucksack and poured some water into the flask's cup for him. Alfred lapped. His long white fur was muddy and sooty and singed so he was no longer pure white but white and grey.

Toby applied the ointment to each of his own burns on his hands and arms and chest and, using his reflection in a window pane as a guide, dabbed each burn on his face.

When he was finished, he stepped inside. The table stood on the left, with the half-eaten bread. A brick fireplace was in the back wall – the rest of the house was wood – and there was no ceiling; the struts and timbers of the pitched roof were visible. On the right, washing lines had been strung across the room and from them hung torn blankets or sheets. There were several fake deerskin rugs on the floorboards – then Toby realised they were real. Then what the hanging washing actually was – recently cut deerskins. He felt queasy.

On a bench on the right were cages, in which creatures moved – hedgehogs, ferrets and rats. There were glass jars of water attached to the cages, with teats, so the animals could drink. Propped in the corner was a longbow with a quiver of arrows. Capes and coats hung on pegs on the wall by the kitchen, and beside them hung a scabbarded sword with leather strapping around its steel hilt.

It was a very odd house.

Quietly, avoiding the deerskin rugs, Toby crossed the room. There were two doors at the back, one shut, which presumably led to the bedrooms, and the other open to the kitchen. The kitchen was neat and tidy, and a pot was on a stove. Something seemed odd about the kitchen but he wasn't sure what. Through the glass in the back door, Toby could see the yard, the vegetable patch and a fenced area of meadow. A herd of deer grazed in the fenced area, and in the yard were pens for chickens and goats, and kennels for dogs. In the next to last of these huddled several tatty-looking badgers and, in the last, a wolf, his fur burned. The bearded man was scrubbing down the yard, sluicing blood into a drain. The dogs were devouring the carcass of a deer. Toby understood at once – it was the deer that had screamed when the man killed it. The man finished scrubbing blood off the ground and came towards the kitchen.

Toby hurried back into the main room and when the man came in a few minutes later, drying his hands and arms, Toby was hovering by the front door with Alfred back in the rucksack, ready to escape. The man popped back into the kitchen and returned with a plate of meats and cheese and bread and a mug of water which he put on the table for Toby. Toby's stomach rumbled.

'Eat,' the man said.

Toby didn't move.

'Where are you from?' the man said.

'Over there,' said Toby, indicating with his thumb over his shoulder. 'Can I use your phone?'

'You live in the forest? No one lives in the forest but the Regent's deer. I make damn sure of that.'

'I live on the other side of the forest, obviously,' Toby said sharply. Perhaps, Toby decided, the man wasn't very bright. 'Can I use your phone?'

'Can I use your phone?' the man said, with a different intonation, as if he was trying to make sense of the words.

'Are you just going to sit there and repeat what I say?' said Toby, sighing with forbearance exactly the way Dad would. 'I need to use your phone.'

The man jumped up, shooting his chair backwards. 'Who do you think you are?' he roared. 'A Dreamer, to speak to me like that? No. You're not old enough. Think you're better than me?'

'I'm no dreamer,' said Toby. 'My dad says I have no imagination whatsoever. My mum's the dreamer, not me. Or so Dad says. Mum says I'm more practical.'

'High and mighty little shi – Well, you can bog off.'

'I want to get back to my mum. Over *there*.' He pointed in sarcastically exaggerated fashion. 'The other side of the forest.'

'Over the mountain?' the man said, astonished.

'Yes,' said Toby, shaking his head at the man's stupidity. 'Over the mountain. Now, can I use your phone?'

The man stared, his mouth open.

Toby sighed. He was dealing with an imbecile. Someone who had lived off grid so long he had lost all understanding of the civilised world. One of Mum's friends was like this. She had lived in a tree for two years. He gently put down the rucksack and took out his mobile.

'Do you have wi-fi? I can't get a signal.'

The man stared at the mobile phone.

'Over the mountain,' said Toby.

'Impossible,' said the man.

'Well, I just walked here so it can't be impossible, can it? If a phenomenon occurs, it can't be impossible.'

The man grunted.

'Well, if you don't have wi-fi, how do I get home? Where's the nearest town? I can catch a bus.'

'A bus,' repeated the man.

The man seemed unable to do anything but repeat what Toby had just said. 'What's your name?' Toby asked.

'Widgeon.'

'Well, Widgeon, I'm Toby. How else can I get home except by bus? Train? Or perhaps I can fly in a Bristol Boxkite.'

'So you *are* a Dreamer.'

'Tell me how I can get home!'

'Well, you can't walk. The fire is still raging.' The man glanced to the window, his thoughts going to the forest. 'It's the worst fire season I've known.'

Brilliant, thought Toby. Mum had brought them to a town where there were annual fires.

'I was lucky,' murmured the man, walking to the window and looking up at the sky. 'The wind changed at the last moment.' As if to himself, he said, 'There's still enough to burn if the wind changes again.'

Toby couldn't resist any longer and sat at the table and took a bite of cheese, which tasted odd, and tore at some bread.

'Go to the Regent,' said Widgeon, returning to the table. 'I've never met a soul from over the mountain.' He peered at Toby closely. 'You don't look like a shleg. They're paler. Maybe you are from over the mountain.'

'What's a shleg?'

'A refugee, now anyway.'

'And how far is this Regent man?'

'A walk of two days, I reckon. In the city.'

'Can't I get a bus?'

'A bus?' the man said.

'All right, all right,' said Toby, patting the air, not wanting to hear him repeat any more. Toby felt sorry for his daughter, having to live in the middle of nowhere. She must have been so unused to seeing strangers she'd run away to hide. It struck Toby then what it was that was odd about the house – there were no devices, no electrical items at all, not even lights.

'I'll go right now. My mum'll be worrying. But could Alfred have something, too?' Toby lifted his bag, and Alfred miaowed on cue.

Widgeon fetched some dried fish. While Toby and Alfred ate, Widgeon explained he was the forest ranger, looking after the animals for the Regent, who liked to go hunting there with his friends. So it wasn't a national park or nature reserve but a large private estate belonging to some sort of rich aristocrat – which would explain the coat of arms above the door. Widgeon was his gamekeeper and those others Toby had seen who had killed the teenage boy must also work for the man. Well, not for much longer, if Toby had anything to do with it. Because they'd be in prison. But, he thought, eyeing Ranger Widgeon who was now talking about the fire season, it would be best not to tell the gamekeeper anything about what he'd seen, in case the killers were his friends.

Each year there were fires, Widgeon explained, but these last few years had been the worst anyone could remember. This year, Widgeon had rescued some of the animals, nursing back to health the injured ones and keeping them all until it was safe enough for them to be released – if anywhere remained sufficiently alive for them to forage or hunt once the fire season ended. Entire regions of the forest had been destroyed. It would take decades for the earth to recover. The fires had also burned farmland further down the mountains, where the shlegs lived – and turned many of them into refugees. Some of them, starving, had been poaching in the Regent's forest, which was illegal. 'The punishment for poaching is death,' boomed Widgeon in his animal-like voice, 'so you're lucky I didn't take you for one and chop your head off.'

'You can't go round killing people,' said Toby.

Widgeon slapped the table. 'That's the law.'

'No, it's not.'

Widgeon stood up, furious, and Toby thought it wasn't a good idea to antagonise him any more so he said, 'Well, I wasn't poaching, anyway.'

Widgeon, his pride assuaged but not his anger, went to prepare some food for Toby to take with him on his journey.

After Toby had finished his plate of goat's cheese and delicious veal and pork, without thinking too hard about the origins of the food because it made him queasy, he went over to the single armchair by the fireplace. His feet were sore, and he eased off his shoes and massaged his feet. He wasn't sure he'd be able to walk for two days to the city to find the Regent. But he was bound to find a farm before that or come far enough down the mountain to get a phone signal. Then he could phone the police and Mum and Dad and everything would be resolved.

Toby sat back in the armchair. As soon as Widgeon brought his packed lunch he would be on his way.

*

Toby woke. He was still in the armchair, a deerskin rug over his knees and a low yellow light shining in his eyes, which is what had woken him. It was a reflection in the glass of the half-open kitchen door. It must be sunset, he thought. He rubbed his eyes and yawned. He must have

86

slept the entire day. He could hear a wooden trundling sound and the creak of machinery, and rain pattering on the thatched roof. His shoes weren't where he'd left them. He found them by his rucksack. They had new, leather soles, neatly sewn. Beside them were clean woollen socks and a woollen jersey, which he put on. The jersey was far too big for him. It was one of Ranger Widgeon's. He put on his shoes and tied the laces. In his rucksack were parcels of food, his flask and an earthenware bottle, corked. Tied to the rucksack was a roll of leather – some sort of blanket or mat. Alfred sat in the open front door.

'Hello, Alfred,' yawned Toby and stroked the cat's head. Alfred was different. Cleaner. Widgeon had washed him. The man had also cut, and in places shaved, Alfred's long fur to access the burned skin. He had applied ointment. The result was that Alfred looked a patchwork animal of very long white fur and bare skin.

'We've been in the wars, Alfred,' said Toby.

Alfred looked at him in agreement.

It was then that Toby saw the low yellow light. It was not the sunset at all and he had not slept the whole day – it was the forest fire. The wind must have changed. The fire had returned and was surging down the mountainside towards them.

Widgeon stood by the rust-brown iron tree. The wheel – that large hamster-wheel – contained Widgeon's dogs,

87

and he was urging them on. The faster the dogs ran, the faster the wheel turned. It was turning some kind of pump housed inside the iron. From the tree's branches that opened like an umbrella over the thatched roof, water was spraying. Each branch had hundreds of little holes in it and, the faster the dogs ran, the harder and further the water sprayed.

'Go now!' Widgeon bellowed at Toby.

Toby looked at the giant fortress of fire that seemed to be striding down the mountainside.

'Go, Toby!'

Toby stood not knowing whether to help or run. He raced to the kitchen, where he found a bucket.

'No!' yelled Widgeon when Toby began filling the bucket in the stream, so angrily Toby thought the man was going to strike him. 'Go to the Regent in the city.'

Toby looked between the racing fire and Widgeon.

'Go!' roared Widgeon. 'Go to the Regent in the city. He will get you home.'

Toby fetched his rucksack and hurried to Alfred. He laid down the rucksack with the top open, like a drawbridge, and Alfred sauntered in and sat amongst the packages of food. Toby put his arms through the straps so once again Alfred rested against his chest, peeking out of the top, then he was ready to leave. Widgeon charged past him into the house and returned with a cape which he pushed into Toby's arms.

'You'll need this if the rains start. I hope they start for real this time. Save our souls. Save all our souls. Follow the track. Eventually, sometime tomorrow, you'll come off the mountains. You'll have to walk all day tomorrow. You should reach the city the following morning. This will keep you dry and warm.' He tapped the roll underneath the rucksack. 'Watch out for shlegs.'

'Thank you, Ranger Widgeon.' said Toby. 'Good luck to you and your daughter.'

Widgeon frowned confusedly at him.

'The girl. The girl who lives with you.'

'I live alone, Toby.'

'But I saw a girl. I spoke to her.'

'I haven't seen another person in weeks. Must be a damned shleg, thieving like they do.' Widgeon ran back to his dogs. 'Hurry, Beeswax! Faster, Coalsmoke!'

The iron tree sprayed the thatched roof and his animals. The fire ate its way towards the ranger's house. Toby set off.

CHAPTER 6

The Shepherd's Hut

Toby followed the path from Ranger Widgeon's house across the scruffy meadow. On the far side it met the meandering stream, which broadened to a ford. Stepping stones took Toby over bronze-coloured water to a path which joined a well-used track. This he followed, and after half an hour he came to a wood. The trees had not been touched by the fire and were winter-bare, which surprised Toby because it had been a hot September day only yesterday, and autumn barely begun, but he concluded that the bareness had some other cause than a change of season: a gale, or disease, or perhaps some effect of the fire's smoke.

He felt he was far enough from the fire to let Alfred

out. He warned him not to wander off or he'd put him back in the rucksack, and the pair walked for several miles, the wood on their left and the stream on their right. The mountain air was chill. Toby was wearing only his shirt and the ranger's oversized jersey so he stopped to put on the cape. It had a warm fleece lining and immediately he felt cosy but when he came to button it at the throat, he discovered the metal clasp bore the symbol of a white swan and he dropped the cape from his shoulders as if the garment was the tall, thin killer himself.

Toby did not want anything to do with the symbol of the swan. Whatever it signified to the people who wore it, to Toby it signified murder. But the light and heat from the sun were draining fast and darkness and cold were coming. Toby and Alfred were going to have to walk all night or sleep outdoors. So once more he lifted the snug fleece-lined cape and put it around his shoulders. But when he touched the heavy clasp with the symbol of the swan standing out hard and proud on the disk, it sickened him and he tore it off and drew back his arm to throw it. He hesitated. He should keep it. It would be evidence for the police against the tall, thin killer with the cruel mouth. He also had worn the symbol of the swan. Toby put it in his rucksack.

Perhaps it was the swan in his rucksack or perhaps it was the memory of the killer but the feeling of another presence grew as Toby and Alfred hurried along the track, Toby clutching the unfixed cape at his throat to keep it from slipping from his shoulders. Fallen leaves hissed and scraped along the ground and a cold wind lightly touched his upper back and the nape of his neck, taking delight in running over his scalp and whispering to him that someone was watching. It made him check behind him a dozen times as he made his way beside that darkening wood.

The light had turned grainy and objects become indistinct in the dusk, and somewhere behind him a twig snapped. Toby spun. There, about twenty metres along the track, stood two deer. They were like statues. They stepped delicately down to the stream and drank. Toby had never seen deer close-up before like that. He shivered with the cold and was about to walk on when he saw a person.

It was the girl from Ranger Widgeon's house. He could hardly see her. Alfred had spotted her too, and miaowed. She didn't move.

'Hello, friend!' called Toby.

The girl did not respond but the two deer, startled by his voice, bounded up the slope and clattered into the wood. After they'd gone, the place felt empty and alone. Then, slowly, faintly, the girl came towards Toby. Her face was narrow and her nose bony and long. Her hair was pale. Not blonde or even white but simply pale. She didn't have any jacket or jumper and the neckline of her navy-blue dress stopped at her collarbone and he could see how skinny she was. The bottom edge of her dress was ripped and frayed and she was barefoot.

'Aren't your feet cold?' Toby said.

Perhaps her hair did have a colour, he decided – the colour of winter mist.

'I'm Toby,' he said when she didn't answer. He wondered if she'd been in some kind of accident, and was suffering from shock. She seemed dazed. 'What's your name?'

'I'm lost,' she said. Except she didn't say it, she breathed it so softly that Toby thought she'd said her name and he'd misheard it, and he asked her to say it again.

'I'm lost,' she breathed.

'I'm lost too,' said Toby. 'I'm going to the police. I saw a –' He decided not to tell her about the murder. 'The police can get us home. And if I can't get the police then I'll go to the Regent in the city.' Something flickered in the girl's eyes at the mention of the Regent. 'He owns all this estate,' Toby went on. 'Where do you live?'

She stared at him.

Toby sighed. 'Were you in the fire?' She didn't answer, so he continued. 'I was in the fire. I live over there with Alfred. This is my cat.' Alfred slinked round her bare shin, and miaowed. The girl's eyes focused and she crouched and gently extended a pale, thin finger and, equally gently, Alfred extended his head and sniffed. 'Oh, he likes you. Well, Alfred doesn't actually belong to me. He doesn't live with me, either. He used to, before we moved. He's Mrs Papadopoulos's cat, only she's stayed in London and we moved because Mum wants a divorce. Mrs Papadopoulos can't stay in the house because we're selling it and anyway, Dad doesn't like her. Dad stayed in London. He works for the government.'

The girl's eyes moved to Toby's face, and something flickered in her eyes again. She straightened, holding Alfred.

'What's your name, then?' said Toby.

'I don't know,' she breathed.

'Why not?'

She looked blankly at him.

'Are you a refugee, then? One of these shlegs the ranger was talking about. He said they're pale. You're pale. You're so pale you're hardly there. Aren't your feet cold? And you haven't got a coat. Here, do you want to put this round you, it's some sort of blanket.'

Toby knelt and untied the roll of material from the base of the rucksack. It was a waxed leather, fur-lined sleeping bag with a hood. 'Well, there's no zip but maybe you could wear it round your shoulders anyway.'

He handed her the sleeping bag. Alfred was purring happily.

'You have to have a name. If you don't know it, you can make one up if you like.'

'I'm lost,' she breathed, and searched his eyes with hers, and a trace of feeling seemed to be there – helplessness and confusion.

He took the sleeping bag from her limp hand and draped it round her shoulders. 'You keep hold of Alfred. He's annoying, he keeps running off.'

Toby felt much more cheerful now, and the feeling of fear had gone. So the pair set off into the failing light.

*

They left the wood behind and without the trees' protection the wind was harsher. It slid beneath the cape which Toby clutched tighter at his throat and it penetrated his limbs and they ached. Darkness fell and it became difficult to see the track. There were potholes, and he kept stepping in them and jarring his knees, so he walked more carefully, scared of turning his ankle, because he knew that if he injured himself he would be stuck on the mountain. The girl would not be much help, he reckoned. She did not walk beside him but a little behind, following him as if he was her mother or father, when she was older than him. She seemed to think he knew what he was doing. Yet in spite of her reliance on him, she wasn't having the problems with the surface of the road that Toby was – Toby stumbled while she seemed to float along serenely, cradling Alfred in her arms.

When he walked off the track for the second time and fell into a ditch, he'd had enough.

'Listen,' he began. He didn't know what to call her because she didn't have a name. 'I'm sick of leading the way,' he said. 'You do it for a change.'

He couldn't see her expression but he could tell from her stillness she was staring blankly at him. She floated away into the darkness, but not along the track.

'Where are you going?'

He was already losing her, her navy-blue dress and the sleeping bag round her shoulders blending with the dark. He could just make out her pale calves moving over the ground.

'Hey!' The ground was boggy and he squelched. 'Come back! The track's over here.'

He couldn't see her any longer.

'You've got Alfred. You've got my cat!'

A faint gleam made him adjust his direction. He hurried but one shoe sank ankle-deep in mud. He pulled his foot out and took another step, which went even deeper, but rather than retreat he decided to go on, trying to run across the sucking ground before it could snatch him. But by running, the stronger downwards force of his steps only drove him deeper into the mud and in less than ten seconds he was sunk up to his knees. He could not lift either leg. He was stuck in a bog.

'Help!' he called. He could just see her, floating across the bog as if she knew a secret path. 'Help!'

When he strained to lift one leg, he lost balance and fell forwards. His hands sank in the mud. Standing up straight, his cape slipping from his shoulders, he swung his arms and struck a post. Grabbing it, heaving, terrified he was going to die, sweating with the effort, he pulled one foot out with a smacking sound, leaving behind a school shoe. Now, wrapping his shoeless foot behind the post, he got more leverage and the other leg came out, eventually. He leaned over and grabbed the cape. His school shoe had been swallowed by the bog. The ground on the other side of the post was firmer, and he limped across the grass. He could see the pale shape of the girl. He walked tentatively, testing the ground the whole way. The girl and Alfred were waiting for him outside a stone hut.

The girl opened the door and went in. Toby hobbled after her.

Batting through a thick curtain that hung inside the door, he entered a cold, dark dry-smelling place. He turned on his mobile-phone torch. There were four single beds with no mattresses or bedding, a wooden table and chairs, a fireplace with two wooden easy chairs before it, and a chest of drawers. Stacked against the back wall were logs and kindling. Toby investigated. The fire was swept. Beside it were cooking implements and saucepans but no matches. The chest of drawers held cutlery, cups, crockery, and in the bottom, blankets. In the table another drawer contained candles and candle-holders and a small wooden box. Hoping for matches, he found needles and reels of thread. Turning back to the fireplace he had to manoeuvre around the girl who, annoyingly, insisted on following him. He scanned the walls with his light. On a recessed ledge was a tin in which he discovered flints and tapers. With the girl kneeling beside him at the fireplace, the tapers spread in her hand like cards, Toby cracked the stones together, firing sparks at the papery card. All Toby's will was narrowed to that single point, wishing for a spark to catch. One landed and the taper smouldered but it didn't flame. Toby struck the flints again. The wind whispered on the outer walls.

Flame.

It rose quickly, yellow and bright, and Toby snatched a candle and lit it, then another, and fixed them in the candle holders. Next, he built a fire, ferrying kindling and logs. The girl didn't help. She was like his shadow, and about as useless, Toby thought to himself.

'Help me, then!' he finally said, annoyed, and she unhelpfully lifted a few bits of kindling between finger and thumb like they were something she didn't want to touch.

He showed her how to make a fire, which his mum had taught him when they went on a camping holiday once. The kindling was dry and lit immediately, and they watched the fire grow, the dry logs catching light quickly too. When he was sure it was burning well, he moved the easy chairs and they brought the table nearer to the fire. He took out the packages of food and the flask and corked earthenware bottle and brought plates and cups. His trousers were soaked below the knee and his feet were numb. He was angry with himself about his lost shoe. He didn't know what to do about that. He wrapped a blanket round his waist and took off his wet trousers and socks and hung them on the back of an easy chair by the fire. The girl watched him do all this. She watched him eat, too. He even had to tell her to eat. She didn't seem to have much appetite. The corked earthenware bottle contained a delicious hot broth. And so with the broth warming their insides and the fire warming their outsides, and the cold wind licking at the door as if it wanted to come in and have some of their food, they had their meal.

Afterwards, Toby took an easy chair and sat before the fire. He stretched out his bare feet to warm them. His socks and trousers were still wet. The girl remained at the table.

'Aren't you cold in just your dress?'

'I'm always cold.'

She didn't say anything else.

'So how did you know this hut was here?'

'I don't know.'

'You must have lost your memory. You're from round here. Or you've been here before.'

She wasn't going to respond to this either, Toby realised. She didn't speak much. 'Do you have parents?'

Something flickered in her face – a memory? – but like the tapers with the flint-sparks, the memory didn't catch. Toby sighed. She was hard work. He was too tired to try talking with her any more. He wanted to be home suddenly. In Arnold Street with his mum. He tried his phone again. No signal and the battery was dying. He turned it off. Mum would be worried. She was having a hard-enough time as it was. She probably thought he'd run away, especially after that fight they'd had. He had cut her hand. He couldn't believe he'd done that. It was an accident, but she had been upset. The fire danced, and he felt tears rise. Maybe she'd phone Dad and he would come and search for him. Yes, that's what would happen. Dad and the police would search for Toby. They'd be waiting for him at the bottom of the mountain. He just had to get off the mountain. Tomorrow.

He hummed the song 'Tomorrow' from *Annie* and looked about.

'What do you think it is, a shepherd's hut? Or for travellers maybe? It doesn't seem to be anyone's home.'

She didn't answer.

His cape lay on one bed. He needed to repair it so he didn't have to keep holding it at the throat.

Retrieving the box of needles and threads from the table drawer, he chose the strongest twine. Then he searched for something to use as a clasp. There was nothing in the chest of drawers and he checked once more in the table drawer, right to the back. Nothing there either. He pushed the drawer shut. It had a flat circular knob. That would be just the right size. He twisted it like a door-knob. There was resistance but he twisted harder and it turned. It was fixed by a screw and he spun it free. Now he had his button.

The cape had been fixed at the throat by a hook on the back of the original swan-clasp but Toby was going to make a button. Using a table-knife, he cut a hole in the hem of the cape at the top, just big enough for the drawer-knob to slip through if he turned it sideways. Then with that same knife he set about gouging out four small hollows at the centre of the drawer-knob, which he pierced with the sturdiest needle. With the four holes pierced in the middle of the knob, he sewed it to the top of the cape with a length of twine. He put on the cape. The knob, now a big wooden button, fit through the slit he'd cut. He smiled triumphantly at the girl, who had been watching him the whole time.

'That's clever,' she said.

'Mrs Papadopoulos taught me. I like fixing things.'

After some seconds, as if it took that long to process any information, she nodded. She turned to the fire, and Toby looked too. Gradually, he grew drowsy. He yawned.

'I'm going to bed,' he said, taking blankets from the chest of drawers. 'You have the sleeping bag. It looks well cosy.' He made a blanket-mattress on one of the beds nearest the fire and, turning to say good night, found the girl standing right beside him. He started.

'You gave me a fright,' he said.

She was holding out the sleeping bag.

'You'll need it,' said Toby. 'It's cold.'

She kept holding it out.

'All right, then,' he shrugged, taking it.

The sleeping bag was fur-lined and deliciously warm. The girl had returned to her chair. Shadows of the fire moved across her face. Her eyes shone in the light.

'We'll be able to find where you're from tomorrow,' he said kindly.

She gave him a hopeless glance, then a sad smile, and he felt bad for her. Alfred seemed to feel the same – he leapt into her lap and curled there. Absently, she stroked him. Toby decided that he could trust her.

'Listen,' he said, 'we will find the police tomorrow. We have to. You see, I saw a murder.'

She seemed to be waiting for him to go on. So he told her everything that had happened to him. It surprised

102

him, but as soon as he started speaking he couldn't stop. The words came pouring out like water over a weir, a jumble he couldn't control, until he came to the part about the murder. Here he stopped. In a quiet voice, he told the nameless girl how that tall, thin man with the cruel mouth had knifed the teenage boy, and how the one with the shaved head had pushed him off the cliff before he fell to his own death. That's what Toby kept saying: 'They just pushed him off the cliff.' After repeating it several times, he fell silent.

'They wore these badges with white swans on them,' he added.

The girl was still. But it was no longer the blank stillness of earlier, when she'd barely seemed able to understand what he was saying, but as if she had been seized by a terrible memory or received shocking news.

'Are you all right?' said Toby. She didn't answer. The firelight played across her face. She seemed to jump in and out of shadows, to dissolve into them and reappear, and before he could get out of bed and find the clasp with the swan to show her exactly what he meant, he felt overcome with tiredness. His eyelids kept closing. Finally his gaze settled on his one shoe propped before the fire, and he thought he should really go out and try to retrieve the other one but he only managed to murmur, 'I need my shoe,' before he fell asleep.

Possibly the cold woke him – the fire had burned

down – or possibly a noise. From the warm glow of the embers he could see the girl was not there, although she had made up another bed and the blankets were scattered; she must have stepped outside. On the floor by his bed something bright was lying on the floor and he could just reach it if he leaned out but when he touched it, he touched bare floorboards, and he saw that it was a moonbeam, shining through the window. He knew he should get up to check if the girl was all right, and in fact pushed himself up to do this, but he was so tired his eyes closed before he could get out of the sleeping bag and he fell back, asleep instantly.

Shadow

The shadow leaned over the boy wanting to destroy something but discovered it was not him she wanted to destroy. She left a splinter of moon on the floor and slipped up the chimney, rising like a wisp of smoke and crying into the night like an ember of fire ascending on an updraft. Higher than smoke, higher than the smoke-polluted clouds (smoke from the forest fires poisoning bats by night and birds by day). But she could not rid herself of the poison of her hate. She felt it in her veins. She flew away from the mountains, away, away. She fled.

She remembered now. She remembered the murdered boy, how he had woven words together like threads in a lovely fabric. He had been knifed, and dropped from the mountain as if he were a pebble. No, less than a pebble. A pebble is precious. He had been treated as if he had no value, as if he were dirt, as if he were smoke from a fire.

The shadow felt now not hate but sorrow; a sorrow that flowed like a song or a river through her, in her, and she was the flowing, the feeling leading to somewhere she did not know through the freezing sky where the stars seemed shrivelled by cold and the moon in need of a fleece-lined cape. She came to a region so cold that even she, the shadow whose body detected no heat, felt the soreness of the cold, felt the intrusive ache in what passed for her body – she who had no body, was a shadow. On, on, she went, hurting herself with the cold, because the cold and the hurt matched the pain she felt over the death of her friend. She cried with the pain of the cold. She cried like a one-year-old cries when winter air touches its sensitive, brand-new skin, wanting only to be let in to the warmth. She cried like this but she could not be let in to the warmth. There was no warmth, no parent, no friend, there was only the cold.

Cormorants cried far below and she dived. She dropped as her friend had dropped, a dead weight, a bag of flour or a bag of sugar let go from the top of a tower, only she was not made of flour grains or sugar crystals but bits of darkness. Yet she had a weight. A shadow with a body, an insubstantial substance. She fell through the clouds. She saw the grey and heaving sea, its white waves. She struck the water like a blacksmith's hammer strikes the anvil. Her brains would have been splattered like a bag of milk hitting the floor if she had been a human being but she was not a human being, she was a shadow, and she dispersed into a billion particles of darkness.

She passed into the water, the salt, the murk, where eels snaked and porpoises slept and seaweed drifted, the giant refrigerator of the ocean in a cold season at a cold hour. Slowly, without will, she felt herself form once again into a near-human shape, disappointed, empty, more a miasma than a form, drifting, nothing:

'Call me nothing,' she said to herself. 'Call me nobody; call me lost.'

Visited by a curious seal, whiskered and warm in the wintry deep, she gazed blankly at its black eyes that gazed back at her.

And what wouldn't she have given then for warmth, for comfort?

CHAPTER
7

The Sea

Toby drifted upwards from the depths of sleep and lay toasty, confident he was back in Arnold Street. But the wall that he usually slept against was on the wrong side and he wondered if somehow he'd shifted right round during the night so his head was at the foot of the bed. Then he opened his eyes and, rather than the roofs on the other side of Arnold Street, he saw a small recessed window in a thick stone wall, showing a milky-blue sky. He sat up with a jolt.

The girl was gone. So was Alfred. He slithered out of the fur-lined sleeping bag and dressed. His clothes were dry. He found – impossibly – not one but two school shoes in front of the fire. The one he'd lost in the bog was filthy. He put them on and rushed out.

The girl stood a short distance away. She turned to him but Toby was already hunting for Alfred. There sat the white cat, on a tussock. Toby felt a wave of relief.

They were in the middle of moorland and the track lay fifty metres away. The mountains stood at a great distance, their stony peaks pink where the morning sun hit them. The range ran from north to south and the unforested mountains to the north, untouched by fire, were green and brown. They appeared almost like giants' bodies, their rocks like bones beneath flesh and their grass and moss and bracken like skin or clothing. The nearest mountains, and those further south, were forested and black, scorched by fire, and some still released smoke, which blew eastwards, away from them. Toby saw that this wind direction meant Ranger Widgeon's house might have been saved. That was good news; what was not good news was that Toby could not recall any mountain range in the part of the country where he lived.

'I remembered my name,' said the girl.

It was strange how faint she was. It was even more obvious in daylight.

'So what is it?' He had to ask because she wasn't going to say.

'Tamurlaine.'

'Tamurlaine,' repeated Toby, getting used to it. 'D'you remember anything more?'

She shook her head.

'You must have had some sort of shock, that's why you can't remember. Thanks for finding my shoe, by the way.'

Again she didn't respond, and Toby wondered whether it would be rude to mention her faintness. He decided that it would be, and went in to have some breakfast.

They had their first disagreement while they were readying to leave. Toby had been taught by his mum always to clean up after himself and leave a place as tidy as he found it but Tamurlaine left her chair pulled out and crumbs on the table and her blankets in a mess on her bed.

'We've got to clear up first,' he told her as she flowed towards the door. 'We're guests.'

She ignored him but Toby decided he wasn't going to do Tamurlaine's work and followed her out. She was crouching to play with Alfred, and he said in a sarcastic tone, 'I'm sorry, Princess, is that too much effort for you?'

Tamurlaine jumped up, eyes flashing. 'Don't *ever* call me that.'

Startled, Toby didn't know what to do. She turned on her heel and walked over to a bank of heather, where she sat.

'Idiot,' muttered Toby, and went inside to clear up.

*

'I remembered something else,' said Tamurlaine after

they had been walking in silence for nearly an hour. The track took a wobbling line over high moorland. Little birds kept starting up from the heather. Alfred trotted along happily beside Tamurlaine. Toby waited for her to elaborate but, as seemed to be her habit, she didn't say anything more.

'Oh yeah?' said Toby, still annoyed about her not clearing up.

'The boy,' she said in her breathy voice, 'the one they killed – I knew him.'

Toby halted mid-stride, shocked. Tamurlaine kept going and Toby noticed again how she hardly seemed to touch the ground as she walked.

'Who is he?' he asked, catching her up.

'His name was Kerten. He was a friend of mine.'

'How'd you know him? Did you go to school with him?'

'He was a friend, that's all I know. And I know because I feel it. It makes me want to cry when I think of him.'

He didn't know what to do or say.

'Then he must be a good friend,' said Toby eventually, feeling both sad for her and a little envious of her having a friend and also wondering what such a friendship would be like. 'I tell you this,' Toby went on, 'as soon as we get off this mountain, I'm calling the police. And they'll find that man with the knife and he'll be sent to prison.' Tamurlaine seemed doubtful. 'They will. I promise. My dad will make sure of it. He works for a government minister. My dad's powerful. He's got what we call "reach". My dad can make a phone call and just like that' – Toby snapped his fingers – 'people will jump. I tell you, my dad's –'

'This isn't a children's game, Toby.'

Toby blushed. They walked on silently. This is what people always said about him, that he was a child. A stupid kid. The wind blew in their faces, bringing a soft, constant roar from somewhere ahead. Toby listened to it and wondered when he would ever meet someone who would tell him that he got something right.

The roar grew louder. 'Can you hear it?' Toby said. 'I think it's a motorway.' He marched past Tamurlaine and soon they reached the edge of the moor. Below lay the source of the noise. It was not a motorway. It was the sea.

There was no sea near the town to which Toby and his mum had moved and Toby knew this for sure – he had studied the map. So in a moment all the explanations that Toby had given himself for everything he had encountered since he walked up Angel Lane were demolished and he was left with reality. Toby, usually a great fan of reality, was not, at that moment, particularly keen on it.

The sea, under the blue sky, was a dark denim-blue. The coastline was dunes and sandy beaches that stretched north and south, broken every half mile or so by rocky headlands. Much further to the north, the mountain range from which they had walked curled round to meet the sea. To the south, the beaches extended for about ten miles before they were lost in a haze. Directly below, a band of fields several miles wide separated the moorland from the coast. A silver road ran south through these fields.

Tamurlaine and Alfred started downhill but Toby could not move. The world he knew had been swept away and replaced by another one. He was alone in this new, unfamiliar land and had no certainty about finding his way home. In a panic, he hunted for his mobile. He emptied his rucksack, searched his pockets, making little moaning sounds, his fingers not working like he wanted them to. He was trying not to cry. He had it. The comforting plastic. He pressed the wrong buttons repeatedly. 'Please, please,' he begged. He found his dad's number. His dad's number did not work. Nor his mum's. No number worked. He tried every number in his contacts list. 'Please.' There was no signal. He was still beyond range.

His chest constricted and he couldn't breathe properly. He was going to die. How could he get home? He had to get home.

Tamurlaine and Alfred were a long way down the slope. He had to hurry or he'd lose them too.

He forced himself to take deep breaths. *Think practically*, he told himself. *Think practically*. How could

114

he get home? The best plan was to do what Ranger Widgeon suggested, and find the Regent. The Regent would get him home. Yes.

Toby dropped to the ground and, with shaking hands, gathered his things together and stuffed them in his rucksack then ran after Tamurlaine and Alfred.

The track zig-zagged down from the heights and it took more than an hour to get to the fields. They saw no people and no farmhouses. It seemed an isolated or even an abandoned region. Crops had been left to wither and die. Yet Tamurlaine seemed more cheerful, her chin rising and her shoulders thrown back and her arms swinging. She halted when their track met the road.

'We'll go this way,' she said finally, pointing at a path that led off through the grass.

'But the road goes this way. Ranger Widgeon said take the road to the city. I have to see the Regent.'

'There'll be more of those men with the sign of the swan. They'll be watching for you.'

And so saying, she flowed off the track and onto the grass. Alfred followed.

'Alf-red!' scolded Toby. He considered the road – really just a wider, more assured version of the track – then Tamurlaine and his cat. If he was no longer in his own world then different rules might apply and the tall, thin killer with the cruel mouth who wore the sign of the swan might not be working independently but have lots of friends. Perhaps there was a gang. The Swan Gang. He dashed after Tamurlaine.

It took them an hour to reach the sea and they met no one, only a few goats who seemed as stunned to see Toby as he was to see them. Then they walked over a dune and there it was.

The surf was big, crashing on the shore in flashing white, and Tamurlaine yelled in delight and pelted towards it, running into the water and away. Now she stood in the shallows, lifting the hem of her dress and enjoying the sea washing round her calves, her heels sinking into the wet sand.

Toby sat and drank from his flask – there was not much water left – and poured a cup for Alfred, who lapped. The cat looked up, alerted by something. At one end of the beach was a bunch of horned sheep eating kelp and at the other end a flock of oystercatchers doing the same but also going into the water, catching oysters, both groups moving towards the middle where presumably they would meet to talk about oysters and kelp. Toby remembered going to the sea with his mum, and felt a rising sadness.

Tamurlaine ran back, grinning at him.

'Do you want to come in?' she asked.

'No,' he said, turning his face away so she wouldn't see the tears in his eyes. Wanting desperately to talk about something else so she wouldn't notice, he said the first thing that came into his head: 'Those mountains look like people.'

Tamurlaine whirled. She put her hands on her hips and looked north to the mountains that seemed to grow directly from the sea.

'You know what?' she said. 'I think I grew up here.'

'On this beach?'

'No, but I know those mountains. That one,' she said, pointing, 'I always thought looked like an old man. And that one like an old woman. And there is a young woman. They're like members of my family.'

'Then we're getting closer to your home.'

'My father used to make up stories about them,' she said, so quietly he had to strain to hear. She spun on Toby and announced in a loud voice, 'I grew up nearby.'

'There's no towns or villages to the north that I can see. So perhaps we'll find your house on the way to the city.'

Tamurlaine peered south, the wind blowing her hair about, and she had a sort of joyful-hopeful expression which only made Toby feel worse. She'd found her home while Toby was further away than ever. He turned to Alfred and stroked him but Alfred had no wish to be stroked and moved out of reach and kept an eye on the kelp-eating sheep. Toby pulled his knees to his chin, wrapped his arms round them and watched grey gannets drop into the sea like stones. A red sail came past the headland.

Toby leapt to his feet and ran down to the shore, waving his arms. 'Help! Help! Hi! Hi!'

Tamurlaine joined him but the boat was moving out to sea and the wind was blowing towards them so their voices did not carry. They watched the red sail for several minutes. Further out, a long way, nearly at the horizon, Toby could see another boat. Or perhaps not a boat, it was too square-shaped for that. It was a rig of some kind.

'Is that an oil rig, do you think?'

'No,' murmured Tamurlaine. 'They're fixing holes.'

'Holes in the sea? I never heard of that before.'

'There are holes everywhere,' said Tamurlaine, speaking slowly, as if the information was only now coming back to her and was difficult to retain, like holding smoke. 'That's how you got here. I think I got lost going through a hole, too, into your world. I remember ...' Her voice trailed off.

'What do you remember?' said Toby, hoping for something, some memory, some bit of information that might get him home.

'No, it's no good,' she said, shaking her head. 'I don't remember any more.'

'But you must do. How did you get from here to my world? Is it the same hole I came through?'

'I don't remember.'

'But you must!' said Toby crossly.

She met his eye with a hint of that same ferocity he'd seen when he called her princess.

The boat was a long distance away by this time and they watched it in silence until it was out of sight, then trudged back up the beach to Alfred and the rucksack. They had only a little food left and Ranger Widgeon had said they would not reach the city until the following day, so while Alfred sat suspiciously watching the sheep they ate a small amount of their provisions and wrapped the remainder for an evening meal.

The horned sheep and oystercatchers did finally meet in the middle of the beach. The horned sheep tore at the kelp, popping bubbles until one oystercatcher flew too close and a ram whipped round and snatched the bird in its jaws. The other oystercatchers flew away, whistling in fear, while the caught bird flapped helplessly. Its bones crunched in the ram's jaws. The ram gulped the oystercatcher down casually then returned to eating kelp. The other sheep noisily licked the blood from the seaweed and sand.

'But sheep aren't predators,' said Toby. 'And they don't eat meat.'

'They do here,' said Tamurlaine.

The sheep were plodding up the beach towards them, docile and woolly.

'Let's go,' said Toby, shoving the remaining food in the rucksack while Alfred stood guard, head lowered, back arched, ready to defend them. The three of them ran along the beach before the sheep could add them to their lunch.

*

Now night drew near and the world grew cold and Toby was glad of his fleece-lined cape. He was weary, hungry and thirsty; the water was finished, and Alfred felt heavy in his rucksack. The cat had suddenly, mid-afternoon, refused to walk another step, and demanded to be carried. Toby didn't like to ask Tamurlaine how much further it was – he didn't want to sound like a little kid. She, on the other hand, hardly seemed fatigued but floated over the sand on her bare feet and hopped over the jagged rocks that formed each headland and waited on their far sides for Toby, who clambered heavily over them, puffing and perspiring. The sun sank beneath the horizon and dusk deepened. Perhaps it was the darkness that made it visible, or perhaps it was only at dusk that it was turned on, but far, far in the distance – it was impossible to say how many miles – a tiny orange light twinkled.

'What is it?' said Toby. 'The city?'

'The castle,' said Tamurlaine, and her voice was different – less breathy, colder, and hard.

'What castle?'

'There's only one castle here.'

Toby peered. In the gloom was a long bank of darkness

that might be hills, and rising from behind the bank of hills and silhouetted against the last of daylight were what might be the crags of cliffs or possibly the roofs, chimneys, battlements, towers and spires of a castle. The castle jutted beyond the bank of hills and there the orange light twinkled, right over the sea.

'We'll camp here,' said Tamurlaine in that same cold, hard voice. 'We'll go no further tonight.'

Abruptly she walked off the beach and into the dunes.

Toby was irritated by her making decisions without asking him but glad they had finally stopped. He wanted to know more about the castle but was too tired and hungry to ask. His head ached, too, and he wished he had more water.

Tamurlaine refused her share of food so Toby put it aside for her for breakfast. She also refused the sleeping bag.

'But I've got the cape. It's only fair you have the sleeping bag. I had it last night.'

'I don't want it!' she snapped.

'All right, be like that,' he said. In a low mutter, he added, 'idiot.'

They sat in the darkness. The wind whispered in the dune grass, and the sea rumbled on the shore. Alfred squirmed in with Toby, and Toby pulled up the fur-lined hood. He was so tired he was already falling asleep when something thumped in the sand beside him and a hand gripped his shoulder.

'Toby,' whispered Tamurlaine in a desperate voice.

The pale oval of her face hovered above him.

'What's wrong?'

The wind whispered in her long hair making a dry rustle like the dune grass.

'You must not go to the Regent.'

'But he's my way back home. Ranger Widgeon said.'

'You can't go to the Regent. He's not to be trusted. He's dangerous.'

'Then how will I get home?'

'I don't know.'

'But who is he?'

'I don't remember. All I remember is that he's no good. No good at all.'

'Then what am I going to do?'

She didn't answer, only thumped away across the sand and sat heavily and wrapped her arms around her knees while Toby fell into sleep, taking the memory of that orange twinkling light into his dreams.

Shadow

The shadow remembered. She remembered all right. She ascended through currents of cold air, kept to the low clouds above dunes and slipped into the city over the long back of Whale Hill. But she kept her distance from the castle's twinkling window. From fear. She skirted it like a dog skirts the animal it's unsure of, that twinkling window where she'd been trapped and caught in the golden net that burned her shadow skin so it fell, peeling and flaking in long strips, from her body – Ai-ee!

She sifted the notes of a sad singer in a tenement on Whale Hill, listened to bathwater draining and gurgling in the drainpipes of a big house, wove the sturdy brick piers of Hogarth's Conduit, the aqueduct that carried the water from the reservoir and the gas from the gasholders into the castle, but when she reached the crags and battlements of the castle itself, she didn't try to get in, despite the fact there were plenty of openings (holes in the crumbling mortar and vents in the kitchen wall and missing window panes in disused wings). Instead she flipped back from the castle wall like a swimmer in the swimming pool at the end of her length and shot through the dark like a seal underwater and, angered by the castle or by her fear of the castle, knocked flowerpots off balconies, dropped down chimneys into apartments and kicked up the corners of rugs to trip grandmothers and poisoned lovers' dreams and made children terrified of next day's school. She lurked in Fredegund's Armpit, the old quarry where the people without homes gathered to drink and talk, bringing desolation into their thoughts. She rocketed down the smelly alley known as Chlothilde's Backside into Padraig's Common and here she flew circuits the way a dog with worms chases its own arse. She entered a disused temple through a bell tower and mixed doubt into the thoughts of scholars who secretly met to discuss the sacred Book of Dreams. Then, almost out of her mind in a whirl of feeling she did not understand, a self-hurting, self-hating, hideous frenzy, she descended upon the colonnades of Theatre Square where the wealthiest promenaded and sat outside by warm fires and the horse-cabs waited with nosebags, and she stampeded the horses so the animals overturned their own cabs, and she kicked dust into the eyes of dogs and sprayed the drinks of the rich with her bitterness, nipping the fingers of the children of the royal family who had come to see a pantomime, toppling burning candles onto restaurant tablecloths, and transforming all the people of Theatre Square into a panicked mob. Finally, both wanting and not wanting to enter it, she skirted the castle once more, found a balcony door open and floated into a ballroom. It was stacked with chairs and wooden trestle tables ahead of a banquet later in the week. She kicked a stack of chairs and *the tower wobbled. She kicked it again and it toppled like a tree in a forest, with a deep reverberating thud, and she raced about, kicking over the other towers. Then she fled. For she was afraid. And in that small office at the end of that dark castle, in the room more like a ship's cabin than an office, its plaster ceiling sagging lower than ever and almost turning it into a burrow for a beast – a heavy beast with sharp teeth – sat the tall thin man with the cruel mouth whose dead eyes, at the noise in the ballroom, twinkled with a strange life.*

CHAPTER 8

Jinky

The dawn air was cold on Toby's face, and his cheeks and nose were numb, but his body was cosy inside the fur-lined sleeping bag. Alfred curled like a warm scarf round his throat. The beach grass rustled. Beads of dew clung to their long blades. Their camp was out of the wind, in a hollow between dunes, but it did not offer much protection and Toby wondered how Tamurlaine, that strange girl, was not frozen. She wore only the navy-blue dress with its low neck and ragged hem. It seemed made of cotton – a thick cotton, but even so – and she was shoeless. She had not even used the fleece-lined cape, which lay flung off half-way between them, and she was turned away in the foetal position, her head pillowed on both hands.

Toby yawned and wriggled out of his sleeping bag. When he stood, he discovered he had a pounding headache. There was no water left – he tipped his flask upside-down and there was not a single drop. Climbing over the dune, he relieved himself, then walked down to the shore. Cloud was low and the wind strong, sea-spray blowing along the beach, hazing the coastline so he could not see the castle. But he knew it was there, waiting for him. How a castle could wait, Toby didn't know, but he felt it. It was not a pleasant feeling. First checking there were no killer sheep about, he washed in the cold surf – so deeply cold it made him gasp – then ran back shivering to their camp. Tamurlaine was awake. She was sat with her knees drawn up to her chin and her arms locked round them. Her dress was coated down one side with sand and when Toby sat to put his socks on, he felt the dampness of the ground spread through his trousers and realised how unpleasantly chilly Tamurlaine's night must have been, and was bewildered by her refusal of a cover.

'Why don't you wear the cape for a bit? Or get in the sleeping bag?'

She seemed to be staring at a point on the ground, a few feet in front of her.

'Are you all right? Tamurlaine?'

She didn't respond and Toby felt suddenly annoyed. He put on his socks and shoes, tied up the laces, and

rolled up his sleeping bag and tied it to his rucksack, his headache banging against his skull.

'Where's Alfred?'

Tamurlaine seemed not to hear him.

'Alfred?' he called. The cat was nowhere to be seen. 'Alfred?'

Toby hurried to the top of a dune. In a panic, he ran up and down all the dunes of the hollow, calling.

'Did you see where he went?'

Then Toby spotted him. He was tucked in Tamurlaine's lap. He ran down and gently lifted Alfred out of his cradle. Alfred, with his small sour mouth, bags under his jaundiced eyes, observed Toby with grumpy disinterest. With his patchy fur he still looked a state. 'You're just a rubbish Aslan, aren't you?' said Toby, putting Alfred down. With great pride and affronted dignity, Alfred sauntered off.

'Why didn't you tell me you had him?'

Tamurlaine didn't respond.

'What is wrong with you?' Toby said. 'Are you deliberately being stupid?'

She lifted her head slowly. 'I had an odd, vivid dream.' Her voice had that breathy quality she'd had when they first met. Something about this response so incensed Toby, he shouted at her. 'Well, I'm sorry to disturb you from your dreams, Princess, but I was worried about my cat.'

'I told you never to call me that.'

'Well, I'm tired of being everybody's last thought. I'm tired of you making decisions without consulting me – taking that path to the sea, camping here. Taking my cat! I'm tired of everyone pushing me around. *Princess.*'

Tamurlaine sprang up and with a single firm thrust pushed him. Toby rocked on his heels, taking a step backwards to steady himself. She'd pushed him! Well, he'd show her. He shoved her so hard she dropped on her bottom with a bump and an expression of wide-eyed surprise.

'Ha!'

A deep growl came from Tamurlaine's chest and, scrambling to her feet, she charged him. Her shoulder hit him in the stomach and he fell on his back with her on top and all the air left his lungs. He couldn't breathe. He couldn't get up either. She was kneeling on his chest and her icy hands gripped his wrists. It wasn't just her hands that were icy; it was as if her body was made of ice. He twisted and flailed and she bared her teeth like an animal then he kneed her in the soft part of her back and she cried out and flung her arms up. Toby rolled sideways and got to his feet.

For a moment they faced each other before Toby marched over to his rucksack, scooped up Alfred and headed for the road.

He kept checking behind in case she tried to attack again, and soon he saw her. She was following him. He kept an eye on her as she travelled over the sand in that irritating, barely-touching-the-ground way of hers. After ten minutes of her silent, distant stalking, he stopped.

'What do you want?' he shouted, his voice hoarse from being winded.

She approached.

'Stop right there!'

She stopped.

'What do you want?'

'Well, you helped me get this far and I've a feeling you can help me find out where I'm from and who I am.'

'Well, I've got a feeling you're an annoying person.'

She didn't rise to this. Instead, she said, 'You've been in my dreams.'

'Oh,' said Toby, not expecting this.

'You've been guiding me in them.'

'Oh,' said Toby again, feeling quite pleased about this job that he had – even if it was in someone else's dream.

'Like I've been guiding you,' said Tamurlaine.

Toby frowned, perplexed.

'I found the hut for you to sleep,' Tamurlaine explained. 'And kept you off the road so you wouldn't get caught by those men with the swan.'

The business with the hut was true, Toby decided,

although he couldn't know for certain if their detour along the beach had helped him avoid the killer or the Swan Gang or whoever they were. He only had her word for that.

'I can guide you to the city,' said Tamurlaine.

'Well, it's pretty obvious. I just follow the road.'

'Yes. That's true. But I seem to be remembering more about this place and that could be useful to you.'

'That's true.'

'I think something happens to me when I dream. I've seen the city in my dreams, as well as you. Only now, the dreams seem to be getting more real, as if the dream world and real world are joining. Or something like that. I'm not sure.'

She looked at him helplessly and Toby felt a wave of pity for odd, lost, fierce, cold, faint, angry Tamurlaine. For a moment, he had the strangest thought that perhaps she was a dream herself, then dismissed the idea. He was distrustful of her, though. He chewed his lip. Then he decided.

'We'll go to the city together,' he said, and so they took to the road.

*

The mountains curled inland and in places their slopes descended to the road and Toby could see that the fires that had taken hold on the forested peaks during fire

132

season had swept down and spread across the fields. The harvest must have been lost. In fact, it wasn't only that year's crops that had burned. Vineyards that had taken decades to cultivate were wiped out and earth that had once grown potatoes, broccoli, maize, barley and wildflowers had turned to ash, its nutrients destroyed. Farmhouses lay abandoned, hedges razed. The people who farmed the land no longer had a livelihood, or hope of a future income. They had to leave their homes. It was a wasteland.

Toby, Tamurlaine and Alfred came to a stream. Here they drank, then filled the flask and washed out Ranger Widgeon's earthenware bottle that had contained the broth and filled that too. Toby was already hungry. Above them on the road at the top of a rise was a stand of charred trees and a scarecrow on a post. It wasn't a very good scarecrow as crows sat on the cross-piece and took it in turns to flap down and peck at the figure. A child sat on the bank below the scarecrow.

'There's someone there,' said Toby, pointing.

'It's a girl.'

They walked up. The girl was about nine or ten years old. She had skin the colour of paper, hair the colour of sunlight on glass, and eyes as staring and hollow as moon craters. She was filthy and cuddled a filthy doll. One arm ended in a dirty bandaged stump. She was missing a hand.

Toby tried not to look but the stump kept drawing his eyes back.

'Are you all right?' he said.

She looked at him blankly.

'Where's your parents?'

She didn't answer.

'I'm Toby. This is Tamurlaine.'

The girl's eyes didn't move from him.

'What's your name?'

'Jinky.'

'Do you want some water, Jinky?'

She drank the water, and burped.

'Where's your parents?'

She pointed and they turned. The limp scarecrow wore an outfit of old sacking spattered with bird droppings. The face was dark blue and hideously swollen and the hands had fingers like sausages. One crow was tugging at the tongue, which is when Toby realised it was not a scarecrow but a person – a dead person.

Jinky was talking. She must have been talking for some time, but Toby had been too stunned by the hanged person to hear.

'... and we was so hungry Dad said he'd get me some food then the Watch knock at the door and take me out and there's Dad and they're holding him and they say he's stolen someone's chickens and they takes us up here. "Be brave, little Jinky," he tells me, and they hangs him.'

Toby wondered if she was joking. They had killed her dad?

'Where's your mother?' said Tamurlaine.

Jinky pointed across the burned fields.

'What's over there, your house?'

'Graveyard.'

'She's dead?'

Jinky nodded.

'Is there anyone else?'

'Anyone else dead or anyone else alive?'

'Alive.'

'There was a woman what watched me when Dad went out to the fields. Mrs Maudlin.'

'Where's Mrs Maudlin?'

Jinky pointed up the road.

'How far?'

The girl shrugged.

'Where did she go, this Mrs Maudlin?'

'Why, the city, naturally. Have you got any food?'

'No.'

'We'll get you some,' said Toby, and Tamurlaine made a face at him like this was a bad idea. 'Do you know whereabouts in the city this woman is, Jinky?'

'Naturally.'

'Where?'

'Nine Fields Lane.'

'We'll take you there,' said Toby. He could feel Tamurlaine staring at him. 'What?'

She shrugged. 'We've got our own journey. People are searching for you. I'm trying to find home. Jinky's not our problem. Sorry, Jinky. No offence.'

'None taken.'

'We're not leaving her. Jinky, we're going to the city. Do you want to come with us and we can take you to Mrs Maudlin?'

'Dad says not to go with strangers.'

'That's good advice,' said Toby. 'But you can't stay here, can you?' They all glanced at Jinky's dead dad. 'We'll take you to Mrs Maudlin and you'll be safe with her.'

'Is that your cat?'

'Well, not strictly mine, it belongs to Mrs Papadopoulos, but he's in my care. His name's Alfred.'

'Can I hold him?'

'Yes.' He handed Alfred over and Jinky stood up and they set off.

'What happened to your arm?' asked Tamurlaine as they left the burned trees.

'They chopped it off,' said Jinky blithely.

'Who did?' said Toby.

'The Watch.'

'Who are the Watch?' asked Toby.

'The Order of the Swan.'

'And who,' said Toby, his mouth dry, his heart thumping slow and hard, 'are the Order of the Swan?'

'The law of the land. They work for the Regent.'

Tamurlaine raised an eyebrow at Toby as if to say, *See, I told you the Regent was no good*.

'Why did they cut off your hand?' asked Tamurlaine.

'For being daughter to a thief.'

What sort of world was this where people cut off the hand of a ten-year-old girl when their father stole to feed his starving family?

'I'll take you to Mrs Maudlin,' said Toby firmly.

Jinky said, in that matter-of-fact way of hers, 'But they cleaned the wound and bandaged me up afterwards.'

CHAPTER 9

At the City Gates

Coming from the north as they did, most of the city was hidden by the long back of Whale Hill. On its flat top tottered the city's cheapest and most dangerous housing. Buildings here frequently burned down or collapsed, killing the families who lived in them, and the steep grassy slope to the fields showed skid-marks where badly built brick, crumbly stone and cheap timber had slid down the hill. The collapses left gaps, like missing teeth in the crookedest and longest mouth in the world. This mouth smiled at them with its bad dentistry from several miles away.

'Nice place,' remarked Tamurlaine.

'It's not nice at all,' said Toby, then realised she was being sarcastic.

Their route skirted Whale Hill, passing several large country estates with mansions. Toby could see gardeners at work in the fancy gardens and wished he had a hat or scarf so he wouldn't be recognised, then they joined a large avenue, busy with people flowing towards the city. Entire households seemed to be on the move – families with small children and babies, elderly couples, large groups made up of cousins and aunts and uncles and grandparents, nearly all of them with luggage, and all of them weary. Toby watched for anyone wearing the symbol of the swan.

The houses on the avenue were big and looked like wedding cakes – white, with lots of columns – but the ones on the left had been flooded. Toby could see the river behind them. It had broken its banks and turned the gardens into large ponds where ducks and seagulls floated. The water had been higher. River weed covered plants and low branches and the high-water mark was visible on the houses. They were filthy below the ground-floor windows and clean above it. A lot of the houses were empty, their doors and windows boarded. The ground sloped gently up to the road, which the flood had not reached, and the houses on the right side of the road were pristine, with flower baskets on their porches, and chimneys smoking, and here and there a finely dressed person watching from a window the crowds tramping towards the city. When Toby sensed that he was being observed by one of these rich folk he had to resist the temptation to duck his head or shield his face; he knew if he did it would only draw more attention. Each house had tall railings, and each had at least one guard, and Toby saw an old woman, who wore a square fur hat with big ear-flaps, go up to a gate and put her hand through for money. The guard shouted at her and she rejoined the stream of people.

'These people have got the money to help but they don't,' said Tamurlaine. 'I'd chop *their* hands off.'

The avenue ended at a crossing and after that it became an unbroken, narrow road between tall townhouses and shops. It was like being in a ravine. Or a trap. The buildings grew dirtier, the windows dustier. On the pavements of this neighbourhood, the people seemed tired, their clothes drab, and they ignored the travellers as if they were used to seeing them.

'Tch!' said Tamurlaine, nodding at a notice in a shop window. NO SHLEGS, it told customers. Further on, Toby saw a similar notice on the door of a dingy hotel: SHLEGS NOT WELCOME.

'What's a shleg?' asked Toby, remembering Ranger Widgeon's mention of 'dirty shlegs'.

'Me,' said Jinky blandly.

Toby looked at her, confused. 'But what's that?'

'The people who were here before Colin.'

'Colin? Who on earth is Colin?'

140

'I don't know. I haven't met him. Dad said Colin and his friends are cruel bullies. Calling us names like shleg and scum. Kicking us in the legs. Making laws about what jobs we do.'

'Colin and his friends did all this?'

'Colin Ists, yes.'

'Colin Ists?'

'I think she means colonists,' said Tamurlaine.

'Oh, I see,' said Toby, the meaning dawning on him. 'Where did they come from, these colonists?'

'The sky,' said Jinky.

'Really, Jinky?' said Toby, doubting this very much.

'That's what Dad says. One day it was just us shlegs, then this city arrived.'

Toby decided to humour her. 'Did this happen recently, Jinky?'

'No, in the long ago. Most of these people going to the city with us are shlegs. They don't like us in the city so most of us worked in the countryside and forests and the mines in the mountains. That's what Dad tells me.'

Toby looked more closely at the people around him heading towards the city. Many of them had a similar tall, skinny build to Jinky, and the same white hair and anaemically white skin.

'Where are they going?'

'Come to get help from the Regent after the fires and floods.'

'Ha!' laughed Tamurlaine bitterly. It seemed the more she remembered, the more bitter she became.

The ravine-like road emerged onto open ground and Toby felt a sense of release. Ahead, across a broad ditch, lay the fortified city. The road ran on an embankment across the ditch and pierced the city walls at a gateway. A large crowd of people queued at the gates, the line reaching back almost to the buildings. On the open ground, the refugees had set up camp with whatever they had brought with them or could find – makeshift tents of old posts and bedsheets and blankets, lean-tos with columns of bricks that held corrugated-iron roofs. Campfires burned here and there.

They joined the back of the queue.

'Excuse me, sir,' said Toby, tapping the shoulder of the man in front. 'Do you know how long we have to wait?'

'There's a checkpoint,' said the man absently, peering ahead. 'You need papers.' He studied each of them, and made a face when he came to Jinky. '*She* won't get in.'

It was the way he said '*she*' that was so horrible, as if even mentioning Jinky was disgusting, but Jinky herself appeared not to mind, only shifted her doll under one arm and regarded the man with her usual bland expression. But Alfred, tucked in the crook of Jinky's other arm, bared his sharp pointed teeth at the fellow.

'You vile little man,' said Tamurlaine, and lunged to hit him.

Toby blocked her way.

'You keep that girl in check, boy,' the man snapped, eyeing Tamurlaine with a sneer as if he hoped she would attack him because then he'd have an excuse to punch her.

'Why you – !'

'Tam!' said Toby, shoving her off the road. 'We'll be noticed!'

Tamurlaine spun away and wrapped her arms round herself as if this was the only way to restrain her anger. 'All right, all right!'

'What are we going to do? We don't even know where we're going once we've found Mrs Maudlin.'

Tamurlaine stalked around desperately.

'Right, you pair wait here,' she said finally. 'I'll go and see what we need to get in.'

'We can all go,' said Toby.

'No. They might be watching for you. And as for Jinky – well, they won't let her in. She'll have to wait here.'

Tamurlaine was about to go then her face changed. She'd seen something. Beyond the city walls, perhaps a mile away, the low cloud had blown away, and there rose the castle.

It was as if a baby giant had been asked to construct a castle out of bits of junk from a demolished giant's house and not really thought about it but forced the bits together so hard everything broke, and when that happened he had banged in nails with a hammer to nail it together, and when that didn't work had used a stapler to staple it, and when that had failed used glue, and when that failed, tied it together with wire. The building seemed to be trying to escape these fixings either sideways or upwards. It had a lot of pinnacles, turrets, towers, chimneys, toilet down-pipes with air vents at the top to carry away the smells of toilets, also curved vents like ship-funnels or birds' beaks, a water-tower that squatted like a sumo-wrestler, lots of weeds and even some trees, a windmill of dirty sails, turning swiftly, and a weathervane in the shape of a gold swan spinning as if it didn't know which way to go. Oh, and it also had a great glass dome in the middle of it, like a boil.

A body gives an involuntary gasp when plunging into icy water – and what Tamurlaine's soul experienced when she saw the castle was like that – a sudden plunge into icy spiritual waters. She gasped. When she recovered, her eyes darted from side to side as panic rose in her. Toby noticed all this, and recognised it. He had felt it nearly every time he saw the classrooms when he arrived at school each morning, so he put his hand on Tamurlaine's wrist and, as had happened when she gripped *his* wrists on the beach during their fight, he was shocked by her coldness.

'It's all right, Tam,' he said. 'It's all right.'

She locked eyes with his, almost pleading with him,

as if he could release her from her fear. And while he couldn't release her, he could help her a little, just by being there. Gradually, her panic subsided. She felt her breath grow deeper and slower. The panic now was controllable and she gave a curt nod and snatched her hand away, almost angry that he had seen her weak like this, and once more she fixed her gaze on the castle, then she left them. Toby watched as she moved up the queue and over the broad ditch until she was lost among the crowd swelling before the gates.

'Don't!' said Jinky.

Alfred was trying to jump from her arm.

'Ah!' said Toby, taking the cat. 'He's smelled food.'

They could smell it too and tracked it down to a makeshift stall. Chicken and peppers sizzled on a grill. People were gathered round, hungrily watching a little old woman stirring a pan. They were prevented from helping themselves by a big man who stood before her stall with thick, folded forearms.

'Can I have some?' whispered Jinky.

'Haven't got the money, Jinky. Not that they would accept. I'm sorry.'

Above the city walls, in the distance, a motion caught his eye. At first he thought it was a large bird. Then, a drone or small helicopter. But it wasn't that. Over the castle, a blond teenage boy hovered beneath what Toby took to be a hang-glider, its wings billowing round his shoulders

145

and flowing out behind him. He carried a gleaming gold net that was bright in the dull day, and he held steady like a seagull riding the thermals. He slid sideways and down and ascended again and took up a new position, searching the ground below. He was above the city walls but further along. Perhaps there was another gate there.

'It's a Dreamer,' said Jinky.

There was a loud *bang*, like someone popping a balloon right next to Toby's ear, and he jumped. Jinky opened her mouth in a silent scream. Alfred leapt from his arms. Toby stuck out a hand and grabbed a handful of fur and flesh and Alfred bit him with small, sharp teeth. White embers, grill, chicken and peppers were flying through the air, along with people's hats, scarves, shawls, the torn pages of a book, a nappy, and the little old cook, holding her wooden spoon. The big man with the big forearms staggered. Toby found himself lying on the dusty ground ten yards away, Alfred tight in his hands. People were treading on him. He began to rise but a knee struck him and sent him back to the ground. He fought to his feet. People were running as fast as they could from the city gates. One slipped on the embankment and tumbled down into the ditch.

Tamurlaine! he thought, and charged forward.

People were coming in a panicked wave toward him and he lowered his head and with Alfred following at his heels, sidestepped and shouldered and pushed. Then he was at the city gates. People lay dazed on the ground, including several men wearing dark capes, all with the clasp at the throat showing the symbol of the swan. The men of the Watch. The Order of the Swan.

'Tam!' he shouted. 'Tamurlaine!'

He almost didn't see her. She was even fainter than usual, nearly transparent. She clutched his hand and her wintry touch threw an icy jolt up his arm.

'Are you all right?'

She solidified somehow. Dazed guards from the Watch were getting to their feet. She was saying something he couldn't hear. She was pulling him by the sleeve.

'What happened?'

She said something but he couldn't hear. His ears were ringing.

She tugged on his arm harder.

'Wait! What happened here?'

'Explosion.' She shouted this but it sounded muffled. 'An air-blast. Come on!' Again she pulled him towards the gates.

'Wait!' he said. 'We've left Jinky!'

'There's no time,' she said, her voice muffled. She pointed at the sky. The blond boy with his net of gold was flying fast towards them, the tails of his coat streaming.

'Quick!'

They ran through the gates, Alfred at their heels.

'Where are we going?'

147

Tamurlaine pulled him along a narrow passage that wiggled along behind shops from which floated smells of pies, past stables smelling of horse and hay and dung, then an inn smelling of beer where a couple of gaunt servants sat on crates. Here the overhanging roofs hid them almost entirely from the eyes of the flying boy with the golden net. Alfred with cunning eyes fell back to try his luck in one of the pie-shops until Toby grabbed him by the scruff of the neck and put him in his rucksack. Alfred protested.

'Wait!' Toby called to Tamurlaine. 'We have to go back for Jinky.'

'The Watch are there.'

'I don't care.'

Tamurlaine's eyes flashed and he thought she was going to lose her temper again. 'Toby,' she said, controlling herself, 'Jinky's old enough to look after herself.'

'She's *ten*.'

'She's not your responsibility.'

'She's *nobody's* responsibility and she's got to be somebody's responsibility so I'm making her mine.'

He sped back along the passage towards the main street and had just reached it when something cold grabbed his wrist and swung him round so sharply he heard the socket of his shoulder pop before he was released to find himself standing with Tamurlaine now barring his exit from the passage.

'I told you I'd get you home,' she said in that cold, hard voice that meant *Don't mess*.

Whether Toby would have had the courage to fight with Tamurlaine a second time after what happened the first time, is unknown, because at that moment two men in long capes swept past the entrance to the passage and one happened to glance in. He grabbed his companion and the pair – short, chunky middle-aged guards from the Watch – clapped heavy hands on Tamurlaine and slammed her to her knees.

'You!' one shouted. 'Do not move! Do not speak!'

The other yelled, 'You're under arrest for causing an explosion at the city gates.'

CHAPTER 10

Crossing the City

Tamurlaine's eyes widened with that same terror that Toby had seen in the eyes of the murdered teenager in the forest fire. Toby knew what the men of the Watch would do to Tamurlaine yet he did not move – he knew what they would do to him, too, if they noticed him. The two men began dragging Tamurlaine away. She thrashed in their arms but the Watch held tight so her kicks could not connect. One of the men glanced up, locking eyes on Toby, and Toby's stomach dropped as if he was riding a roller coaster which had passed the summit and plunged. But the man's glance switched back to Tamurlaine and Toby was released. He had escaped. Tamurlaine had not. She dug her bare heels in the earth and gouged a pair of tramlines as they dragged her from the passage then her heels banged the street cobbles. The men – and the moment for Toby to act – were about to vanish.

'Wait!' he shouted.

They stopped. Beneath their capes, on big belts, metal creaked.

Toby didn't know what he was going to say. 'She's my sister,' he exclaimed. 'She hasn't done anything wrong.'

The men of the Watch examined Toby with such close scrutiny he struggled to stay still. His heart beat loudly and his skin grew hot. He hoped he wouldn't blush. He hoped he wouldn't start trembling. His lie was stupid, so obviously a lie – *you idiot, Toby*, his own mind screamed at him. One of the men, who had grey ringlets that fell to his shoulders, said, 'She's wanted for causing a blast at the city gates.'

'I've been with her all day.'

'Sounds like you're an accomplice, then,' said the second man. He was bald and had bulging eyes, like a frog. 'Besides, she doesn't look like your sister.'

'We've got different dads,' Toby said. 'And my dad works for a minister in the, in the ...' Toby trailed off because he knew his dad carried no weight in this world, then he rallied and finished triumphantly, '... in the castle!'

The two men exchanged an uncertain glance.

'You'll be in trouble,' Toby added.

They exchanged another glance.

'What's your names?' said Toby, 'I'll tell the Regent exactly who you are.'

The bald one with a face like a frog seemed suddenly terrified, and murmured, 'Barry Cheyn.'

'Billy Winch,' said the one with grey ringlets, reluctantly.

Shaking, Toby dug in his rucksack, produced a school exercise book and biro, and in wobbly handwriting wrote their names. Tamurlaine hung limp in the men's grip.

'It's Cheyn spelled with an E-Y,' said Barry Cheyn. 'Not chain like a dog chain.'

'Wait a minute,' frowned Billy Winch. 'How do we know you're telling the truth?'

Toby once more dug in the rucksack, pulled out the sign of the swan that he'd torn from the cape that Ranger Widgeon had given him, and held it high, hoping his hand wouldn't shake so badly they'd notice. The two men dropped Tamurlaine and she banged her nose on the ground.

'No harm done, Miss,' said Billy Winch, helping her up.

'You won't tell the Regent, will you, Miss?' said Barry Cheyn.

Massaging her nose, Tamurlaine glared. For a moment Toby thought she was going to bite them.

'I think you should leave,' he suggested.

Barry Cheyn and Billy Winch hurried off.

A wave of dizziness overcame Toby. He closed his eyes and swayed. Then it passed.

Tamurlaine rolled her shoulders and rubbed her arms where they'd gripped her. 'Come on,' she said, marching past him.

'No,' said Toby, starting in the other direction.

'Toby!' Tamurlaine yelled. 'The boy in the sky!'

'Jinky!' he called.

Glancing up constantly for any sign of the flying boy and not finding any, Toby hurried back towards the gates. He spotted the orphaned girl just inside the city walls, sitting on the step of a stationery shop. She had her doll under one arm and was gnawing at a chicken bone, red sauce smeared on her face.

'Hello, Jinky.'

'Hello, Toby.'

'We're taking you to Mrs Maudlin.'

Tamurlaine was waiting for them, pacing up and down in the covered passage. She asked for directions to Nine Fields Lane from the gaunt servants at the back of the inn. They stared at her as if she was from another world – which in a way she was – then told her the lane was by the harbour, and the three travellers set off.

'They gave you a funny look,' said Toby.

'Tch!' scoffed Tamurlaine.

'Can I carry Alfred?' asked Jinky.

'I'd better keep hold of him now, Jinky. He keeps trying to escape. I think he's hungry.'

'I should have saved him some chicken.'

'He'll be all right. My dad says he's too fat.'

Toby was hungry too, and wished he was home. Perhaps he would be soon, once he'd taken Jinky to Mrs Maudlin. They stopped at a junction of passages, peered upwards through the gap at a vacant sky, and ran across.

'How does that guy manoeuvre his hang-glider so easily,' said Toby, remembering his books on flight. 'The wings aren't big enough, either.'

'They're not wings, they're his coat-tails,' said Tamurlaine.

Toby thought she was being sarcastic, and snorted, then saw she was being serious.

'He dreamed himself the ability to fly,' Tamurlaine explained.

Toby would have asked more but they came to the end of the passages. Before them lay what appeared to be a rubbish tip, including several demolished houses, and on one side of it ran a broad road beside the river. Toby checked the sky for the flying boy. He couldn't see him but that didn't mean he wasn't up there somewhere, waiting for them. Or more precisely, for Tamurlaine. It was Tamurlaine the men of the Watch had wanted, and Tamurlaine the flying blond boy wanted, too. They thought she was responsible for that explosion at the city gates. Tamurlaine was peering upwards, her mouth a thin line, her eyes narrowed in concentration – or perhaps hatred – and Toby was hit by the idea that Tamurlaine *had* caused the blast.

Tamurlaine felt him looking, and met his gaze. 'What?'

'Did you cause that blast?'

Her eyes seemed extraordinarily clear. But she didn't answer the question.

'The Watch are after you now,' he said. 'Not me. They don't know I'm in the city.'

She looked coldly at him.

'I can take Jinky without being noticed. If I go alone.'

There was a flash of understanding between them and she gave a sharp, pragmatic nod. 'I'll draw the Dreamer away,' she said. 'Meet you at Nine Fields Lane. All right?'

They exchanged a nod of agreement and Tamurlaine ran onto the open ground, spun and faced the passageways. Toby's heart thumped. He clutched Jinky's warm, chicken-greasy, sauce-sticky hand.

'Ready, Jinky?'

'Yes.'

The flying boy must have been waiting out of sight above the roofs for Tamurlaine, because she raced back towards them. The boy swooped, his net skating over the ground, but Tamurlaine accelerated and escaped into another passage and the boy had to soar upwards.

'Come on,' said Toby and stepped out. He felt exposed, the way a field mouse feels as it scurries across open ground when an owl is hunting nearby.

It was hard terrain to cross. Their feet sank into soft earth and they had to negotiate obstacles. The flood had done a lot of damage. Wooden houses had been tipped off their foundations, their contents littering the ground – broken bed-frames, a splintered mirror, a toboggan. Children played in the rubbish. On the left, across the river, rose the high castle. Ahead was the aqueduct; men worked from scaffolding repairing a gap in the middle. As Toby and Jinky passed underneath, one workman put down his tools, turned to the rail and lit a cigarette.

'It can't be,' said Toby.

But it was – the old man from the roadworks at home. He saw Toby and waved.

Jinky waved back.

'Do you know him?'

'Works and Buildings,' said Jinky. 'Everyone knows them – they fix everything.'

The old man put his roll-up in the corner of his mouth and leaned with both hands on the scaffolding rail.

'Helloo,' he yelled down.

'Helloo, McGinty!' Jinky yelled back.

'I saw you in Angel Lane!' shouted Toby.

'Ah, it's you. All right, Chief? What are you doing on this side?'

'I'm trying to get home. Can you help?'

'Ooh,' said old McGinty, wincing, as if this was a difficult project that Toby had in mind. 'Both of you trying to get over?'

Toby looked at Jinky. She was gazing up trustingly at McGinty. Toby looked back the way they had come. There was no sign of the flying boy or Tamurlaine. He looked onwards, along the river. Beyond large sheds and warehouses he could see the harbour. Then he looked at Jinky again. Toby wanted badly to say to McGinty, *Get me home right now*. But he couldn't just leave the girl in the middle of a rubbish tip.

'Don't go away!' shouted Toby. 'I'll be back. I need to talk to you.'

McGinty waved.

'Come on, Jinky,' said Toby. 'Let's get you to Mrs Maudlin.'

The warehouses and sheds along the quays had fallen into disuse, like so much in the city, and the harbour contained only rotting hulks, their ribs poking from the low tide's mud like the ribs of a long-dead whale. An actual whale – or something similar – swam in the middle of the harbour, its sleek back wheeling through black water.

Nine Fields Lane was oddly named – it was not beside any field let alone nine of them. A narrow road off the quayside, it seemed a friendly place. Everyone knew Mrs

157

Maudlin and when she came to her door, her mouth fell open.

'Oh my days! Jinky! Have you come all this way on your own? Where's your father, Jinky? Who's this?'

'Dad's dead,' Jinky said blandly. 'This is Toby. His cat's Alfred.'

Mrs Maudlin's eyes brimmed and she clutched the girl to her, then she saw her bandaged stump and stifled a sob.

'Maisie! Moody! Rain! Come see! It's little Jinky come to live with us!'

*

Toby waited for Tamurlaine at the opening to Nine Fields Lane, sitting on one of the quayside's stone bollards. He felt suddenly tired, slightly sick and faint. He hadn't eaten since the previous evening and it was now the middle of the afternoon. He wanted to go back to the aqueduct immediately to see McGinty and learn if the old man could get him home but he was worried he would miss Tamurlaine.

If she was caught, he didn't like to think what the Watch would do to her.

In the harbour, the large swimming creature broke the surface. It was not a whale. It had a smooth, sleek back yet it was too wide to be a whale, and was the wrong colour, an ill-looking green. It vanished. The harbour was formed by a wall on the right, and on the left by the headland and castle. It was a hideous building, covered in graffiti along the lowest section of its walls. Nobody seemed to like the Regent much; the comments about him were extremely rude. Toby hoped he would never meet the man. Above the graffiti were many patches of black mould, and under the windows, white stains. There were cracks everywhere, some so deep they had opened into fissures. At the tip of the headland was scaffolding, and up there, amongst it, must be the room where he'd seen the light twinkling.

Some castle servants came onto a terrace to hang washing. White tablecloths flapped, scaring some crows away. A whole murder of crows was making a kerfuffle around some wooden posts. Not posts, Toby saw, but gibbets. From them hung dead bodies.

Toby wished he was home. Right that moment. He had had enough of this world. He pictured Arnold Street, the sunlight warming the stairs, Mrs Papadopoulos singing through an open window, Dad tap-tapping at his keyboard, Mum working on her thesis.

'Hey.'

Tamurlaine stood before him. He jumped up and went to hug her but there was something forbidding in her so he said, 'You all right?'

Tamurlaine eyed the castle. 'It's a mean-looking place, isn't it?'

Toby agreed, telling her about McGinty from Works and Buildings as they hurried back to the aqueduct. Tamurlaine didn't utter a word as Toby explained how McGinty had been in his world and might know how he could get back; she seemed preoccupied. Toby didn't like to ask what had happened with the flying boy – he was scared to find out. Tamurlaine seemed capable of anything.

But when they arrived, the men from Works and Buildings had finished for the day.

'I don't believe it!' said Toby, putting both hands on top of his head and interlinking fingers. 'What am I going to do now? How am I going to get home?'

'I want to get out of here as soon as I can, too,' said Tamurlaine, and set off across the rubbish heaps towards Whale Hill. 'Come on!'

'Wait! Did you set off that explosion at the city gates?'

She stopped and faced Toby. 'Why?'

'You did, didn't you?' said Toby.

'So what if I did?'

'People were hurt.'

'A few bruises. Burst ear-drums. It was only an air-blast. It got you into the city, didn't it?'

'Well, yes.'

She marched off.

'That's not the point,' he called. 'People were hurt. People were frightened.'

'The same people who sneered at Jinky for being a shleg,' said Tamurlaine, whirling on him. 'Who chopped off her hand and killed her father. Who stabbed Kerten. The same people,' she said, pointing at the castle, 'who hang dead bodies from castle walls.'

'Not all of them,' said Toby, but Tamurlaine was flowing away across the rubbish heaps.

He didn't want to follow her now but didn't want to wait on the rubbish heaps. The Watch might come past at any moment. Besides, who knew how long it would be before the old man from Works and Buildings returned? Toby went after Tamurlaine.

'Where are you going?'

On the far side of the rubbish heaps lay a vast square. At one end tall sheds echoed with mooing and grunting and at the other end a crowd stood round a platform where a woman was making a speech. The square was so large and the woman so far away, Toby couldn't hear what she was saying, but he heard what the crowd chanted in response: 'Down with the Regent! Down with the Regent!'

'Where are we going?'

'Hurry!' said Tamurlaine. 'It's not safe here.'

They skirted a sinkhole large enough to swallow a bus, passed a woman who frowned oddly at Tamurlaine, and arrived at the bottom of Whale Hill. In a road that ran parallel to the big square, a squadron of cavalry waited.

The horses were restless, as if they sensed something was about to happen. One rider cantered towards them, horseshoes ringing on the cobbles in the cold afternoon air. The horse was strong and tall and broad and blinkered and the rider wore a dark cape with red flashes, fixed by the emblem of the swan at his throat, different from the symbol Toby carried because the rider's white swan was on a red background. A long club hung from a leather loop around his wrist.

'You children,' he barked. 'Get off the street if you don't want a broken skull.'

They hurried on.

'Wait!' the horseman called. 'You, girl, what's your name?'

'Jinky,' said Tamurlaine.

The man peered uncertainly at her, then wheeled his horse and cantered away.

'What were they doing?' said Toby.

'Waiting.'

'What for?'

'For the order to attack those people in the square.'

'But why?'

'You're not allowed to say anything against the Regent.'

Twice more, as they climbed Whale Hill, people did a double take when they saw Tamurlaine. Toby assumed it was because her description had been given out as the

person who had caused the air-blast at the city gates, but couldn't understand why the horseman of the Watch had not arrested her, because he too had seemed to recognise her.

'I think people here know you,' he said after it happened another time.

Tamurlaine didn't answer.

The afternoon was growing gloomy as they turned into a drab street.

'There's someone here who can help you,' said Tamurlaine, stopping before a stone building with pillars and shadows. 'The Dreamers will get you home.'

'The Dreamers? Like the boy we saw flying?'

'He's one of them, yes. He won't help you but the other Dreamers will.'

'Who are they?'

'They have the power to dream things into reality. They will be able to dream you home.'

Toby was so tired now, he no longer had the energy to question such statements. 'And they live here?'

'No. They're in the castle. There's someone here who can take you to them and introduce you. His name's Burston. He works here but he knows the castle and where the Dreamers are quartered. He also knows the Dreamers. He's friends with them. They'll help him. And you.'

The building was not an inviting place.

'Toby,' she said.

He faced her.

'I'm not going.'

'Why not?'

'I can't go to the castle. I can't be in the city. I'm remembering more all the time. It's too dangerous ... I hate this place.'

'I don't like it much, either.'

A smile – a surprising one – twitched at the corners of her mouth, and she shook her head. 'I can't take you to the castle,' she said. 'I can't.'

He saw she was frightened. 'It's all right.'

'I'm sorry.'

He felt suddenly alone but he battled down the lonely feeling and grinned at her. He took her cold hand and felt that bolt of ice fly up his arm. 'Thank you for helping me. I hope you remember everything, and find your home.'

She looked lonely herself then, and as if she was about to cry.

'Burston Shimpling,' she said, almost angrily, pushing his hand away. 'That's the name of the person you have to see.' She started to go then turned back. 'And if he makes any excuse, tell him this – if he doesn't take you to the Dreamers I'll destroy his life.'

She wasn't joking. She flowed away along the street, not the way they had come, but onwards, as if she could not get away fast enough.

The lonely feeling grew stronger. The dark shadowy building waited. Toby crossed the road and went up the steps into the darkness.

So he did not see Tamurlaine when she halted. She had heard the distant sound of a hundred men roaring like a football crowd when a goal is scored, and the thundering hooves of their galloping horses, and the screams of the protestors – women, men, and some children. Tamurlaine faced the wall and rested her forehead against its cold surface and shut her eyes as if she could shut out the pain in people's screams. In her mind she saw the bloodshed, then the place which had ordered that bloodshed – the castle. Tamurlaine breathed out. She exhaled so deeply she seemed to shrink, then she drew a breath and straightened and even though she did not want to, she was frightened, she made her way back along the street to the dark building, to wait for Toby to come out so she could help him. And as dusk fell and the outlines of buildings and objects began to disintegrate, Tamurlaine's body also began to disintegrate, became particles, insubstantial, dark, a darkness – the shadow.

CHAPTER 11

The Bureau of Broken Dreams

There were no lights in the portico of the dark building but a soft glow came through the small, thick panes that pierced the upper part of the entrance doors, illuminating a brass plate that read:

BUREAU OF
BROKEN DREAMS

The swing doors were so heavy Toby had to lean his whole body against them, and they swung back hard afterwards, hinges gulping at the effort and a thick draft-excluder sighing deeply, as if with weariness.

Warm air rose through an iron grille in the floor and Toby stood on it for a few seconds, glad of the heat. The light came from a porter's lodge. Toby went up on tiptoe to speak over the high counter.

'I need to see Burston Shimpling.'

'Personal or official business?' the old porter asked, giving Toby a shrewd look.

Toby, who had been on plenty of visits to the ministry where his dad worked, knew the best if not the true answer to this question.

'Official business,' said Toby, producing the emblem of the swan that Ranger Widgeon had given him. Its cold heavy metal clunked on the wooden counter.

The old man lifted a tube with a brass mouthpiece and called into it. 'Anon! Visitor!'

Toby waited. The glass panes of the entrance doors reflected the hallway and for a moment Toby had the urge to run back into the street, then an athletic figure, standing at over seven feet tall, came softly from the darkness. When he stepped into the light from the porter's lodge his head remained in the shadows above the lodge window, and all Toby could see was the gym-worked muscles of his body.

'Take this boy down to Records,' said the porter. 'He wants to see Burston Shimpling.'

'This way,' said the tall figure in a young, wavery voice at odds with his size, and Toby followed him into a gaslit corridor, careful not to step on the young man's cape, which was an extraordinary garment. It was skin-tight across the shoulders so Toby could see the definition of his muscles and it tapered to a narrow point that was so long it swept the floor behind him. It was made of something soft and each time they passed a light its colours changed, from turquoise, to deep-sea blue, to rose.

They descended to the basement where the young man escorted Toby to a door then turned to go. Toby had never seen anyone so mournful. The young man could not meet Toby's eye, and for all his size and splendid cloak, seemed horribly self-conscious. Toby felt so sorry for him, he patted him as if to say *there-there, it's all right*. He would have patted him on the shoulder but the young man was so tall, Toby tapped his elbow. The boy looked like he was going to burst into tears then suddenly gave a broad smile which lit up his face and his cloak lifted and opened from his shoulders, becoming a pair of iridescent wings that he beat several times, filling the width of the corridor and wafting air against Toby's face so forcefully it blew his hair backwards.

'Burston's in there,' he said in his young, wavery voice before rustling away, dragging the long feathers of his folded wings behind him along the floor.

Toby watched him go. What a strange world he had entered.

When Toby went in, he was not sure what the place

might be. An animal sanctuary perhaps, or the engine-room of a ship overrun by cats. It was, like everywhere else in the bureau, dimly lit, and it was the size of a tennis court and whizzing with movement. The movement was mainly inside dozens, perhaps more than a hundred, glass tubes that ran from the ceiling with curves and steep angles and sharp bends, where mice were shooting at tremendous speeds. The mice exited at the mouths of these tubes onto a sort of spongy landing area in the middle of a broad counter from which they scampered off to various points around the edge. It was like the most ingenious water-slide complex ever constructed, only without water, and for mice.

The mice wore harnesses so they could carry cylinders on their backs, and on their heads appeared to be cyclists' helmets, presumably so they didn't brain themselves on the sharp corners of the glass tubes. They were not scampering aimlessly about the counter but running to specific stations, at which stood cats. Blue cats, grey cats, Japanese bobtail cats, even a bald cat. These cats were using their teeth to tug the cylinders from the mice's harnesses, then using their claws to unroll the cylinders, which turned out to be scrolls. Once they had unrolled the scrolls, and read what was written there, they put a paw in an ink-pad and stamped the scroll and let it roll itself up. Other cats transferred the scrolls to pigeonholes that covered an entire wall, ascending via ramps. The mice, once they had made their delivery, were exiting along the counter via various neatly cut mouseholes in an end wall. There seemed to be no friction between mice and cats, although Alfred had sniffed out the rodent couriers and was furiously trying to escape the rucksack to chase them. 'Stop it, Alfred!' Toby hissed. 'Why can't you be more like this lot?' Alfred did not respond to such a stupid question. He was a cat, after all.

At the head of the counter, sitting in what looked like a tennis umpire's chair, was a bored teenage boy, slumped so low his lanky legs spilled far beyond the seat. His head was the only vertical part of his body and he was pulling his fringe straight and gazing at it, as if counting how many hairs he could see. There were no other people in the room and Toby, after a long time watching the mice and cats at work, amazed at their intelligence but unable to work out the purpose of their task, approached the teenage boy, whom he presumed was Burston Shimpling.

'Excuse me,' said Toby.

'Who the hell are you?' said the boy.

'Toby Porter. Are you Burston Shimpling?'

'Why?'

'I was sent here by Tamurlaine. She said Burston Shimpling would take me to the castle to see the Dreamers.'

The boy turned very pale. 'Tamurlaine?' he said. 'Tamurlaine?'

'So you are Burston?'

The boy didn't answer. His boredom had been replaced by a sort of stricken expression and he was biting his lip.

'You must be Burston,' Toby said decisively. 'Tamurlaine told me you'd take me to the castle. To see the Dreamers. So they can dream me home. She said you know them.'

'You spoke to her? You're sure?'

'Yes. Can you take me?'

'When did you see her?' said Burston, coming down the ladder, worried.

'Just now. Outside.'

'Outside?' said Burston, whirling to the door.

'She's gone now.'

'You're sure? You're absolutely positive she's gone?'

'Yes.'

Slowly, Burston relaxed, then gradually resumed his bored air. He yawned, and spent a great deal of time adjusting the position of the umpire's chair, as if that was the reason he had climbed to the bottom of the ladder.

'So you'll take me, then? We can go? We can go soon?'

Burston leaned against the umpire's chair and studied his fingernails, murmuring, 'Not a chance.'

'But she said you'd take me.'

'Out of the question. I'm too busy here.'

Toby, infuriated, was about to say *You don't look very busy* but stopped himself; there was nothing to be gained from a fight. He said instead, 'What do you do here, then, Burston?'

'Look around,' Burston said obnoxiously, still leaning against the chair, studying his fingernails.

'Well,' said Toby, turning to the tubes and mice and cats and trying to work it out, 'I don't know but it looks extremely important.'

Burston looked at Toby, startled, then stood upright. 'You're right. It is important. This is the Department of Records and I,' he concluded, tugging straight the jacket of his suit (which was threadbare, Toby noticed), 'am the Head of Records.'

'How old are you?' Toby asked.

'Fifteen.'

'That's impressive,' said Toby.

Burston pushed his shoulders back, proud and pleased.

'Tell me, Burston, what are the cats and mice doing?'

'Well,' said Burston, indulging his visitor and clasping his hands behind his back and pacing behind the cats, 'upstairs in Sorting they receive the dreams that didn't work and send them on to the various departments in the Bureau. The departments try and work out what's wrong with the dreams. Suggestions are sent back to the castle to improve the work of the Dreamers and the dreams are disposed of. The details of each case are brought down here – the mice bring them – and the bureaucats sort them.'

172

'Bureaucats?'

'The cats, Toby Porter. The Bureau's cats.'

'Ah, I see,' said Toby. 'It's amazing. Can you really not take me to the castle, Burston?'

'No.'

'Please?'

'Out of the question.'

Toby tried one last time: 'I've got to get home. My mum's worrying. Please.'

'Nope.'

Toby changed tack. 'Well, you'd better.'

'Oh yeah? Why?'

'Because Tamurlaine said she'd destroy your life if you didn't take me.'

The colour drained from Burston's face until it matched his very white shirt.

The door flew open and a man swept in, papers in one hand and in the other a steaming cup of tea with a chocolate bar balanced across the top.

'What are you doing, Mr Shimpling?' the man said. 'Less than an hour I'm gone. Lazing about like a hippo. You're the most useless clerk I've had.'

'Sorry, Walid al-Walid,' said Burston, immediately squatting on a low stool among the bureaucats.

'And who the hell is this?' said Walid al-Walid, climbing the umpire's chair from which he gazed down at Toby.

'No idea, Walid al-Walid,' said Burston. 'Who are you, boy?'

'But I just tol –'

'Who are you, boy?' shouted Burston.

'Toby Porter.'

'He's Toby Por –'

'I heard him, Mr Shimpling! No non-Bureau personnel in the Records Room. Get rid.'

Burston grabbed Toby by the collar.

'Oi!' called Toby. 'Let go!' He was roughly steered to the door and pushed out. Toby put his shoulder against the frame, wincing as Burston bashed the door-edge against him. 'You have to take me, Burston. I've got to get home.'

Burston leaned all his weight against the door. Toby's shoulder was agony.

'If you don't take me, I'll go to Tamurlaine right now and tell her. She'll destroy your life!'

The pressure eased slightly.

'I swear I'll tell her!'

The pain vanished.

Burston studied Toby. He chewed his lip, looking over his shoulder several times. Then he said, 'Pah!' and yelled back to his boss, 'I'm going to chuck this kid out, Walid al-Walid!' and stepped into the corridor.

'So you'll take me?'

'Ruddy Tamurlaine,' said Burston, striding away.

'Burston?'

'Yes, yes. I'll take you.'

They ascended stairs. Toby kept a close eye on the boy in case he tried to trick him. They entered a hallway. The signs on the doors were strange:

LUCID DREAM DEPARTMENT

PROPHECIES AND VISIONS

DEPARTMENT OF RECURRING DREAMS (A-SECTION)

A bulky figure approached. He was only vaguely human, his flesh a fatty brown substance he was generously shedding in drips and smears and footprints. Burston pressed himself against the wall to make room and pegged the end of his nose with forefinger and thumb, saying, 'Evening, Sludge,' and sounding like he had a bad cold.

Toby gagged at the wave of warm stink that emanated from Sludge. Sludge held in his muddy paws a glass case containing a cloud of what could only be dreams, galloping animals and faces that kept dissolving into one another.

'Interesting,' said Burston, nose still pegged, still sounding like he had a cold. 'Where are you taking it?'

Sludge waved a muddy paw, flicking brown goo that splatted on a door-sign warning AUTHORISED PERSONNEL ONLY and, beneath that, DEPARTMENT OF NIGHTMARES.

Sludge went inside and Toby briefly heard wailing, then the door was shut.

'Whatever you do,' said Burston, walking on, his cold cured, 'do not go in there.'

Toby continued to look at the door, then ran after Burston. 'Who is Sludge?'

'Sludge is a dream. He would have been disposed of but he's superb at fixing other dreams. So he survived.'

They passed the DEPARTMENT OF RECURRING DREAMS (B-SECTION) and stepped into the back garden.

A thought suddenly struck Toby. 'Is Tamurlaine a dream?'

'Tamurlaine?' said Burston, stopping. 'Why do you ask?'

'Well,' said Toby, 'she seems a bit faint sometimes, as if she's only partly there.'

'That's interesting. Well, when I knew her she was a person all right. Definitely a person. Unless the Tamurlaine you met is a dream-version of herself. Anyway, I know she'll destroy my life if I don't take you to the castle.'

'I'm sorry to get you into trouble with her. And with your boss.'

'You think I'm scared of my boss? I just act like that to humour him. He's insecure, is old Walid al-Walid. I'm scared of no one, not even the Regent.'

Toby thought Burston was either very brave or not telling the truth. They crossed the garden, following a wire

fence. Behind it, illuminated by the Bureau's windows, stood several chilly figures. There was something so forlorn about them; standing silently in the dark, they seemed more like ghosts than living people.

'Are they dreams too?' Toby asked.

'No. Retired Dreamers.'

'Then they can dream me home,' exclaimed Toby excitedly.

'No. They retired because they lost their powers. See her?' Burston pointed at a miserable-looking girl in pink pyjamas, shivering, a steaming mug in one hand, a cigarette in the other. 'She was responsible for dreaming the city's naval defences – a giant ulcer. It swims about the harbour and no one's dared attack us by sea since then. Saved the city but what it took for her to dream an ulcer wrecked her own mind. And see him?' Burston pointed to a heavy figure in a dressing-gown who, although he was only eighteen or nineteen, was already bald. 'He dreamed the new generation of cows and pigs. A genius. If it wasn't for him, the city would have starved to death.'

'What's wrong with him?'

'Same as her. Same as all of them. Their minds don't work any more. All the Dreamers are finished by the time they hit twenty, twenty-one anyway. A few rarities get to twenty-four or -five. Most of them go on to do something else, or live on the adulation or fame. But some, it simply destroys them. Like this lot. The reserves of energy they've drawn on leaves them with nothing. They can't even look after themselves. If it wasn't for the Bureau letting them live here, they'd be on the streets. Sad, isn't it?'

The young Dreamers seemed drained of vitality, sapped, their eyes sat in their sockets like water shrunk from great ponds of life to become dried-out puddles.

CHAPTER 12

Raven Yard

It was growing dark as they made their way down Whale Hill, a cold wind blew, and across the other side of the city the castle waited. So Toby was going to have to go there after all. As long as he didn't have to meet the Regent, he could just about face it.

'How do you know the Dreamers in the castle,' he asked, 'if you're only a clerk in the Department of Records?'

'I'm the Head of Records, mate,' replied Burston as if Toby had insulted him.

'Yes, of course,' said Toby, not wanting to upset the older boy.

'I went to school there, if you must know.'

'The castle? What's it like?'

'Cold.'

Shop awnings were being cranked away, gas lamps were being extinguished and shop shutters being slammed down. People were wrapping scarves round necks and pulling collars up necks and tugging down hats against the wintry wind, and rushing off. Even the birds were rushing to get home, crows and ravens cawing as they flew overhead. A bell clanged a rapid repetitive rhythm from a nearby tower, and other bells answered across the city as if to say *I quite agree, it's time to go home.*

'We'd better hurry,' said Burston, and broke into a trot.

Toby felt a wave of dizziness and had to stop so he didn't fall over.

'Don't hang about, Toby Porter. I don't want to be out after dark. Especially tonight.'

'You haven't got any food, have you? I haven't eaten since yesterday.'

'You want me to feed you as well? I'm risking my job taking you to the castle when I'm meant to be at work. I'm not even meant to go to the castle at all – I've been banned.'

'I'm sorry.'

'Get one of the Dreamers to dream you a sandwich when we get to the castle.'

'You can't eat dreams.'

'You can if you cook them properly.'

They crossed the great square. It was empty except

for a few scraps of newspaper scooting over the ground. The protestors were all gone – in gaol, or nursing broken limbs, or hiding from the Watch, or in the mortuary. The sky was full of crows, all of them heading towards the castle, and perching on the roofs of the houses around it. Burston led Toby past the animal sheds, and Toby saw huge creatures – pigs the size of cows and cows the size of elephants.

'They're enormous!' Toby exclaimed.

'That boy we saw in the Bureau? They're the ones he dreamed. Well, not these exact ones. He dreamed the originals and they breed them all to this size now.'

'So Dad was wrong,' said Toby, 'you can live on dreams.'

'Well, if you're from the castle you can. All these are for the royal family. And members of the government, and their hangers-on. Not the likes of you and me. We're the lowlies.'

An elephantine cow mooed. It sounded like a giant truck engine bursting into life. They left the square and crossed the rubbish heaps and then a bridge over the swollen river. Everyone seemed to have gone home. It was dusk yet no streetlights had been lit, and the curtains and shutters of the buildings showed no light. They climbed a steep, narrow street towards the dark castle.

'Why are you banned from the castle, then, Burston?'

'Because I'm a rebel, mate. I eat rules for breakfast

and throw regulations on the fire of my independent thought.'

Toby doubted this so only grunted in response.

'Are you calling me a liar?' said Burston, stopping and looming close in the dusk.

'No. I was agreeing with you.'

'Good,' said Burston.

They reached a small square and here Burston halted under a tree with a dark canopy, out of breath after the steep climb. He sat on the circular brick wall that housed the trunk.

'I could have been a Dreamer,' he said in a faraway, disappointed tone.

'Really?'

'What, you calling me a liar?'

'No, of course not, Burston.'

'I could have been one of the great Dreamers. Maybe the greatest the kingdom's ever known. If it wasn't for that Tamurlaine. Now look at me, a stupid clerk in the Department of Records.'

'I thought you were Head of Department.'

'That's what I meant. A stupid Head of Records.'

The loud ding of a handbell came from a nearby street, and two figures approached.

Burston groaned. 'That's all we need.'

'Who is it?'

'We're breaking curfew, aren't we?'

'I don't understand.'

'You really are an innocent, Toby Porter.'

Toby said nothing, annoyed at the patronising tone.

'Such a little kid,' Burston went on. 'Well, the shadow came back last night so the Regent's ordered a curfew. Everyone inside by nightfall.'

'The shadow – you mean the shadow's here? In the city?'

'Since last night. It used to terrorise us but disappeared a few months ago. Now it's back.'

'But I've seen the shadow.'

'Yikes! What's it like?'

Toby shuddered at the memory, how the shadow had passed through him, how he'd felt its iciness, its hatred. 'Terrifying.'

When the two figures entered the square, by the last glimmers of daylight Toby recognised the grey curls of Billy Winch and bald skull of Barry Cheyn. He grabbed Burston's arm and pulled him behind the tree, crouching down behind the brick wall.

'What are you –'

'Shh!' hissed Toby.

The two men of the Watch plodded across the square, bald, frog-faced Barry ringing the bell.

'I'm taking a breather,' he said, arriving at the brick wall. He sat on the edge with a deep sigh and lowered the bell, the clapper muffled on the ground.

'Come on, we've the round to complete by six,' said Billy Winch.

'Well, you take the bell, then. It's heavy. I've got another shift in a bit.'

Billy joined his colleague on the wall. The square was very quiet, and Toby hoped neither man would hear them, crouched a few feet away. He wished that Alfred would stay very still in the rucksack but he was stirring as if something was wrong.

'I've been thinking, Billy,' said Barry Cheyn.

'Wouldn't do that if I were you. You might hurt something.'

'No, seriously. Do you ever worry about what we do, Billy?'

'How'd you mean?'

'Working for a tyrant.'

'Shut the flip up, you brainless berk,' said Billy, looking about guiltily. 'You want to end up hanging on a gibbet?'

'No.'

'So shut up, then.'

'But it's a rotten job, isn't it?'

'If you don't like it, leave.'

'In the middle of a recession? I've got three children to feed.'

'Well, shut up then.'

'It's school holidays too so they're not getting school lunches which means the weekly food bill's gone up. I've got to do extra shifts. I can't leave now. I can barely pay the rent as it is.'

'I told you to shut up, you prat,' said Billy Winch, running his fingers worriedly through his long curly hair.

There was a faint scratching sound as Alfred clawed at the inside of the rucksack.

'Can you hear that?' said worried Billy.

'Hmm?' said Barry, brooding on his job.

Toby slipped his hand into the rucksack.

'It's coming from somewhere nearby.'

Toby held Alfred tight. The cat stayed still.

'It's stopped now,' said Billy.

'It's not right, though, is it?' said Barry. 'What we do. Take that incident at lunchtime. That girl, and the boy.'

'I told you we're not telling anyone about that.'

'You think that boy was the one we'd been told about? The one that was seen in the forest?'

'Yes, I do. And I think that girl was responsible for the air-blast at the city gates. And if anyone knew we had apprehended not one of them but both of them then got tricked into letting them go like a pair of idiots, we'd both be executed. So shut up.'

Drawing this conversation to an end, Billy Winch picked up the handbell, and the two men of the Watch went on their way, dinging.

'You're wanted by the Watch?' said Burston after they'd gone. 'Oh, brilliant. Absolutely brilliant. Are you

185

trying to get me killed?' And so saying, Burston marched away. Not towards the castle but back downhill.

Alfred was once more scratching, and now also bashing the sides of the rucksack. Toby let him out and he sprang onto the wall and tried to jump up into the tree. There must be a bird up there, Toby decided, and grabbed him. 'It's not the time for hunting, Alfred!' he said, putting him back in the rucksack and running after Burston. 'Wait!' he hissed. 'Please, Burston. Please.'

Burston kept marching. 'Stay away from me, you're wanted by the Watch!'

'I've got to get to the Dreamers. I've got to get home.'

Burston broke into a trot.

'Tamurlaine will destroy your life if you don't help me.'

'Yeah, and if I do help you the Watch will destroy my life. So I'll take my chances with a sixteen-year-old girl, thank you very much, not an armed militia.'

Toby was frantic as he trotted alongside Burston. How was he going to get into the castle now? 'You're not scared, are you, Burston?'

'Scared?' said Burston, stopping. 'Scared?'

All across the city the bells stopped ringing. The crows began to cry and caw. Both boys turned to see rising from every roof and chimney of the district, and from the castle itself, hundreds, then thousands, then tens of thousands of crows and ravens, swirling and circling and more coming from all over the city until there were perhaps a hundred thousand birds flocking round the castle like night itself. The sky was a screen of beaten air and screams and caws and flickering blackness. Then all of them converged, like some great darkness, upon the building, and settled down for the night.

Burston murmured, as if the sight had calmed him. 'Follow me,' he said, and led Toby up a side street.

Behind them, in the square, the dark canopy of the tree under which they had sheltered began to move. It was not crows, late for the evening roost, but dream-creatures – tree-wolves. They climbed and dropped, almost dripped, like some heavy, oozy substance, from the limbs of the tree, landing heavily with a thump on the cobbles. The tree-wolves worked for the Watch. They were its spies. One trotted off to the castle to report that Toby, the only witness to the murder of Kerten, had finally been located (it also intended to denounce Barry Cheyn and Billy Winch for not reporting the capture then release of Toby and the girl who caused the air-blast at the city gates). The rest of the pack followed Toby and Burston at a discreet distance, sniffing the air and the ground for Toby-scent, their claws clicking on the cobbles, their teeth ready to crunch and rip.

In turn, the tree-wolves were followed. By a nearly formless being, a darkness, kept together only by its own emotions – vengeance, loyalty, friendship, and hate.

*

Burston stopped at an archway where a sign read: RAVEN
YARD.

'In here,' he said, opening a door in the archway wall.
'After you.'

As soon as Toby stepped inside Burston slammed the
door and Toby heard his footsteps hurry away.

'Wait!' Toby yelled, taking a few seconds to find the
handle. By the time he got out Burston was nowhere to
be seen. 'Come back!'

From the gloom, Burston called faintly, 'He'll help
you.'

'Who will?'

But Burston had gone.

A wooden staircase rose between narrow, greasy walls.
The treads of the stairs were worn thin; many people had
climbed this way before. At the top, a gas flame hissed in
a glass shade and cast a dull glow onto a name painted
on the plaster: Mervyn Sump Esq. Toby put his ear to
the door and wondered if he could hear something. A
scratching sound. Perhaps Mervyn Sump Esq. kept a pet
hamster.

Toby knocked.

There was no answer and no answer again when
he knocked half a minute later, only the sound of that
hamster, so he sat on the top step, propped his head on his

hands, and waited for Mervyn Sump Esq. to return. Toby had been away from home for three days now. His mum would be sick with worry. She'd think he was dead. He remembered once when he was small he had got lost in a department store and when his mum found him she had been so scared something awful had happened to him she had crushed him with her hug. And Dad? How would he be responding? Toby told himself his dad would be worried too – but Toby didn't entirely trust what he told himself; a lot of what he told himself lately was turning out to be untrue. He stood and knocked on the door once more, just in case.

'Yes?' boomed a man's voice.

Toby needed some courage so he put his hand in his rucksack and stroked Alfred, who had forgiven Toby for shoving him inside and nuzzled his fingers.

'Okay, Alfred,' whispered Toby, and opened the door. The light dropped as the draft from the stairs blew out two candles. Loose papers rustled. There was paper everywhere, pinned to the wall, carpeting the floor, in piles on a desk. Toby shut the door and the extinguished candles flared up brighter than before.

The scratching noise was being made not by a hamster but a quill, which was in the hand of a large man at a desk, his broad back to Toby. He wore a long mac with the collar up, over which straggled greasy hair. The scratching noise was also being made by the fingernails of the man's free hand, vigorously working at an itch on his scalp. The man reminded Toby of his dad. Not physically, as the man was much bigger, but for some other reason. Perhaps it was because he did not turn round. Toby fought the urge to say 'Dad?', instead saying, 'Mr Sump Esq.?'

The quill hand continued to scratch but the scalp hand stopped. Not for Toby, but for something the man had discovered in his hair. Forefinger and thumb tweezered out a minuscule object which was placed on the desk and examined before being crushed. The shell of the thing made an audible *crack*. All the while, the quill wrote, only pausing to be refreshed by a sip of ink from an inkwell.

'Mr Sump Esq.?'

The hand that held the thirsty quill froze half-way to its pool, put down the quill and gripped the back of the chair as the man twisted round to see his visitor. The hand was, like the man, large and pale, with dark hairs and ink stains. Mr Sump Esq. looked nothing like Toby's dad – his head was bigger, his jaw, nose and forehead were bony, and his eyes were sunk deep. He looked mountainous – wild and craggy.

'Mervyn Sump will do,' the man said. 'Who are you?'

'Toby. Toby Porter.'

'And what do you want, Toby Porter?'

'I want to go home.'

'Which begs the question,' said Mervyn Sump, 'why on earth you have come to see me?'

'Burston said you could help.'

'Burston Shimpling? The notorious liar and coward?'

'Well … yes.'

The man gave a scoffing laugh then scratched at his scalp, though whether that was to find a bug or because he was working out how to respond to his uninvited guest, Toby wasn't sure. The matter was finally decided. 'Come in properly and sit down.' Toby was surprised by the offer. He couldn't see anywhere to sit. 'Over there. There's a stool.'

It was by the stove. Toby was glad of the warmth. Candlelight wavered shadows across a row of tall bookshelves topped by scrollwork, reminding Toby of the ancient gravestones at Highgate Cemetery his dad had shown him once, and the light gleamed on the gold lettering of the books on the shelves, like so many inscriptions to the dead. Papers pinned to the wall by long metal pins reminded him of butterflies in display cabinets. On the desk lay a large manuscript.

'My dad's a writer like you,' said Toby.

'Where are you from?'

'I used to live in London. Then we had to move. And I went through a tunnel and ended up here.'

'You're from the other side? You've come through a hole?'

'Yes,' said Toby, with an unexpected rush of emotion. He remembered crawling through. The forest fire. Going down to the cliff-edge after Alfred. He saw again the teenage boy, Kerten, his frightened eyes, and the man with dead eyes plunging the knife into Kerten's stomach, the silent fall of the body ... He shut his eyes to make it go away. 'I just want to go home.' The wind gusted on the window panes and Toby opened his eyes and still saw the dead boy. 'A boy got stabbed and thrown off a cliff.'

A tin can rattled along the street and once more Toby felt the knife at his throat, the heel of the thumb against his windpipe. He started up, grabbed his rucksack, and rushed for the door.

'Toby Porter!'

Toby froze.

'Wait. You're safe here.'

Toby hesitated, then returned, and Mervyn poured Toby a cup of water. Toby drank. When Mervyn refilled it, Toby drank a little more then put the cup on the floor and took Alfred out to give him a drink. But the cat was unsure of his new surroundings and sat behind Toby's legs and peered and waited.

'Tell me what happened,' said Mervyn.

'The Watch killed him.'

'This boy?'

'Yes. His name was Kerten. There were two of them. In the forest. Men of the Watch. They had the sign of the swan here.'

Mervyn rushed to his desk, found a new sheet of paper, dipped his quill in ink, tinked quill against inkwell, and scratched. 'There were two of them?'

'Yes.'

'Tell me what happened. Exactly.'

'There was a forest fire. There was Kerten and two men standing by a cliff. One man held Kerten and the other stabbed him in the stomach.'

'The one who stabbed him, what did he look like?'

'Tall and thin, with a high forehead, and grey hair at the temples.'

'What was he wearing?'

'He had the badge with the swan. He was from the Order of the Swan. And a long leather coat. All the way to his boots.'

Mervyn twisted in his chair to look at Toby. 'Not a cape?'

'No. The other one wore a cape. The one who held him. He dropped him over the cliff.'

'But the one who stabbed Kerten, the one with the knife, he wore a long leather coat? You're sure?'

'Yes. With the badge of the swan at his throat. And leather boots.'

'Did he say anything?'

'To me he did. He said something like, "I'm going to slit your throat", then he started to pull his hand across and –' He couldn't go on. 'The shadow saved me.'

'The shadow was in the mountains?'

'Yes.'

'That's strange. Do you remember anything else about the man? The killer.'

'No. Except ...'

'Yes?'

'His mouth was cruel and his eyes were dead.'

Mervyn breathed a half-laugh of discovery. He looked to the window. The glass reflected a bud of candle-flame. Alfred lapped water rhythmically.

'I have to get home. The Dreamers can dream me home. Burston said you'd help me get to them.'

Mervyn's only response was to scratch his scalp. Toby, for many reasons – that he had finished telling his story, that he was hot from the stove, that he was weak with hunger, that he had finally been able to relax after the dangers of the day – was overcome by dizziness. Once it had passed, he said, 'Can I have some food?'

'Mmm?' said Mervyn. 'Yes, of course.' He came over and took a pot off the back of the stove and poured hot plopping broth into a bowl. 'Not much.' Oily, watery, with a few shreds of unrecognisable meat, the soup nevertheless tasted delicious. Toby saved half and when it was cool enough, put it down for Alfred.

'What are you writing?' Toby asked Mervyn, who had returned to his desk and was reading back what he had written.

'This? An account of what happened to you. I'll include it in my history.'

'Of what?'

'The kingdom.'

'My dad's writing a novel.'

'You know,' Mervyn said, turning once more to Toby, 'I have never met someone from the other side. I've read about you. I've even written about you. But met you: no. But it's something I've thought about. For a future project – a study on the influence of the other side on our art, language and customs.' The man narrowed his eyes. 'I can't help you get home, Toby, I'd better tell you that now. I used to work in the castle archive but I wrote a history of the Regent's family. He didn't like it and I was sacked. So I'm not allowed in the castle any more.'

Toby felt a tightness in his chest, a sickness in his stomach. 'But I have to get to the Dreamers.'

'I'm sorry.'

Toby stood and went to the window. The castle was up the hill, a fearsome-looking place.

'How can I get in without the Watch seeing me?'

When the archivist didn't respond, Toby turned. Mervyn had started to scratch – at both paper and scalp, chasing thoughts and bugs. He was more interested in his writing than Toby getting home. Toby felt a rush of impatience.

'I mustn't *disturb* you from your important business,' said Toby crossly.

The broad back was once more his dad's back.

'Not when you could do something that might actually help another person. Another human being.'

Both nib and fingernail stopped. Toby thought he had somehow reached the kind bit of Mervyn, then Mervyn let his thirsty quill drink from the ink-pot and continued to write.

Mervyn Sump wasn't interested in Kerten's death so he could find justice for the boy. He was only interested in the story. In putting another tale in his big history. Toby shuddered. He actually shuddered. He couldn't stand to be in the same room as this horrible man. It was the man's selfishness he couldn't stand. He scooped up Alfred and slipped him gently into his rucksack and put his arms through the straps. Alfred poked his head out to see how this encounter was going to end.

'It's not Burston who's the coward, Mervyn Sump Esq., it's you. You're the biggest coward in, in, in – in whatever this stupid place is called.'

'Balthasar,' said Mervyn.

Toby spluttered, then spent half a minute coughing. Mervyn watched him.

'Balthasar,' said Toby, when he'd recovered himself. 'Balthasar?'

'Yes. Balthasar.'

'But it can't be. It can't be Balthasar.'

'I assure you it is. The Kingdom of Balthasar.'

'This isn't a real place,' Toby said, as much to himself as Mervyn. 'It's from my dad's novel.'

For Balthasar, as Toby knew, as he had heard from almost the day he was born, was the name of the world in his dad's novel.

'I can promise you it's a very real place, Toby Porter. People are born here, people suffer here – at the hands of the Regent's men who are known as the Watch – and people die here. And you're right, in the face of that, we're all cowards.'

'This place was invented by my dad.'

'So your dad's creator of the universe, is he?' said Mervyn Sump, and Toby heard the sarcasm. 'You think the universe revolves around you and your dad, do you?'

'He's a better man than you are. He's a better writer than you are, *Mervyn*.'

'Oh, is he?'

'Yes, he is.'

'How would you know, Toby? You haven't read anything I've written.' Mervyn went over to one of the bookshelves, found the book he wanted and, leafing through its pages, brought it across. 'Read that before you go.'

'I don't want to read any of your rubbish.'

'It tells you all about how Balthasar came into existence. And it wasn't invented by your dad.'

Torn between anger and curiosity, Toby snatched the book and sat by the stove. Alfred wanted to get out so Toby lifted him and he curled in Toby's lap and the pair sat together as they had once sat in Arnold Street on Toby's duvet with its pictures of sailing boats, reading about engines and aeroplanes. But they weren't in Arnold Street any more, they were in Balthasar, and Toby was not reading about aeroplanes but how Balthasar came to be:

M. Sump A History of the Early Years of Balthasar

HOW THE QUEEN OF BALTHASAR GOT THE POWER OF DREAMING

It is not easy to live on a border, it often leads to confusion. Especially when the borderland has very little in the way of character, like mountain ranges or lakes or a certain kind of cheese. The region called Balthasar was this type of place. Even worse, it had no famous actors or singers, no renowned scientists, and it had no amazing architecture, any of which might have helped to define it. Its weather was nondescript, its geography vague (though it did have a very fine river running through it), and its language was a borrowing from all the various languages used by its neighbours. Like most border country it was landlocked, and sometimes it seemed that all you could say about Balthasar was that it was surrounded on all sides by much bigger kingdoms and empires.

These other territories liked to define Balthasar. In fact, Balthasar had at one time or another been inside these other territories, and under their political rule. But only for short periods. Then it returned to independence or to the control of another of its neighbours. Being border country, it went the way of whichever power was the strongest, and with as little fuss as possible. In doing this, it was trying to protect its people from violence and war.

But there was one good thing about Balthasar's location in between powerful neighbours: it was the ideal spot for trade. Goods from the neighbouring lands began to be traded in Balthasar. The taxation on this trade by the Balthasarian government, and the arrival of merchants who wanted to spend money, meant that over a long period Balthasar became wealthy.

It was at this point in the history of Balthasar that *something happened*. This often occurs in history: *something happens*. What happened was, a certain person noticed that if Balthasar had at least one proper border, then it would be less likely to be bullied by the other powers that surrounded it. It would also no longer have to put up with invasion and war, which are generally pretty nasty things. The certain person who noticed this was Edwige, Queen of Balthasar. She argued her case very forcefully (she was a very forceful woman). But many people argued against her, saying there had not been a war for some time, and that actually all the trade had made the people of Balthasar prosperous. So don't start any trouble, Edwige! But Edwige wasn't about to give up her argument. She responded that Balthasar would always be at the mercy of whichever neighbouring power was the stronger, and just because there wasn't a war at the moment, didn't mean there wouldn't be one in the future. In other words: wake up and smell the coffee!

There followed the nastiest internal conflict in Balthasar's history (before this, people generally got on). At the time Balthasar was what's known as 'a clan-based society', which meant families had lots of political power, and these families or clans turned against one another as everyone argued over this border-business. The anti-Edwige clans finally won the argument and Edwige was removed from power. She was locked at the top of a tower in the capital city. (BTW: the capital city of Balthasar was named, unsurprisingly for a region that is generally low on originality, Balthasar.)

The traditional myth says that Edwige walked round and round the tower for years, dreaming of the perfect Balthasar. And this myth is TRUE. She *did* walk round and round the tower for years. She was composing her one known work, *To the Sea*. In this book (and I'll paraphrase because it's pretty long, and also pretty boring) she argued that the only way for Balthasar to survive was for it to have a border with the sea. As Balthasar was surrounded on all sides by land, this was impossible. Her opponents were delighted when they heard all this, because it meant that Edwige had gone mad, and this meant she could no longer be a threat to them.

Edwige would probably have been consigned to the history of the mad queens of Balthasar,[1] if it was not for the fact that a war between Balthasar's two largest and most violent neighbours became a real possibility. This possible war soon became a probable war, then finally it became an imminent

---

[1]   See my brilliant book, *A History of the Mad Queens of Balthasar* (Balthasar, 1541).

war. Meanwhile, Edwige continued to circle her tower. Each night for six months she pictured the coast, then she dreamed it. People said she was madder than a mouse that thinks it's a cat.

And as she prowled the battlements, the armies of the two neighbouring powers mobilised. The dust from their manoeuvres darkened the skyline, the metal of their weapons winked in the distance. It seemed that the war to end all wars was about to start.

The night before the start of the war, Balthasar's political leaders received some visitors. Envoys from the two opposing armies arrived. They told the politicians that Balthasar had to choose a side or it would be destroyed. Around midnight, the envoys left. The ministers didn't know what to do. They argued, they fretted, some bawled their eyes out. Everyone was going to die! Finally, the queen who had been imprisoned all these years was brought from her tower and asked for her opinion. Which side should they choose?

Edwige, who was fond of drama, did not answer for a long time. She savoured the moment after her years locked in the tower. Then she spoke. 'You should choose,' she said, and paused for effect while looking about at the politicians, 'Balthasar!' To general uproar, Edwige swept out.

What help was a mad old mongoose like Edwige at a time like this?

It was a quiet, still night, and a thick fog hung in the air, but around dawn, a strong wind rose. The smell of the two armies reached the city of Balthasar, where all the kingdom's citizens had gathered for protection. The people were terrified. They knew that it was likely to be their last day on earth. They smelled that frightening mix of woodsmoke, sweaty horses, gunpowder and horse manure that belongs to an army camped right outside a city's gates. Soon the sound of infantry and cavalry reached them, that deep reverberating rumble. And as the crash and thunder descended, the fog cleared.

But what greeted the people of Balthasar was not two armies descending upon them. It was something else entirely. People who had never seen it didn't know what it was, they had to have it explained to them. People spoke of its greyness, the changeability of its surface, but mostly of its size. It went all the way to the horizon. And it is difficult to imagine, for those of us who have always known it, what it was like for them to see it for the very first time: the ocean.

It wasn't understood at the time whether the ocean had moved to Balthasar or Balthasar to the ocean, but everyone knew its appearance was the result of Edwige's dreaming. Somehow – no one knew how – Edwige had changed Balthasar. She had dreamed up a border with the sea.

CHAPTER 13

Escape from Raven Yard

Reading the word 'Balthasar', even more than learning about its mad origins, made it easier for Toby to believe that the world he had entered was actually the one in his dad's novel; the archivist might be a coward but he was not a liar. How it might be that the world of his father's novel was in the real world, or, alternatively, how Toby had entered his father's novel, Toby did not know. Over the past two days he had received so many odd shocks that he no longer quizzed too closely the causes of what occurred, he only knew that they did occur.

'So am I in some sort of … fairy tale, then?'

'No.'

'A dream?'

'Balthasar is not a dream or a fairy tale,' said Mervyn.

And as if to prove it, the wind rustled across the roof and rattled the window frame and a draft slipped in, stirred the curtains and flapped the candle flame, and touched Toby's face, bringing with it a scent of burning wick. Alfred sat up on Toby's lap and, straightening both front legs and digging his claws into Toby's thigh, stretched, then settled back down. Toby wished now that he had read his dad's novel but his dad had never let him read it. His dad had never let Mum read it, either, not since he showed it to a book editor he knew, who told him to stick to writing newspaper articles. Toby had learned about some of the novel, details that his dad mentioned from time to time, but it was like knowing a few corners in a great city – a lamp-post and a small park, a particular shop – but none of it would help Toby get home.

If only his dad was here, Toby thought, he would know where to go and what to do. He knew Balthasar. But his dad was not here, and Toby was alone.

'So how can I get home, then?' he asked, subdued.

'I don't know. There's no other way into the castle apart from the main gate. And I'm not going to march you through the main gate. You're right about one thing, Toby – I'm a coward. The Regent understands that. He doesn't even have to kill me. He understands I'm too frightened to do anything against him. We've known each other our entire lives. We grew up together. I've discovered all his family's secrets. But he knows I'd never do anything with the information.'

'How about Works and Buildings, can they help me?'

'Hmm?' said Mervyn, roused from distant thoughts. 'Not sure. The holes go to a lot of different worlds. And the Department of Works and Buildings don't make the holes, they only fix them. Once a hole is sealed it can't be reopened.'

'How are the holes made?'

'They just happen. Because of dreaming.'

'I don't understand. Explain it to me.'

'It's the Regent again. It all comes back to him. At first, generations ago, dreaming was rare. It happened under great pressure on the individual. Then, gradually, people learned how to do it. I wrote a book on its development. Here, I'll show you –'

'No, no, no. Just tell me, Mervyn.'

'Dreaming became an art. Not everyone had the power to do it. But those that did, could develop it. These were the Dreamers. They had to want the thing they dreamed, to the core of their being. So what was dreamed was individual to them. But the dreams didn't always come out as planned. Dreamers dreamed hybrid animals, strange buildings. But also people they loved who had died, or people they loved who didn't love them back. Most importantly for Balthasar, in time of danger to everyone in the city – say, during a war, or an earthquake

207

– then the Dreamers were able to dream something that could save Balthasar.'

'Like Queen Edwige in your history.'

'Yes. But then the people of Balthasar started to make specific requests of the Dreamers. And the Dreamers developed their abilities to dream more precisely, and to dream whatever was requested. Dreaming stopped being an art and became something else. When the Regent first grew powerful in the government, he saw he could use dreaming to consolidate his position. So he angled to take control of dreaming. And he did. Now it is learned by children who are trained according to a strict syllabus. And the Dreamers dream what the government tells them to. What the government wants. And the Regent is head of the government. The Regent has made dreaming like a machine – he churns out dreams. He gives the people what they want – fabulous clothes, exotic furniture, fancy food, shampoo.'

Mervyn paused to scratch his scalp, found something in his greasy hair, and snapped it between his fingers.

'But dreaming drains the Dreamers. It drains the entire world. It seems that in some way, dreaming takes its energy from the world. At first, the world could recover, but now that it's in constant use through continual dreaming it no longer has time to recover. And the holes are part of this. The holes are caused by dreaming. That's why there's forest fires and floods. Earthquakes and tidal waves.'

The wind in the street blew the tin can rattling away into the distance.

'Kerten, the murdered boy, was a Dreamer. He had just graduated. He would have been one of the great Dreamers. He could dream a garden from a grain of sand. But he opposed the Regent because he saw the damage that dreaming was doing to Balthasar. He believed the purpose of dreaming had been corrupted. So the Regent decided to get rid of him. Kerten had been on the run for months. And you saw his murder.'

Toby remembered that look of helplessness in the boy's face – that plea for help.

'The Dreamers are so tightly controlled by the Regent, you see, they have to do exactly what he says. And even if I could get you into the castle, I couldn't get you to the Dreamers – they're closely guarded by the Regent himself. Especially now, after Kerten's treachery. And, I'm sorry, I cannot face the man. I haven't the courage to go against him. It's a shame the queen can't do anything.'

'Queen Edwige?'

'No, she was many generations ago. There's another queen now. But she can't do anything.'

'Why can't she? She could help me, couldn't she? If she's queen, she must have more power than the Regent. I could go to her. Go to the top if you want something done, Dad always says.'

'In theory, you're right, Toby, but in practice, she's –'

But Toby didn't find out what the queen was, because a commotion began in the street – it sounded like a pack of dogs falling upon their prey. There were squeals of animal pain and ferocious snarls like motors being started, a human shout, the sound of galloping, then a loud bang as the downstairs door was thrown open and its handle hit the wall, and another bang as it was slammed shut, then somebody thumped up the stairs and the door was launched wide and there, face rivered with sweat, stood Burston Shimpling.

'The shadow,' he gasped. 'It's out there.'

He kicked shut the door and pressed against it. Then he rushed to the window, cupped his hands against the glass, and looked out. Mervyn joined him.

'Tree-wolves,' said Mervyn. He turned. 'Toby, you have to go. The Watch will be here in a minute. The tree-wolves must have followed you here.'

A hollow boom came from downstairs.

They all froze.

'What was that?' said Toby.

'It's here,' cried Burston. 'The shadow.'

'Lock the door!' yelled Mervyn.

'It's too late for that.'

'I said,' the archivist shouted, running across the room, 'lock the door!'

The door blasted open.

In the first rush, Toby saw nothing but a pair of eyes, a mouth. Both wide, both screaming. Then the shadow hit him. A wave of sickness passed through him and he hunched over and vomited. The room went dark – the candles must have been blown out – and when he straightened snow was tumbling everywhere. The stove door had been flung open and its glow sent shadows across the wall. Something dived into the flames and flew out with a scattering of sparks. There were thuds, bangs, furniture overturned, a terrible scream. Paper pinned to the wall caught fire. Another scream, and Toby watched as the shadow grew, grew further, took up the entire room, had to lean over to fit in the space. It hulked above Burston who cowered before it. The shadow's face lowered, its black mouth opened, its long curved teeth closed about Burston's skull.

'No!' shouted Toby and the shadow turned to him and for a moment, Toby saw a face. A human face.

Burston sailed sideways and dropped unconscious to the floor. The shadow shrank from its giant shape, grew smaller and smaller, concentrated itself, became more dense, narrowed to a long fluid form with eyes of malice – a weasel – and launched itself.

Toby did not have time to move. It poured into him.

All the blackest things that it seemed possible for the world to have – hate and hurt, pain and rage – shot through him and Toby stood dazed, his brain immersed.

211

Something cracked. Wind roared. Opening his eyes, Toby saw the curtains pouring in the open window and had an after-feeling, almost a taste on his tongue, or an idea that he couldn't quite formulate, or a memory of something that he couldn't quite recover. Of what? He didn't know but he wanted suddenly to cry. Then Mervyn was rushing past him with a blanket and beating the flames on the wall. Wind was whipping round him, the flames were spreading across the papers on the floor and on the wall, and Burston was rolling in the corner, hunched, moaning.

'Quick, Toby,' called Mervyn, 'or the building will burn down.'

A small island of fire lay on the floor near him. He jumped on it. It escaped from under his foot. It was like trying to flatten a particularly cunning rat. He squashed it. He saw another flame, squashed that, then another, and another. From the corner of his eye, he could see that Mervyn had extinguished the fire on the wall, and was tackling another on the door.

Meanwhile, Burston had got to his feet and, seeing Toby's fire-fighting, joined in. Soon the three of them were stamping about in a heavy jig. Finally, all the fires were out.

Toby stood dizzy, nauseous, trembling with cold after being touched by the shadow. Mervyn shut the window and the room quietened.

'It's gone,' said Mervyn. 'Are you all right, Toby? It went right through you.'

'Yes. I – I think so.' He wasn't quite sure *how* he felt. In the window glass he saw the face of Tamurlaine, floating off in the distance. He rubbed his eyes to clear his vision. He hoped she was all right, out there in the night at the mercy of the shadow.

Mervyn locked the door and lit a candle. 'Quick. The Watch will be here any moment. The tree-wolves will report you. You have to go. There's a fire escape outside the window.' He went to re-open the window. Toby crouched to see if he could locate Alfred – he would be hiding somewhere.

'Er, people,' whispered Burston.

'Now!' said Mervyn, opening the window. 'You have to go now.'

'I have to find Alfred.'

'There's no time.'

'Um, people,' insisted Burston.

Mervyn was peering out into the darkness for the coming Watch. Toby searched under the bookshelves.

'Um, people, I hate to tell you this, but, um … I think you should take a look.'

Burston was standing flat against the wall, his eyes trained on a point on the ceiling. They followed his gaze. There, small and crooked, hung the shadow. For a few seconds, no one spoke.

'What are we going to do?' said Burston in a whisper.

'I think the main thing,' said Mervyn, 'is not to annoy it.'

'I wasn't going to annoy it,' said Burston.

The shadow had taken the form of a bat. It fluttered a shadow-wing and they all ducked. It seemed to be washing itself, pushing its head under its wing and licking.

'Perhaps it'll leave on its own,' said Mervyn.

'Oh sure,' said Burston.

From behind a box of books, Alfred appeared. He sashayed out into the middle of the room until he stood right below the shadow, then he sat, oblivious to the darkness above him. The shadow-creature's head popped downwards, and its ears pricked up and its tiny eyes peered.

'Alfred!' hissed Toby.

'It's moving,' said Burston. 'Do something!'

'Alfred!'

There was a rumble on the stairs and it sounded like an entire football team was running up them. Alfred strolled over to Toby and allowed himself to be lifted. The shadow-bat twitched. The door handle was tried then heavy fists boomed. 'Open up for the Watch!'

'Toby!' mouthed Mervyn from the window.

'Uh-oh,' said Burston. 'It's changing.'

And indeed, it was. Deepening its shade. Almost to black, perhaps even purple. Then it definitely was purple, then it grew purpler than purple, the whole thing had gone a disgusting puce. At the same time it was swelling and Toby had the horrible feeling it was about to explode.

'We're looking for a boy,' shouted the voice, trying the door handle again. 'And we understand he's here. You're sheltering a fugitive. Open up!'

'I'll be with you in a minute,' called Mervyn, then whispered, 'Quick!'

More bangs on the door. 'Let us in or we'll kick down this door!'

Bent double beneath the shadow, Toby hurried to the window. But he needed his rucksack to carry Alfred.

'Toby!' hissed Mervyn as Toby rushed back across the room, picked up his rucksack and put Alfred inside.

'Unlock this door now!'

Toby slipped the rucksack onto his back. A boot struck the door. The door shuddered but didn't give way. Toby couldn't get onto the sill so Burston linked his palms and Toby put his foot on them and was heaved onto the ledge. Wind tousled his hair. Burston hauled himself up beside Toby. 'Up there.' Above the window two legs of a ladder projected beyond the sloping roof. Carefully, Toby got to his feet and grabbed the bottom rung. Wooden, slippery.

'I can't –'

Something tapped his shin, and Toby saw Burston's hands were a stirrup again. Lifted, Toby gripped a further rung and hauled himself up and over the lip of the roof. The wind howled and he heard a sound like a car backfiring, then screams, and he knew that the Watch had entered and the shadow had attacked them. Then Burston was tapping his leg again so he began to climb more quickly up the so-called 'fire escape'. He reached the apex of the roof and straddled it. Buffeted by the wind, he waited for Burston to come up the ladder.

'Where's Mervyn?' Toby called.

Eyes narrowed against the wind, Burston simply jabbed a finger for Toby to keeping going down the other side. A second ladder descended to a flat roof. Toby turned and lowered himself down, rung by slippery rung, Burston following. From the flat roof they descended an outer stairway and a minute later they were on the street behind Raven Yard. They ran. The rucksack was heavy on Toby's back. The sound of their steps was covered by the roaring wind. After ten minutes, they stopped.

'What happened to Mervyn?' asked Toby, out of breath.

'I don't know. I only heard the bang.'

'Where are we going?'

This question seemed to take Burston by surprise because he glanced down the road the way they had come, then the way they were heading. He opened and shut his mouth a few times then said, 'I don't know.'

'I have to get to the castle.'

'Well, you're on your own there, Toby Porter.'

'I have to see the Dreamers.'

Burston regarded him strangely.

'What?'

Burston continued to stare.

'What is it?'

Burston's expression changed to one of revulsion.

'Why are you staring at me like that, Burston? I know you don't want to go to the castle. You just have to point me in the right direction. Please, Burston. I have to get Alfred home. I have to get myself home. Mrs Papadopoulos will be worried about Alfred and Mum will be worried about me. I don't belong here. This isn't my world. It's my dad's but it isn't mine.'

Burston's expression had shifted to one of horror.

'What is it?' said Toby. 'You're looking at me like I've got the plague!'

Actually he felt not so much as if he had the plague as that he needed a bath. He was grimy, and he had an itch on his neck, and he wondered if one of Mervyn's hair-bugs had migrated.

'Don't move!' hissed Burston.

Toby halted with his hand half-way to his neck.

'Why?'

'Because,' Burston whispered, 'the shadow is sitting on your shoulder and I think it wants to kill you.'

CHAPTER 14

The Coffin

Toby did not move or breathe. Now, on his shoulder, he could feel the dreadful weight of the shadow. He pictured it in the form it had taken in Raven Yard, with its sleek face and sharp teeth.

'Get it off me, Burston.'

Burston started towards him but stopped.

'What is it? What's wrong?'

The shadow's claws dug into Toby's skin then one paw pushed on his neck and he wanted to disappear. Right that moment. He wanted to be in the new flat with Mum and he promised whatever divine power there might be in the universe that he would never say anything horrible to his mum again if he survived the shadow. The shadow climbed onto his scalp. It was so heavy, about the weight of half a bag of potatoes, that Toby had to strain his neck muscles to keep his head upright.

'What's it doing?' Toby breathed.

'It's … sitting there.'

They stood waiting for something to happen. Toby tried not to move. The wind blew. After about five minutes, Burston yawned.

Toby glared. 'What's it doing now?'

'I think it's gone to sleep.'

'What are we going to do?'

'I don't know,' said Burston. He grew alert. 'Though we should probably do something soon because there's the Watch.'

'Where?'

'End of the street. I'm getting out of here.'

And, so saying, Burston ran away.

'Burston!' seethed Toby, and felt a stirring on the top of his skull.

'Hoi!' a man shouted and Toby ran. It was an upright, stiff-backed jog, as if he was balancing a bucket of water on his head. The shadow growled, and Toby let out a short scream and ran faster. The shadow scrambled down the side of his face to his shoulder, a claw jabbing his nose.

'Eeeugggh!'

The streetlamps had been extinguished in this part of town. He ran through dark courts and passages. Behind him, the men thudded and jingled, and one repeatedly blew a loud whistle. A paw moved on his shoulder. Toby emerged onto a street and pelted along it. And there, at the end of a lamplit bridge, hulked the castle.

The archway into the castle beneath a gatehouse was as black as a cave. From behind Toby came urgent whistles and shouts. He was cut off from retreat. Slipping his rucksack from his shoulders gingerly so as not to disturb the shadow, he fetched out the emblem of the swan and gripped it in his palm. If it worked once, it could work twice. He started across the bridge.

A blast of wind blew him sideways. The castle sang a high note as if it was excited he was coming. It accompanied this with a *ting-ting-ting*, like an orchestra's triangle being repeatedly struck. The bodies of hanged men swayed from the bridge's lamp-posts, their ravaged crow-eaten faces swinging into lamplight, grimacing at him. From the cave of the gateway stepped a figure. Toby's heart accelerated into a drum-roll and suddenly he needed to pee. Behind him the men of the Watch were thundering onto the open space before the bridge. The figure from the gatehouse stepped into the light and Toby saw it was Barry Cheyn.

Toby couldn't trick his way past Barry Cheyn. Barry knew Toby was a fugitive. Toby faced about. The Watch were coming onto the bridge. Toby walked to the parapet. It was not a man-made bridge but a roadway built along a thin strand of cliff that ran from the hillside neighbourhood he'd come from to the headland on which the castle sat. A long way below were rocks, a bit of beach, and harbour water. The wailing castle climbed up the musical scale as if it knew something had changed, locating a murderous note. The troop of men were closing in. Barry was coming towards him. Toby gripped the cold stone of the parapet.

The shadow climbed onto Toby's head, across his scalp and, clinging by its two arms to his hair, hung before his face. Toby gazed into a pair of dark, gleaming eyes. They looked as if they could see inside him to all the feelings he had. *Do as I say*, the eyes seemed to say. In fact, they did say this – not out loud, but the words formed in Toby's mind, not in his own voice, but the shadow's. It was a whispery voice. The shadow let go of his hair and dropped to the parapet then to the ground where it formed itself into a mini-human shape, a ninja. It held Toby's hand.

The sensation of being touched by the shadow was strange. It had touched his skin while it moved from his shoulder to his head but that had been a cold paw and claw; also, it had fired into him, including once when it had made him vomit, but this time it held him intentionally and … carefully. There was no other word for it, the touch was careful. It was also clammy and cold, as if he was being touched by a sea creature, or something like … moss. A feeling of wanting to cry rose in him but he didn't have time to start crying because the mossy hand of the shadow tugged and he understood it wanted him to crouch and, as Barry and the men of the Watch converged, the shadow rose, grew larger, and covered Toby completely.

'He's disappeared,' said one of the men.

'I don't understand. He was right here.'

'Did he get past you?'

'No.'

'Well, he's not jumped for it.'

'He must've got past you, Barry.'

'No one's gone past me. You can see for yourself.'

'Well, I never.'

'Totally bizarre.'

'He must have got past somehow. Must have done. Right, you two stay with Barry at the gatehouse and the rest of you come with me. He's trying to get to the Dreamers. That's what Mervyn Sump told us.'

So Mervyn had betrayed Toby at the first opportunity. Well, the man was right about one thing – he was a coward. The shadow was clearly furious about the betrayal too, grabbing Toby's wrist and digging its nails into his skin.

Toby remained on his haunches, watching as the men from the Order of the Swan jogged to the gatehouse. They vanished inside, leaving Barry Cheyn and two others on guard. The shadow withdrew itself from Toby and stood. Then it moved back along the bridge, away from the castle. Toby followed, crouching low by the parapet, checking behind several times. At the end of the bridge was an opening in the wall over the harbour and here the shadow went down steep stone steps. Toby followed.

The lower steps were sandy and on the last one the shadow, still in its ninja form, stopped. Ahead lay the inlet and its small beach. The tide was coming in fast and only one small corner, about the size of a beach-towel, was dry, but the water was shallow enough to cross. On the other side of the inlet rose jagged, inhospitable rocks, and above them stood the castle walls, too high to climb. A short way along the headland, among the rocks, was a sheer brick wall as high as a house and at its top a terrace. The semi-circular wall looked at risk of collapse. It was studded with anchor plates and tie-rods like giant washers and screws, that Toby supposed fixed the crumbling wall to something solid on the far side of the terrace. Timber buttresses skirted the wall, black from being continually soaked by seawater. In spite of these attempts to contain the terrace, its wall tilted crazily outwards. One area was not at risk of collapse – it had already given way and bricks and black earth and broken wooden boxes containing long white stones had spilled down into the sea. Through this gap, Toby could see what the terrace contained – a graveyard. With a shiver of revulsion he realised that the long white stones spilling down towards the sea were actually human bones.

A darkness moved beside him – the shadow, pointing. At first he thought it was pointing to the graveyard, then he saw it was indicating much further round, to the tip of the headland, where there was scaffolding. Toby remembered that the scaffolding covered the castle all the way up to that golden window he'd seen the night before. Was the shadow suggesting he climb and get in through that window?

'The scaffolding?'

The shadow pointed again, more emphatically, and Toby could make out, above the graveyard terrace, a dark door in the castle wall. Of course. There had to be a way for people from the castle to reach the graveyard. Steps descended from that door to the burial ground and on its seaward side a gate opened to another set of steps, hewn from the rock, which Toby hadn't at first noticed, and which led down to the inlet. All Toby had to do was wade across the shallow water to reach the steps.

Taking off his shoes (the leather soles that Ranger Widgeon had sewn on were holding out well), he tied their laces together and hung them about his neck, pulled off his socks and stuffed them in his shoes, then rolled up his trousers. He checked on Alfred, who was eager to climb out, and zipped him up again, causing a frenzy of scratches and miaowed complaints. Finally he threaded his arms through the straps so the rucksack sat once more against his chest. Checking what the shadow was doing – it seemed to be waiting for him – he stepped into the sea.

Cold seized his ankle. He lowered his other foot and gasped. He felt that half potato bag of weight climb up his jumper and wrap its arms round his neck. The shadow wanted him to carry it? Exasperated, wanting to tell the shadow to wade across on its own but knowing it wasn't a good idea to antagonise a shadow, Toby hesitated. It tapped him on the shoulder: *Get moving!*

The steps were around sixty metres away. But the beach shelved and the water came up almost to his knees. Each time a wave rolled in he had to stand on tiptoes so his trousers did not get wet. The waves swept swiftly past him and struck the cliff with a splash, smaller ones making a clucking sound, catching in the hollows and clefts of rock, and the wind blew spray off the surface of the harbour; Toby had left his cape at Mervyn's apartment in his hurry to escape and he was getting soaked.

Although he pulled his trousers further up his thighs, and held them as he waded, each wave now soaked the bottoms. After a dozen or so paces he gave up any hope of remaining dry and pushed, slowly, onwards. He kept his eyes fixed on the steps – his destination, and the only way home.

A big piece of flotsam scooted with a wave and Toby fended off what turned out to be a long wooden chest, or perhaps it was a boxily shaped kayak, although he couldn't see the hole where a person would sit. Either the tide had risen or the beach shelved more steeply at this point, but whichever the cause, one wave climbed over his waist and he shuddered with the cold. He had travelled only twenty metres. He wondered if it might be easier to paddle on the box to the other side because at the moment he was in danger of being lifted off his feet and thrown against the cliff. Placing both hands on top of the box, he tried to open it. He felt the lid loosen. There were nails, but the wood must have rotted or the nails worked free in the water, because the top came off without any trouble. A bad smell – of cabbagey farts and a sort of yellowy rot – rose up and communicated in a flash what the box held.

Toby pushed the coffin away and stumbled backwards and lost his footing. The next wave sent him towards the rock wall, the coffin coming with him. The shadow scrambled onto his head. Toby regained his footing. The shadow sat on his shoulders. Toby moved out of the path of the coffin. The rucksack was soaked. He raised it, dripping, and undid the zip. Alfred was squirming frantically and Toby lifted him out. He was a drenched cat. No longer able to use his arms for balance, Toby waded on, the sea up to his stomach, each wave rising to the lowest of his ribs. The smell of death would not leave his nostrils.

He was about half-way across when he heard voices above him on the bridge. He could feel the shadow pressing against the back of his skull but didn't know whether to go on or stop or wade up to the cliff face, out of sight. If someone glanced over the edge they would see him in the lamplight. Alfred miaowed. Someone appeared above. Toby froze. Barry Cheyn. Barry's back was against the parapet and he was leaning backwards. If he turned round he'd see Toby. Toby clamped shut Alfred's mouth. Alfred swiped at him with his paws. Toby heard a snatch of speech. '.... do that,' Barry was saying. The other person's reply was taken by the wind. Barry said '... never did.' Alfred scrabbled against his chest. He was trying to warn him of something. Toby looked about. A broad shape was lolloping through the harbour beyond the inlet, its smooth back rising and falling as it crossed to and fro in the deeper water. It kept turning to come into the inlet, rising from the surface then catching on the shallow seabed as, wriggling and jerking, it tried to get to Toby. Its frustrated repetitive ramming, the blind stupidity of it, scared Toby. A wave rose up Toby's chest. The creature – it was the whale-like thing he'd seen earlier in the day – raced back and forth.

'... assisted a fugitive,' a voice said from the bridge above.

The creature slipped beneath the water. Toby, his body numb with cold, watched the broad back approach from far out in the harbour, as if taking a run-up for a long jump. What was it Burston said had replaced the ships of Balthasar's navy? Some dreamed thing. Whatever it was, it was coming for him. At speed. The creature breached and revealed itself as a gross-bellied ulcer. Swollen and eyeless, it had a white tip that looked ready to burst. It leapt as if Toby was lunch and the ulcer was starving. It fell short and splashed about, stranded. Toby backed up towards the cliff face. He bumped the coffin as the ulcer flopped and lunged at him. Above, Barry Cheyn shouted, 'I didn't help him. The kid tricked me. I promise I didn't do it on purpose.'

The ulcer wriggled, the coffin bumped, and Toby pushed the lid off and popped Alfred inside. The shadow jumped in and, as the ulcer dragged itself painfully over the sandy bottom of the beach towards him, Toby managed to pull himself into the coffin too, landing in something mushy.

He rolled over onto his back and directly above saw the frog-like face of Barry Cheyn, hanging over the parapet. Two men of the Watch were holding him. It seemed to be the Watch's favourite game, dropping people from heights. Barry saw Toby lying there beside the rotting corpse stinking of cabbage and dustbins, and Toby guessed what Barry might be thinking. He would be thinking of himself, just like Toby's dad always did, and would betray Toby immediately. No, he would be thinking not only of himself but also of his three children on their holidays who would not eat unless he did extra shifts, and of those children losing their father and his wife losing her husband, and Toby knew that if their positions were reversed, and Toby could save his own family – Mum and Dad and Alfred and Mrs Papadopoulos – by denouncing Barry, then Toby would do it because, for Toby, love was stronger than honour.

But Barry was not Toby.

'I'd never help an enemy of the Regent,' insisted Barry loudly to his two captors, his eyes locked on Toby.

The two men of the Watch pulled him off the parapet and, with shouts and raised voices, marched Barry Cheyn away for some dreadful punishment.

Toby could not believe it. The man had chosen to help *him* even though it meant he would be hurt, possibly executed.

The ulcer was thrashing through the shallows towards Toby. Alfred was standing on the corpse, front legs on the side of the coffin, hissing at the ulcer, ready to fight. Toby, rolling over on the dead body, which softened and collapsed under his weight with an audible crumple, grabbed the unwieldy coffin-lid and sat up. Immediately the wind tried to rip the lid from Toby's hands and hurl it away, and Toby wrestled for control while the ulcer, with a helpful push from a wave and the rising tide, bumped the coffin, nearly capsizing it. Alfred swiped with a claw, scratching the ulcer. The sea boiled as the ulcer went into a frenzy of rage and pain. Its skin must have been super-sensitive to feel Alfred's scratch. Holding the wider end of the coffin lid, Toby plunged the thin end into the water. He paddled as fast as he could.

Soon, they were in shallower waters and the ulcer could not reach them and now Toby made his way more steadily towards the far side of the inlet. The corpse, its flesh putrefied by rot and seawater, its thin hair waving in the wind over the empty sockets of its once-seeing eyes, looked upon clouds sweeping across the sky and felt without any sense of touch the lovely sea air, and silently thanked Toby for this ride across the inlet, while the ulcer spewed its poisonous liquid, wanting to devour human flesh and that damned cat.

But Toby left the ulcer behind and paddled to the castle of Balthasar.

*

Toby plodded with his bedraggled cat between gravestones up to the castle wall. There was no handle on the door. Toby strained against it with his shoulder but it sat in its frame as solid as stone. He put his head against the wood and struck with his forehead three times. How could he have been so stupid as to think he could just walk into the Regent's fortress? The shadow, which had raced up the rocks and through the graveyard like a greyhound, moved to the side of the door then narrowed itself until it was as thin as a sheet of paper. Then it simply poured itself into the door's black edge, like liquid.

Toby waited, soaking wet, teeth chattering, body shaking, beside the castle which had lowered its murderous wail to a moan. Alfred hunched, shivering.

A bolt clunked, a lock *thunked*, and the door opened. Before Toby stood a figure – but not the shadow. A teenage girl. She wore a dark dress with a ragged hem and a low neckline that showed bony collarbones. She was slightly faint and she beckoned him inside.

Toby did not move. 'What – ?' he said. 'How did you get here? Wait. Are you – ? Are you the – ? You're the shadow?'

'Hurry up and come inside,' said Tamurlaine. 'Or you'll catch your death of cold.'

CHAPTER 15

The Storeroom

Toby and Alfred stepped inside the castle and Tamurlaine locked the door. They were at one end of a stone corridor that ran away towards the heart of the building like a tunnel. The castle's weight felt oppressive and gloomy.

'Come on,' she whispered.

Toby was going nowhere. 'Y-y-y-you're the shadow!' he said, shivering with cold.

'Shh!' she hissed, stepping close.

'Don't t-t-t-t-t-t-touch me!'

'I'm not going to touch you. Come on!'

'Y-y-y-you are, aren't you? You're the shadow.'

'Well ... Yes,' she said, as if she hadn't really thought about it before. 'I suppose I am.' Her features barely visible, the faint light behind her, Toby couldn't see the expression on her face. She moved away.

'You hurt me!' he said, his voice booming off the stone walls.

'Shh! Are you trying to get caught?'

'You m-m-m-made me vomit. You s-s-s-scared the life out of me about seven times.' He wanted to hit her. His body was juddering with cold and he couldn't stop it.

There were the sounds of steps outside the castle and Tamurlaine seized his shoulder. Toby managed to control his shaking. The steps were heavy, boot-like. Neither spoke. The boots clumped past.

'A patrol,' she whispered after a minute had passed. 'Come on.'

He remained where he was. 'It all s-started with you,' he hissed. 'C-coming to Arnold Street, ruining our lives. We were happy.'

'Come *on*!'

'You ruined my life.'

'You weren't happy, Toby, you were miserable. You were all miserable.' She took his hand. His flesh was as cold as hers. So now he was as cold as a shadow, he thought. She pulled, gently. 'Come on. This is how you get home.' She waited for him. And where else was he going to go? She knew the way to the Dreamers. He went with her. But he didn't like her.

At the end of that dark, dank corridor lit by a dim

233

blue stone in a cage on the wall, a spiral staircase took them dizzily up into a darkened room of chunky shapes – tables and counters. Beyond, way down a hallway, shone firelight. Tamurlaine headed for it and Toby squelched after her.

An old man was coming down the hallway, half turned to grumble at several boys behind, shuffling and puffing with the effort of keeping up some heavy object they were carrying. It was the carcass of a pig – one of the giant pigs from the sheds in the city – partly wrapped in a blood-stained sheet. The little procession hadn't seen them. Tamurlaine plucked Toby's sleeve and they slipped into a side-room. Its acoustics suggested a crypt or cellar but it was too dark to see properly what it was. Toby knocked into something that clanged. As he reeled away, he toed something which was heavy and tripped, landing on what felt like a sack of sand. He managed to get up, only to bash his head on a shelf. He sat back down with a thump.

'Shh!' Tamurlaine whispered as outside the old man hobbled past with the straining, shuffling boys and that dead pig.

Toby tried to sit still but couldn't stop shivering. His sopping clothes clung to him. He could hear the seawater dripping off him onto the flagstones. His teeth chattered.

'Shh!'

'I c-c-c-can't shh,' he breathed. 'I'm freezing to death.'

Her eyes gleamed. 'Here,' she whispered, and put some rough material into his hands. It felt like a sack, and smelled mustily of grain. 'Take off your clothes and get dry.' He did while she brought more sacking, and he dried himself as best he could, the coarsely woven material rough on his skin. His eyes began to adjust to the darkness – there was the faintest of light from a narrow window near the ceiling. He lifted Alfred, who looked like a cartoon electrified cat, fur on end, wet-through, and dried him too. Tamurlaine crouched at the door, listening.

Who was Tamurlaine exactly, Toby wondered? *What* was she? A person or a shadow? Both? Whoever or whatever she was, she knew the castle. Had she lived here then? Perhaps she had been an opponent of the Regent, like the murdered boy Kerten. Yes! She had been a friend of Kerten, she had said. Was she a Dreamer, then? She was the right age – the Dreamers were teenagers. No. If she was a Dreamer, she would have been able to dream Toby home herself and she was taking him to the Dreamers. But if she was able to become a shadow, perhaps she was a dream, then? One of Kerten's dreams maybe. Toby wondered if she would stay in this form as Tamurlaine now. Part of him wanted to ask, part of him was scared to, but mostly he wanted to go across to her, put the sole of his shoe on her back, and push her over so she'd bash her head on the door, he was so angry with the way she'd treated him when she was a shadow, twice frightening him in his world, then firing through his body, first in the mountains and then in Mervyn's room. Although, he suspected it wasn't wise to push over a person who sets off air-blasts and transforms herself into a shadow-animal that can pass through people and make them throw up. He sighed loudly and she turned, her eyes bright with warning.

Stupid shadow-Tamurlaine!

Toby leaned his head back against the wall and thought of home. His mum would be worrying badly. This would be the fourth night he had been away. She would think he was dead – murdered, or killed in an accident. He wished their last conversation, in the car outside school, had not ended like it had. He'd been horrible to her. He had cut her. He shut his eyes and said to her silently he was sorry. Sorry, sorry, sorry.

In that silent place of his mind, Toby heard his dad snort a sarcastic laugh at him for apologising to Mum. *The sooner you realise things don't work out for the best,* his dad had said, *the better.* He said it on the day Toby and his mum had left Arnold Street for the new flat. And things hadn't worked out for the best.

No, that wasn't it. His dad had said something else. He'd said *in this world.* Things don't work out for the best in this world. And Toby wasn't in *this world* any more, he was in Balthasar. And things could work out differently here. Dreams could become reality. So maybe things could still work out for the best. Maybe what Tamurlaine said, that none of them had been happy in Arnold Street, could be changed. Maybe all Toby needed to do was get the Dreamers to dream everything right again. Make his family intact.

In fact, it occurred to Toby, the Dreamers didn't even need to dream his family back together. Toby had an idea. Not one to do with the Dreamers at all. And his idea was this – if he made a mental note of everything he heard and saw in Balthasar, if he learned about the rulers of the kingdom, and how the place worked, then maybe he could take this information back to his dad and help him finish his novel. That was it – Dad would be happy if he finished his novel and would stop being mean to Mum. Toby would fix his parents' marriage himself. He would fix the family. And if there was one thing Toby was good at, it was fixing things. It would be easier than any repair of a window or chair he'd done. All he had to do was notice, and when he got home, tell his dad what he'd seen. He would bring his family back together.

He felt elated.

Suddenly Tamurlaine was beside him and Toby sat bolt upright. He hadn't heard her move. By the faint light from the window, he saw her place her finger to her lips – *shh!* They were almost touching and Toby was super-aware of her. She sat in profile, facing the window, straining to hear noises outside in the hallway, and he saw her nose and the pursing of the lips, her shining eyes. Her chin was tilted upwards. He wondered if this was the real her or if the shadow was the real her. Or perhaps both of them were the real her. Why couldn't people be two things? She made a noise. Was it a ... sniffle?

Did shadows cry?

But why would she cry?

In a flash he understood – she was lost. Like him, she was lost and trying to remember who she was and where her home was.

He patted her shoulder. It wasn't a very sympathetic pat; Toby didn't totally like her right then and also he anticipated the unpleasant feelings he'd experienced when she'd attacked him before – fear and sadness and hate – but he touched her shoulder anyway. It was firm and bony. She turned to face him and her expression softened and she seemed ... ordinary. An ordinary, somewhat faint girl who was very sad. He wanted to comfort her. He wanted to ask her questions too. Who she was, *what* she was, *how* she was whatever she was. Why she had come back for him and got him into the castle. Why she had ... It occurred to him then, in another flash, that actually she had helped him. Even when she was the shadow. She had saved him when he was caught by the killer in the forest fire. Then she had saved him again, by chasing him off the cliff so he fell through the fir-tree and out of the path of the fire. And even recently, after she had left him at the Bureau of Broken Dreams when she was Tamurlaine, she had come back for him as the shadow and saved him from the Watch in Mervyn Sump's room, and saved him from the Watch again on the bridge. And got him into the castle. Even here, she had led him to this hiding place.

'You've helped me,' he whispered. 'Why?'

'Why'd you think?'

Tamurlaine moved and her hand grazed his. She was icy, colder even than Toby. He flinched, and she sat upright and they both seemed separate again as if there had never been any closeness.

It was lonely being a shadow, Toby decided.

The sounds of the old man and the boys grew loud then faded away – they had taken the carcass of the pig wherever they were going and passed back along the hallway.

'Let's go,' said Tamurlaine.

Toby went to put Alfred in the rucksack but the cat point-blank refused to get inside.

'You have to, Alfred.'

Alfred miaowed a firm *No*.

Toby sighed and warned the cat to be absolutely silent. He shoved his wet clothes in his rucksack. His shoes and socks were the only dry things, still tied together by their laces and strung round his neck. He put them on, and so, with one sack wrapped round his middle like a towel, and another round his shoulders, the three of them slipped from the room.

CHAPTER 16

A Game of Cards

The firelight came from the kitchen, a place of shadowy vaults and blackened brick, busy with preparations for a great feast. Pastry chefs were rolling dough and others spooning fruit jellies into strudels and Danishes, tray after tray of them being pulled from big ovens. The servant boys who'd carried the pig were hefting cases to a table where the old man counted out bottles of wine. One chef, a woman with a mop of dark hair, glanced up towards Toby and Tamurlaine. They froze but she had only stopped to wipe sweat from her brow with a forearm and returned to plucking feathers. Toby, Tamurlaine and Alfred kept to the kitchen's darkest edges, under the half-moon windows and hanging copper saucepans and black frying pans.

The fireplace was wide enough for a class of children to gather inside to thaw out from a winter afternoon of standing around pointlessly on a frosty playing field, and Toby wished he could get in there and warm up. He felt jealous of the pheasants rotating on a clockwork spit, getting nicely cooked. But he couldn't go over, a *saucier* was there, stirring about a dozen pots hung over the flames, pausing every so often to decide if her recipes tasted right. The three of them went on past the end of a counter and there, on the hearth, lay a pack of dogs. Tawny, white, speckled, grey, fawn, with long, slender snouts. They were so intertwined it was impossible to see how many there were. The exit was on the far side of the hearth so Toby, Tamurlaine and Alfred would have to sneak past dogs and *saucier*.

They waited until the *saucier* had her back to them then moved slowly across the flagstones. The bellies of the dogs rose and fell in their sleep. One lifted its head. Toby stopped. Alfred stopped. Tamurlaine stopped. The *saucier* moved to the end of the fireplace so she could go round and taste the sauces at the back, at which point she would see them. But they couldn't move because the dog was growling at them. 'Shh,' Tamurlaine breathed softly. The dog growled more loudly. Alfred shot forward, arched his back, and hissed. The dog dropped its head and whimpered. They crept on. The *saucier* tried the final mixture at the front. They would have to be quick. From her apron, the *saucier* took a packet, pinched out some powder and sprinkled it into the pot. They were nearly past the fireplace. They were going to make it. Another dog stirred. They halted. It clambered to its feet, stepped across and blocked their path, a low rumble starting in its chest. Alfred crouched warningly but it made no difference, then Tamurlaine slipped past and offered her hand. The dog sniffed and wagged its tail and she gently led it back to the pack. It settled down with a sleepy groan but when Tamurlaine stood, the dog tried to follow her and Tamurlaine had to crouch and pet it. The *saucier* moved round the back of the fire. Toby wanted to shout *Hurry up, Tam!* From deep in its chest the dog let out a long happy growl, and the *saucier* looked up.

Toby felt naked on the flagstones. He *was* nearly naked, wrapped in sacking; he certainly wouldn't pass for a servant boy. But the *saucier* moved on as if she hadn't seen him. Toby and Tamurlaine exchanged a glance. They hurried for the door. As Toby left the kitchen, he saw that the flames were so close to the *saucier*'s eyes, and so bright, she had been blinded. The fire had effectively hidden them.

'That dog knew you,' whispered Toby, as they hurried down the corridor. 'I think you're from the castle.'

'So do I.'

They passed a cavernous furnace-room in which dream-figures were shovelling coal. Bears and a demon, who had a monkey-tail and folded wings, worked together with men, who looked like professional wrestlers. Blackened by coal dust, soot and shadows from the fire, their actual shadows playing about the ceiling, they were transferring lumps of coal from a hillock via wheelbarrows to the furnace doors, where they chucked them inside. On top of the hillock, naughty chimpanzees tossed lumps of coal to one another like juggling balls, and one of the wrestlers kept shouting at them to stop.

Further along the corridor Tamurlaine opened a door to a staircase as dark as a mine and so steep and narrow it might have been made for mountain goats. Toby went first. They climbed silently in the dark until Toby bumped into two servant girls who were rushing down. The first one shrieked and the girls turned back, giggling, and waited on the next floor for Toby to come up. 'Sorry,' the first one began as Toby emerged, then she saw him properly and burst out laughing. 'It's a street kid!' she announced. 'Go on, back to Fredegund's Armpit, you filthy beggar.'

'These are the royal apartments, you daft nut,' said the second girl.

'You can't come in here dressed like that.'

'Not dressed at all, is he?'

'But for a sack.'

'Daft lad.'

Toby was digging in his rucksack for the swan emblem when the first girl grabbed his earlobe. 'Ow!'

'Get out of here, you son of a shleg!'

Tamurlaine stepped from the staircase and both girls were stunned. The first blushed, the second ducked her head, bobbing, and the pair shot past them and clattered down the stairs, shrieking with laughter.

Neither Toby nor Tamurlaine had to say anything – Tamurlaine had been recognised.

The royal apartments, like everywhere else in the castle, were dimly lit. Candles had been set on tables. There were gas lamps on the walls but none of them were working. The candle flames bowed as Tamurlaine and Toby passed. Tamurlaine's attention was drawn to a framed picture on the wall.

'What is it?' Toby whispered.

It was not a picture but a mirror. What did she see? The reflection seemed strange to her, although it showed herself. She touched her own face, pressing at her cheeks, cheek-bones, lips, jaw, temples, forehead, like a blind person deciphering something never before encountered.

'Are you all right?'

She seemed overwhelmed.

'Do you decide when you change?' Toby asked. 'From shadow to person, I mean.'

After a pause, as if she had to think about this question, she shook her head slowly. 'It just happens. It happened the first time on the mountain. In the fire.'

'I'd find it frightening.'

'I don't really think about it. It feels normal.'

They crept on. Voices came from a room off the corridor, and they stopped. The doors were open and they would be visible when they went past. They inched forwards. Toby indicated he would go first then Tamurlaine ruined everything by entering the room.

'Tam!' breathed Toby but it was too late. He darted to the gap by the door-hinges and peered through. The room was shadowy, neither chandelier nor wall lamps working. Flickering candlelight and firelight illuminated four people at a table playing cards. Two servants stood like waxworks in the darker reaches of the room but Toby couldn't see Tamurlaine.

'Oh no,' Toby whispered to himself when he saw one of the card players. It was the teenage blond Dreamer who had flown after Tamurlaine. He wore a black velvet cloak, its edges decorated with green thread, which was fixed at the throat by an ivory swan on a black field. Toby felt sick. But there was no immediate danger because the boy seemed stupefied – his head lolled sideways, his mouth hung slack, and his eyelids drooped.

But where was Tam?

'You sure you want to play that card, Dreamer?' said a flabby man with grey hair. His hair was so flat on his skull it appeared to have been slapped on. He hunched over his own cards as if hoarding them, or perhaps it was only that he had poor eyesight. Toby looked at the other players. The flabby man's card partner was a gaunt jewelled woman who registered each unkind sound or comment that came from the flabby man (there were many of them) by doodling deep marks on a pad of paper. Most of the unpleasant remarks seemed aimed at the Dreamer. The fourth player, the card partner of the blond teenage Dreamer, was a tiny old lady in a long black dress whose feet barely touched the floor. Her skin was chalky, and she seemed nearly faded to dust, or perhaps it only seemed like that because she used a lot of powder in her make-up. Her hair was as thin as the hair of the corpse in the coffin. Toby thought that the old lady would probably soon join that corpse and go bumping about the harbour in her own casket. She wasn't dead yet though. When she sat back after playing a card, the tips of her toes left the floor and she swung her legs like a little girl, and her lips were moving as she kept up a stream of silent chatter to herself on some mysterious topic.

'You really are playing a pig-thick hand, Dreamer,' said the flabby man to the blond teenager who, despite his stupefaction, had played a card.

'Lord Snow,' scolded the gaunt, jewelled woman – so quietly that Toby wasn't entirely certain she had spoken.

'Yes, Lady Snow?' replied the nasty piece of work. 'What are you moaning about now?'

Lady Snow dropped her gaze to her pad of paper, and scored some deep marks. 'Nothing. It's just ... Ollie will hear you.'

'No he won't – Look at him.' The blond teenage boy drooled, saliva darkening black velvet. 'He's barely conscious. Here lies Ollie Reckless, used-up Dreamer.'

'Please, my love, you'll get us in trouble,' the gaunt woman pleaded. Turning to the old lady and trying to change the subject, Lady Snow went on, 'Mrs Bleverhasset, I'm *so* looking forward to the feast tomorrow night, aren't you?'

The old lady, Mrs Bleverhasset, murmured something to herself on her mysterious topic, but did not respond to the question.

'Hogs' ears!' exclaimed Lord Snow, as if the mention of the upcoming feast had put food into his mind.

One of the servants appeared with a plate of hairy, pink ears.

'Well, I'm looking forward to it very much, Mrs Bleverhasset,' said Lady Snow. 'The Feast of Queen Edwige.'

'The Queen!' cried Mrs Bleverhasset. Roused from her muttering, she gazed at a point above the mantelpiece. 'The Queen!'

Lady Snow caught her husband's attention and rolled her eyes and Lord Snow tapped his temple with a finger and spluttered 'mad' through a mouthful of hogs' ears.

They played a new hand of cards and for a while there was quiet until Lord Snow banged the table. 'We win!'

Ollie Reckless jumped in his seat, waking from his daze.

'Another game?' said Lord Snow. 'Oh, and you, bring me a venison pasty!'

Ollie Reckless wiped his mouth with the back of his hand and looked blinking around the table as if trying to work out where he was. Lord Snow winked at Lady Snow while Ollie Reckless took off his velvet cloak and hung it on the back of this chair. Then he dug in a waistcoat pocket, produced a small tub, unscrewed the top, and scooped out some gel which he smeared beneath each eye. Almost as soon as the gel was applied, he perked up. He sat straight, his eyes brightened and the pupils grew huge, as if he was amazed by everything. Meanwhile, Lord Snow polished off his venison pasty.

'You ready, Mrs Bleverhasset?' said Ollie Reckless.

Mrs Bleverhasset stared at something over the mantelpiece.

'Mrs Bleverhasset?' said Ollie Reckless kindly. 'Shall we destroy Lord and Lady Snow?'

'Urthax.'

'Shall we play?'

'My darling Urthax was only a baby when she was destroyed.'

'I know,' said Lady Snow, taking Mrs Bleverhasset's hand. Toby saw what the old lady's eyes were fixed upon – a painting over the mantelpiece. The light was bad but Toby could make out that it showed a young woman with a toddler on her lap.

'My baby Urthax!'

'Less of this chatter!' said Lord Snow. 'Let's play!'

For several minutes they played in silence. Ollie Reckless was superbly alert, his decisions quick, his movements sharp, his humour good. 'Are you confident of playing that card, sir?' he said to Lord Snow. 'That's a dangerous card to play.'

'Oh really, do you think so?' said Lord Snow. He peered at his cards. 'I can't even see the damn things properly. Bring that candle. Hurry up, man.' A servant brought the candle. 'Tell me this, Dreamer Reckless, when are those damned layabouts in Works going to fix the gas pipes? We're walking around up here like it's the Age of Darkness.'

'I have no idea, Lord Snow,' said Ollie Reckless.

'No idea? But you work for Her Majesty's government.'

'The Queen!' cried Mrs Bleverhasset.

'Shut up! – Blast!'

'He told you not to play that card, dear,' said Lady Snow.

'You can shut up too.' At this latest insult Lady Snow took up her pencil and began doodling again. 'And another three houses collapsed in the city last night. Simply collapsed. I mean, if poor people are stupid enough to live in substandard housing, that's up to them. But three houses? It's getting ridiculous. Well, let's see how you play *this* card.'

The players slapped down their cards until the game was ended by Ollie Reckless spreading his cards on the green baize and smiling.

'Blast!' said Lord Snow. 'Blast! Blast! Blast! Gravy soup!'

A servant appeared with a tray. Slurping. Gulping. Slurping and gulping. Lord Snow squandered much soup down his front. Ollie Reckless dealt.

'What's the government doing about any of it? Fire, floods, sink holes, earthquakes, damned refugees wanting our damned charity. You don't see me asking for charity, do you?'

'Dear, I'm sure they're doing everything they can.'

'*What* are they doing, though? *What?*'

'I wouldn't advise you, sir, to play that particular card.'

'You wouldn't *advise it*, eh? Well, I'll play what I ruddy well like.'

'Dear, he said don't –'

'Blast!'

Lord Snow banged his cards down.

'Dear, you're getting worked up.'

'Shut up!' Lord Snow snapped, and Lady Snow scored savagely on her pad. 'A new hand. Tell me, *what* is the government doing?'

'Mrs Bleverhasset,' said Lady Snow, putting down her pencil and trying to change the subject again, 'Did I tell you, we saw an excellent execution yesterday.'

'The mob are on the verge of revolt. Shlegs stinking up the city. And as if that wasn't enough, the damned shadow's back. I tell you, Regent Malladain's making a right pig's ear of it.'

'Dear!' shushed Lady Snow.

As if mention of a pig's ear had set in motion a new train of thought, Lord Snow yelled to the servants, 'Pickled oysters! Paraguay pie! Collared eels!' before facing Ollie Reckless. 'Regent Malladain's losing the confidence of the royal family. And remember, he rules by favour, not right. *Our* favour. Mine and that of my cousins, aunts, great-aunts and great-uncles, and the rest of the royal family. The Queen is the rightful heir. Not Regent ruddy Malladain.'

'Be quiet, husband!' snapped Lady Snow, her gaunt face now hollow.

'The Queen, the Queen,' moaned old Mrs Bleverhasset. 'And my poor Urthax in her grave.'

'That's treasonous, you know, Lord Snow,' said Ollie Reckless mildly, as if he was enjoying himself, 'what you say about the Regent.'

'Dreamer Reckless,' said Lady Snow, quivering with fear, 'You misheard my husband, I believe. Lord Snow was only reporting what others have said, not what he himself thinks. He would never say a word against the Regent.'

'Don't speak for me, woman.'

'Lord Snow did say a word against the Regent actually,' chuckled Ollie Reckless. 'More than a word. Regent Malladain is not the rightful ruler of Balthasar. That's it, Lord Snow? That's what you said? Lady Snow, please do continue – you saw a good execution yesterday?' He gave the word 'execution' particular stress.

'It's only –' she tried. 'I mean – He'd never – Please.' She clutched the teenage boy's fingers, tears in her eyes. 'Let's not have these dreadful arguments about politics.' Leaning across the table, she said, 'Lord Snow, you didn't say anything against Regent Malladain, did you?'

His temper cooling, Lord Snow blew out a long breath and as he did he seemed to deflate, like a fat balloon growing thin. 'No,' he said, casting his eyes down at his cards.

Ollie Reckless only smiled.

They played on. Lord Snow, now calm, now thoughtful, perhaps even regretful, lightly held his throat between forefinger and thumb, as if imagining a rope being tied around it, and his body swinging from a gibbet on the castle walls while crows pecked at him. Cards slapped on the green baize.

Tamurlaine appeared. She lurked in the furthest corner, and when she stepped forward her features were contorted, stricken, blind almost. Toby held his breath. The four continued to play and did not notice as she came nearer. Her eyes were fixed on the Dreamer, Ollie Reckless, and as she came into their circle of candlelight, she seemed hardly there at all, she was so faint. Toby wondered if daylight somehow had a relation to her form; he had only ever seen the shadow at night, and she was becoming the shadow now. He watched as the shadow-girl – did she even have a name now that Tamurlaine was no longer there? – moved slowly until she was behind Reckless. She leaned close as if she was going to whisper in his ear. Then, slowly, she grew. Toby did not notice it at first because the firelight had burned low and the candles only properly lit the card table, but then he saw that the darkness of the room was *her* darkness and Toby couldn't see where she ended and the room's darkness began. Perhaps she went beyond the room, was the entire castle, and ended only in the wind outside.

'The Queen!' shouted old Mrs Bleverhasset, and pointed. The others turned and saw the shadow. Lady Snow screamed. Lord Snow yelled. The Dreamer Ollie Reckless was astonished. Without his golden net to catch the shadow, he was powerless. He shot out of his seat.

Lord and Lady Snow had already made a run for it. There was a bang. They raced down the hallway, the shadow pouring after them, and Toby was alone.

Toby didn't know what to do – go after the shadow, wait for her, or continue his journey without his guide and hope she'd catch him up.

A blast on a whistle from somewhere nearby decided him. As he hurried past the empty room, he noticed Ollie Reckless's black velvet cloak on the back of a chair. He rushed in and grabbed it and was nearly out again when his head was jerked painfully back. Someone had hold of his hair.

'The Queen!' cried Mrs Bleverhasset in his ear.

She must have been hiding somewhere in the room.

'Let me go!'

She wouldn't release him. 'The Queen. I saw her. Queen Fadranga, the murderer!'

Alfred, watching from the door, sprang at the old woman with a terrifying screech and she shrieked, let go, and tripped. As she struck the hard wood floor, she groaned. Then she was silent.

She did not move.

Was she dead? Had Alfred killed her?

Her eyes opened. 'Urthax. My child. Queen Fadranga murdered her. I saw the Queen. I saw Fadranga tonight. She was here. Stop her!'

Toby knelt beside her. 'Let me help you up.'

She lifted her hand and Toby went to take it but her fingers went past his and dug into his throat like metal claws.

'My daughter must be revenged. My daughter Urthax. I saw Queen Fadranga!'

Toby batted her arm away and hurried out, trembling. From the servants' stairs came raised voices and a blast of the whistle, and Toby and Alfred ran in the other direction.

CHAPTER
17

Central Hall

For a moment Toby thought he was inside a machine. The biggest machine he had ever seen. And the space that housed this machine was bigger than any space he'd been in, than any he knew in London, than the main hall of the Natural History Museum, than the concourse of Waterloo Station, than the dark vaults of Westminster Cathedral; it was a murky void rising from depths far below to a glass dome that seemed printed with odd leaf shapes. Some of the leaves moved and Toby saw they were the webbed feet of dozens of seagulls standing outside on the curved glass, where the wind swept and ruffled the gulls' feathers. Much cosier were the pigeons roosting on the inside of the glass along frilly iron ribs, invisible in the darkness but audible above the rumbling machinery, their coos amplified by the dome. He could also see the white streaks of their crud. It spattered the machinery below.

This machinery: he wasn't sure what it was. He wasn't sure what the entire hall was. Floor after floor of galleries ran around the machinery. There were people moving around on these galleries but it was all so badly lit, presumably because of the repairs being done to Hogarth's Conduit which carried into the castle the gas for the lighting system, that he couldn't see anything properly. The hall seemed a mish-mash of wheelwork, pipework, brickwork, ironwork, stonework, woodwork, glasswork, dreamwork, and unintentional waterworks from cracks in the dome from which water dripped; it was also a mix of decorative shellwork, fretwork and bonework, and finally it was clockwork. This last one because the machinery resembled the interior of a mechanical clock, but on a giant scale. There were dozens and dozens of wheels. The smallest was the size of a steamroller cylinder and the largest the size of a Ferris wheel, and they seemed to be turning together through intermeshing cogs.

Then Toby saw the cogs were not meshing together like they would in gears or clockwork; instead, each cog was passing a few inches short of a cog on a neighbouring wheel, and there were people on the cogs; then he saw that each cog was in fact a platform. The machinery was a transport system, moving people from one gallery to another. The people were stepping from a platform on one wheel to a platform on another, and by changing from wheel to wheel they were ascending or descending from floor to floor and across from one side of the hall to the other.

Further around the gallery on which Toby stood, men of the Watch spilled out from the royal apartments, on their hunt for Tamurlaine and, possibly, Toby. He tore off his rucksack, opened the top and lowered it for Alfred, who jumped in, then he walked to a gap in the balustrade and stepped onto a passing platform which immediately, and with surprising speed, lifted them away.

Toby gripped a handrail. The platform remained horizontal as it rose, tilting a fraction as it turned on its axle. He did not feel particularly safe. The drop was into other wheels below. He'd be crushed, and the platform was completely open at the back. On the gallery he'd left behind, men of the Watch were quizzing people, shining lamps in their faces. Above him, someone stepped across from his wheel onto the platform of a passing wheel. Toby waited to do the same. A passing platform neared. He saw that if he hesitated he would miss his transfer and have to go through an entire revolution of the wheel on which he currently stood. Or he might get a limb trapped between the two platforms and be maimed. The wheels were big, made of wood, and could easily rip and wrench apart a human body. It was a dangerous system.

Toby stepped to the neighbouring wheel, his heart racing, and grabbed the new platform's handrail. This new wheel soared. He was giddy, free. The wheel moved much too fast to be safe. But the people using the wheels did so with indifference; they were office workers journeying home, and the tired mechanical rumble of the machinery felt as weary as the workers themselves, who were dishevelled and barely awake.

The next wheel that Toby approached was out of order and as Toby's platform passed, a head popped through an open hatch in the closed central drum. It was an old man with white hair and stubble.

'McGinty!' said Toby, and, in the moment before he passed, he leapt to McGinty's platform.

Toby didn't time his leap quite right, and tottered. Below, the giant wheels revolved, like mill wheels waiting to crush grain, and Toby was no more than a piece of grain in this giant system. A hand grabbed his collar and pulled him to safety.

'Whoa!' said McGinty. 'What you doing here, Chief? I thought you'd gone home.'

'I'm trying to,' said Toby, peering past McGinty to the hatch. 'Is there a hole in there?'

'In there?' laughed McGinty. 'No. I'm fixing a bust wheel. Not sure if the problem's mechanical or dreamy.'

The old man took a tobacco pouch and papers from his overalls pocket and considered the wheel's interior while several floors below, men of the Watch stepped onto the first giant cog.

'Is there a hole nearby that I can use to get home?'

'RK14 model, you see,' McGinty went on, rolling his cigarette. 'Always get problems with these.'

'McGinty?'

'Standard dreampower, but you don't get the quality of dream these days. Not the way you used to.'

'Please. I have to get home.'

'Hmm?' said McGinty, lighting his roll-up and becoming aware of Toby again. 'Where are you from again?'

'Angel Lane.'

'Angel Lane?' McGinty said, wincing at the memory of Angel Lane. 'Now that job was a son of a –' McGinty sucked on his roll-up so Toby didn't discover what Angel Lane was a son of. 'Middle of a forest fire. All sealed up now so can't help you there.'

'How about Arnold Street?'

'Arnold Street ... Arnold Street ...' said McGinty, trying to place it.

Some of the men of the Watch were fanning out across the wheels that descended the Central Hall, and some were coming up.

'London,' supplied Toby.

'Ah, London,' exclaimed McGinty, 'I remember now.'

'Yes! Can you take me there?'

'No. All sealed up too.'

'Can't it be unsealed?'

'You're having a laugh, aren't you? The only thing that can open a hole after it's been sealed is a Dreamer's dream. A dream's got the power to blow the gates off Alkazabad.'

'I don't want to blow the gates off Alkazabad,' said Toby. 'I just want to go home.'

McGinty pondered. He pondered some more. The men of the Watch rotated and rose.

'McGinty? I need to go. Like, now.'

'There is one hole open at the moment ...'

'Yes?'

'But it's not to your world.'

Toby groaned. 'Can you tell me where to find the Dreamers, then? They can dream me home.'

McGinty winced again. 'Wouldn't venture down that end of the castle if I were you. Regent's office. Queen's apartments. The Dreamers' apartments. Regent keeps the Dreamers under lock and key these days. Except for that pompous Ollie Reckless; the Regent lets him wander about all right.'

The men of the Watch were on the adjacent wheel. McGinty saw them, noticed Toby's agitation, grasped the danger, and said, 'Here you go, Chief!' Then, launching Toby through the hatch, he clambered in after him. 'Up there!'

Toby climbed the hollow interior on rungs which circled the wheel, and which he used as steps, coming out through another hatch onto a platform aligned with a gap in a balustrade. McGinty strode through the gap and across the gallery to a glass panelled door and unlocked it.

'Far side of these offices you'll find somewhere to hide. They catch you, don't tell them it was me gave you access.'

He propelled Toby through the door and locked it after him.

Toby walked along a curved corridor that took him out of sight of the Central Hall. It was carpeted and silent and it seemed safe enough to let Alfred out. They passed deserted offices then took a drafty staircase to the attics. Here Toby found an empty room. He sat on bare floorboards against a wall with his knees drawn up, the black velvet cloak of Ollie Reckless wrapped round him for warmth. How was he going to get to the far end of the castle now?

His mobile rang.

The noise made Toby start. Then he scrambled. Someone was calling him. The phone? It was in his rucksack. He dragged out his wet trousers, Ranger Widgeon's jersey, his shirt, his pants. Among his damp exercise books, pencil-case, the clinking flask and earthenware bottle, he fumbled. His mobile-phone screen glowed and there shone DAD.

'Dad! Dad!'

'Toby?' said Dad, sounding far away. 'Are you all right? Where are you?'

'Dad, I'm in Balthasar.'

There was a quiet at the other end.

'Dad? Dad? Can you hear me?'

'Where are you?'

'In Balthasar, Dad. I'm in the world from your novel. I'm going to tell you all about it when I get home. I've got to get dreamt home first. I'm trying to find the Dreamers. I'll tell you all about it. So you can finish your novel. We can go home to Arnold Street. All of us.'

There was silence on the other end of the line.

'Dad? Are you there? Dad?'

'Do you know we've had the police searching for you?' His dad sounded angry. 'You've been reported as a missing person. Your mum's worried. She thinks you might be dead, you stupid idiot.'

Toby wanted to ask if Dad had been worried but knew his dad wouldn't want him to ask this, it would only enrage him more.

'I'm sorry,' said Toby.

'Where are you? And no more silly games.'

Toby knew that if he said Balthasar that his dad would explode, the way he had when Toby had spilt coffee on his manuscript. *Are you deliberately being stupid?*

'Toby? Toby? Are you there?'

264

'Yes.'

'Where are you?'

In a voice shaking with the onset of tears that tightened his throat, he breathed out, 'Balthasar.'

'Stop playing the fool. This isn't a game.'

'I know it's not a game,' murmured Toby.

'What's that?'

'I know it's not a game.'

'Where are you?'

'I don't know,' said Toby, not wanting to annoy his dad any more.

'You need to go back to your mother. Right now.'

'I'm trying to.'

'So where are you?'

'I'm stuck.'

'Where? We can come and get you.'

He didn't want to say it. He was scared of his dad's anger.

'Toby?'

'Balthasar.'

'Do you know how much public money you've wasted?' his dad shouted. 'How much of my time you've wasted. I've missed meetings with the minister because of you.'

'I'm sor-sor-sorry.'

'Playing stupid children's games about made-up places. Get home, Toby! Get home to your mother now!'

'I'm sorry, Dad. I wanted to fix things. I wanted to save Alfred. I want to come home. Please.'

'I've got damned meetings. I'm late for one now.'

'I'm sor-sor-sorry.'

Toby's intakes of breath were rough. His dad did not say anything. Toby hiccupped.

'Dad?'

His dad said nothing.

'Dad?'

The line was dead. His dad had ended the call.

He couldn't believe it. He tried phoning back but he had no signal. He tried phoning Mum but it was no good. Then he tried Mrs Papadopoulos but he had no signal and could get no one.

The wind rattled the dormer window and swept over the pitched roof. He was never going to get home.

It happened like a wave he didn't see coming. The sobs rose. His body was under their control. The sobs did not let go for over a minute. The only thing that could cut them out – and that was only for a second – was when he hiccupped. He lay on his side, wrapped in the black velvet cloak, the draft coming through the floorboards, and when the sobs had finished and gone wherever it is sobs go when they're not possessing a person's body, he was left with the hiccups, and the cold.

How hopeless everything was. How useless he was. How stupid he was. And if he had not been so stupid and useless his dad would not hate him so much. And he had made it worse by coming here to Balthasar and not being able to get back. And he would never get back, because the Order of the Swan wanted to kill him because he was a witness to one of their murders.

He was a useless idiot.

A paw cuffed him round the cheek.

'No, Alfred.'

The paw cuffed his cheek again. The paw-pad was as rough as sandpaper.

He put his hand up to push Alfred away but Alfred ignored him and swiped him across the cheek again. Hard. He did it repeatedly. Thankfully he didn't use claws.

'Ow-ow-ow. Stop it!' cried Toby, sitting up, hiccupping.

Alfred was angry. He seemed to have gone mad. He bared his small, sharp teeth, extended his claws and began attacking Toby savagely through the velvet cloak, scratching the material in an effort to get at the boy. Eventually Toby was forced to stand up. Alfred would not bring an end to his attack and swiped at Toby's ankles so he had to move about.

'What is it? What's got into you?'

Alfred emitted a particularly aggressive *mia-OW* and frowned at him with those sick-yellow ancient eyes with bags under them.

'All right, Alfred, all right.'

Alfred stopped. Toby sighed and picked up the wet

clothes strewn on the floor. He untied the sleeping bag and searched for somewhere to hang everything up to dry. There was a coat hook on the back of the door, and the dormer window had a curtain rail from which he hung the sleeping bag.

'Is that what you wanted?' asked Toby.

Alfred miaowed. Toby returned to the wall and slid down it, his knees up before him.

'Happy, Alfred?'

Alfred miaowed again then leaped up and curled on Toby's lap. He purred, the vibrations transferring deep into Toby's body and Toby realised the hiccups had gone. Alfred transferred warmth too. The wind gently knocked the window in its frame. Silently, his lips barely moving, Toby sang the chorus of 'Tomorrow' from *Annie*.

CHAPTER 18

Gasper

When Toby woke, it was light. He tried phoning his mum but there was no signal. From the window, he could see the attic was at the very top of the castle, on the other side of the headland from the city, right over the ocean, with a sheer drop to thunderous waves splintering then slackening and sloshing before gathering again to beat against the rocks. The sea went to the horizon where grey sky darkened to a deep charcoal blur, as if a storm was brewing. The wind rasped like a big tongue across the pitched roof, licking something it was going to eat later. On this sheer edge, Toby couldn't see the rest of the castle fully, he could only see that it extended in both directions. To find out where the Dreamers' apartments were located, he was going to have to explore.

And he was going to have to do it by himself, without Tamurlaine.

Toby put on his heavy, damp clothes and the Dreamer's cloak, lifted Alfred and nuzzled his fur, whispered, 'Sorry, you're going to have to be in the bag again,' an apology Alfred accepted with a miaow, and placed him in his rucksack.

The attic corridor was quiet. Quiet in the way of Sunday mornings in Arnold Street when there was no traffic and his mum and dad were asleep. In fact, it was almost exactly the same quiet as early mornings at home – the heavy, muffled silence you get outside rooms where people are slumbering.

Ahead of Toby, a door opened and a boy in his underwear came out, yawning. He padded along the hallway and disappeared through another door. A tap ran. To Toby's right, another door opened and a freckled boy, a towel slung over his shoulder, appeared. Scratching his arm, he looked Toby up and down, and said, 'How old are you?'

Toby stared at the boy for several seconds, not sure what to say. 'Thirteen,' he said finally.

'That's young for a Dreamer.'

Toby had no idea how to reply.

'Hey, everyone,' the freckled boy called, 'there's a Dreamer here.'

More boys were appearing along the corridor all the

time, in pyjamas, dressing-gowns, T-shirts, and there was a buzz of excitement as they gathered round.

'Go on, dream something,' one boy said.

'Dream us a day off.'

'Dream the headmaster being fired into space.'

There was an air of expectation.

'Go on,' the freckled boy said. 'You *are* a Dreamer, aren't you? You're wearing a Dreamer's cloak.'

'I ... er ...' said Toby. He had a brainwave. 'I dreamt a cat.' He opened his rucksack, brought out Alfred and held him up for everyone to see. Alfred frowned crossly. He did not think much of these boys or of being dangled before them in such an undignified manner. He was a cat, after all, not a toy.

'That's just a cat,' said the freckled boy. 'A regular cat.'

Alfred's frown deepened and his small mouth soured. He was, he seemed to be saying, in no way 'regular'.

'Are you really a Dreamer?' said the freckled boy.

'I ... er ...'

'You're not, are you?'

'Er, no.'

There was a groan of disappointment, and the crowd broke up and the boys went into the bathroom. ''scuse me,' said one, brushing past. More boys were moving back and forth along the corridor but the freckled boy hadn't moved and was regarding Toby with curiosity.

'Why'd you say you were a Dreamer?'

'I ... Well, I was trying to be accepted.'

'That doesn't work.'

'What doesn't?'

'Making stuff up to impress people.'

'Doesn't it?'

'No. Do you always do that?'

'I did it at my last school.'

'Did it work?'

Toby thought about this a moment. 'No,' he said.

'What's your name?' the freckled boy asked.

'Toby.'

'I'm Myles.' He offered his hand. It felt formal and grown-up to be shaking hands. 'Why are you wearing a Dreamer's cloak, then?'

'I ... er ... My clothes got soaked on the way here.'

'Wait a minute. Are you the new kid?'

'I ... er ... well ... Sort of.'

'Then you're in with me. Where's the rest of your gear? Have you come a long way? Have you got a towel?'

'This is everything. No, I haven't got a towel.'

Myles stomped back into his room, returning with a fresh towel. Going into the bathroom, he said, 'Give us some room, give us some room,' elbowing his way to the basins. Gratefully Toby stepped to the free space. His face was dirty. He bathed himself gently in lukewarm water. His skin felt grimy and the water good. Then the faucet had a coughing fit and the water stopped running.

A loud groan broke out among the boys.

'Stupid Order!' someone called.

Several of the boys ran to the frosted windows, flung them wide and leaned out, thumping on the walls and shouting: 'Oi!' 'Get the hot water on!' 'Who used all the hot water?' 'Fire up the furnaces, down there!'

The hot water did not come back on.

Myles took Toby to his room. One half, with Myles's bed and desk, was a landscape of chaos, the other half entirely clear, the bed stripped, and on it a pile of ironed and folded clothes, and on top of that, a hat.

'That's yours,' said Myles. 'They haven't collected his things yet.' He opened the narrow wardrobe by the stripped bed and took out a grey cape. 'Might be a bit big, but it'll do until your uniform arrives.'

Toby took off the Dreamer's black cloak.

'You're soaking wet.'

'I fell in the harbour.'

'You're hilarious. Take some of Gasper's gear. He won't mind.'

'What if he comes back for it?'

Myles was suddenly glum. 'Gasper won't be coming back.'

Toby wasn't sure that Gasper really would be all

right with Toby wearing his clothes, but his own were so damply clinging that he accepted the offer.

'Hang your stuff in front of the fire,' said Myles, putting a chair in front of the empty grate and, while Toby changed, opened the window and leaned out.

'Oi!' he yelled down.

Toby could hear other people banging saucepans, shouting insults, demanding hot water.

'Oi! Petula!' shouted Myles. 'Here, look at this, Toby, it's brilliant.'

Toby, now in Gasper's clothes, joined Myles at the window. Myles's room was on the city side of the castle. Near the bottom, above the harbour graveyard, by the kitchens and furnace room, a chimpanzee popped its head out of a half-moon window and shook her fist at the various residents requesting hot water.

'Oi, Petula!' bellowed Myles. 'Give us some coal!'

Petula let loose a long, chattering scream, vanished, then reappeared, clearly distressed by all the complaints.

'Come on, Petula, we're freezing up here!'

Once again Petula vanished, and this time reappeared with an armful of coal which she started hurling at people's heads. Whether she intended the coal as missiles or gifts Toby wasn't sure but Myles, giggling, knew how he was going to use it.

'Here, catch it,' he said, leaning further out, and together they snatched at the coal as Petula pelted her critics. Myles was laughing loudly and soon Toby was chuckling, in spite of everything. They narrowly missed being brained several times and finally it was only them who remained hanging out of a window, everyone else safely back inside, and Petula, satisfied, shook her fist one last time and disappeared into the furnace room.

While Myles finished the homework he should have done the night before, Toby made a fire and Alfred settled before the flames. Toby hung his clothes on the back of the chair and put on the last item of Gasper's clothes – the grey cape. It was made of a thick, waxed, heavy material, and the neck-clasp showed the symbol of a white swan on a bronze field. When he fixed it at his throat, he remembered the killer with the knife. He wanted to tear off the cape and burn it.

'That'll do,' announced Myles, spinning his exercise book to his satchel and turning to Toby. He laughed out loud. 'Welcome to Dreaming School, then, Toby.'

Toby gulped. So that's what this place was.

'What's wrong? You don't look very happy about it.'

'No, it's excellent.'

'What's the matter, don't you *like* the Order of the Swan?'

'It's excellent. Excellent. Delighted to be a member of the Watch.'

'You're a cygnet in Dreaming School, you dope. Don't you know how it all works?'

'This is all new to me, completely new,' said Toby, glancing desperately round the room, wanting to change the subject before Myles realised he was an impostor. 'So, what happened to Gasper, then?'

'There's only one thing you need to know about the Order of the Swan,' said Myles, in a low, flat voice. 'Shall I tell you what it is?'

'Yes,' said Toby, glad the subject had changed.

'You'd better sit down, then.'

Toby sat on Gasper's bed.

'You know about the Regent, do you?'

'Heard about him. Regent Malladain.'

'Well,' said Myles, 'There used to be a lot of stories about the Regent here. People said if the Regent didn't like someone in Dreaming School, he'd kill them. His favourite way of killing them was defenestration. Do you know what defenestration is, Toby?'

'No.'

'Throwing someone out of a window. Anyway, there was a new kid at Dreaming School who heard these stories and he thought that's all they were – stories. Something to tell the younger kids at night, scare them. And because he'd come from a family where he was encouraged to ask questions, when the Regent visited Dreaming School, this new kid went up to him and asked if it was true he threw pupils out of windows. The Regent looked down at the new kid. Then he bent to speak to him and his eyes twinkled like sunlight on the sea in the early morning and he said, "Do you believe I would throw a child out of a window?" "No," said the new kid, "I don't believe it." The Regent looked into the boy's eyes a moment longer then lifted the boy – who was big, by the way – and walked across the Beebox and hurled him through a closed window.'

Toby wasn't sure how to respond. Perhaps this was supposed to be a joke. He laughed nervously.

'That's not the end of the story,' said Myles. 'This boy, the new kid, fell about ten storeys onto the rocks in the harbour. He lay there, smashed up. He was so bloody you couldn't tell if the sharp points poking up were bones or rocks. His heart lay beating beside him in a rockpool where the crabs nibbled it. His classmates ran down and found him murmuring, "Mother. Father." He lay like that for what felt like hours but was only minutes while the other children stood around him. And when the court doctor scuttled out with his napkin tied round his throat, greasy brown sauce down it, do you know what the doctor did?'

'No,' said Toby.

'He bit his lip. He bit his lip. Can you believe it? He didn't know if he should move the boy to his surgery or leave him where he was. Because he was scared of the

Regent. The Regent obviously wanted the boy dead and the doctor was frightened of the Regent. This doctor had been so worn down by the Order of the Swan that he no longer had any courage or conscience. Even though he had taken an oath to heal people.'

'What happened?'

'His conscience returned and he moved the boy. But it was too late. The boy died within two minutes and the doctor was executed by the Regent for moving him. And no one in Dreaming School has told stories about the Regent since.'

The coals sighed and in front of the fire Alfred's stomach rose and fell with his breathing.

'What do you think about that, then, Toby?'

Toby wasn't sure if Myles had told him this story as a useful warning or if it was a trick and he was tempting Toby to say something against the Regent, at which point he would call the Watch.

'He sounds a dangerous man,' said Toby cautiously.

Myles thrust his face forward and bared his teeth. 'Well, I'll tell you what I think about it – I think the Regent is a murderer. I wish I could kill him. Every night, I try to make a dream to kill him. Every night I dream of stinging him to death with bees. Thousands of bees. Millions of them. Zillions. But when I wake up – no bees. I've dreamed whole hives of bees, and all I wake up with is maybe a single dozy bee. If I'm lucky. Usually I just find honey on the pillow. I've got honey coming out of my ears, literally.'

Myles wiggled his little finger in his ear, rotated it, and pulled out a honey-covered fingertip, which he sucked.

Toby regarded the freckled boy. His eyes were narrowed, his brow furrowed and his jaw stuck out as he sucked his little finger, and Toby decided he was telling the truth.

'Myles, I've got to tell you something.'

His heart pattering with fear, he took a deep breath and blew a long sigh, and told Myles everything. How he'd witnessed a murder by one of the Regent's men. How the Watch had chased him about the city. And how he was trying to escape and get home. He left out the parts that implicated other people he'd met who had helped him – Ranger Widgeon, Jinky, Burston, even Barry Cheyn, and especially Tamurlaine – and when he finished he waited apprehensively for Myles's response.

'If that man killed Kerten on orders from the Regent,' said Myles, 'then that's serious. It means Regent Malladain tried to arrange the murder of a Dreamer. Do you know what that would mean, if it could be proved the Regent ordered the murder of Kerten?'

'Would it matter? He seems to kill whoever he likes.'

'Yes, it would matter. Once you're a Dreamer, that's

it. You're untouchable. The Dreamers are heroes in Balthasar. They're like gods. They're adored by everyone. It's one thing arranging their work, but if he's killed one of them, if people knew this, it would turn everyone against him.'

'But who would believe me? Or even investigate? The Regent's got all the power. Anyway, I don't want to be involved. I just want to go home.'

Myles rubbed the back of his head. 'You're right,' he said finally. 'There's no evidence. And who would believe it?'

'So can you get me to the Dreamers? To get me dreamed home.'

'The Regent keeps the key to their apartments. He only lets them out occasionally. He's got them dreaming continuously. They're like farm animals kept in stalls, dreaming whatever he wants. It's horrible.'

'I've got to get to them.'

'Not necessarily. There's another way.'

'What is it, a hole? Is there a hole here?'

'No. *I* could try to dream you home.'

'You?'

'This is Dreaming School, after all.'

'This is superb!' said Toby. 'Can you do it now?'

'Right now.'

And so saying, Myles sat up straight in his chair and promptly fell asleep.

Toby wasn't sure what to do. He didn't like to ask, either, in case he woke Myles. He picked up Alfred and held him in his lap, ready.

He waited.

In the other rooms, the boys were getting ready for school, chatting noisily about lessons and timetables and homework, laughing, kicking a ball up and down the corridor. Outside was that faint high-pitched moan he'd heard on the bridge leading to the castle gates.

Something on the windowsill buzzed. A bee. It buzzed again. Then, groggily, it buzzed into the air and headbutted a pane of glass and Myles opened his eyes.

'Big pants!' he exclaimed, and turned towards the window. 'A single damned bee.' He opened the window and let the creature sail away. 'It's all I seem able to do – bees. One at a time, which is no good. Not to worry, we'll go to the older kids at break-time. They're stronger at dreaming. There's a couple of older girls who are really powerful. They're graduating to Dreamers in a few months. They'll be able to dream you home. No problem.'

'Can we trust them?'

'Most of the Dreaming School love the Order of the Swan. A few don't. These girls hate him as much as me. We don't agree with murder.'

'That really happened, then? Exactly as you told it? About that boy being thrown through a window?'

Myles was going to answer but couldn't. He was choked with emotion. He nodded vigorously.

'You were there?'

Myles nodded.

'Was he a friend of yours, the boy who was ... defenestrated?'

'No,' said Myles, and pointed at the stripped bed. 'He was my room-mate.'

'Gasper? Gasper was the one who was killed?'

Myles nodded.

Toby looked from the pile of clothes on the bed to the ones he was wearing. 'Then I'm wearing a dead boy's clothes.'

Myles and Toby exchanged a glance, and Myles nodded again.

In the corridor, someone began ringing a bell.

'Leave Alfred,' said Myles, heading out, 'we're coming back in ten minutes.'

They gathered in pairs and soon a column of caped boys stood ready. An older boy appeared, with a tall man. The tall man warned everyone to be careful because there was an escaped murderer at large – a teenage boy. A murmur broke out among the cygnets and Toby felt his body tighten with self-consciousness but Myles just snorted at the news, turned to Toby and curled his lip. The man barked an unintelligible command, and they were off.

They travelled staircases and hallways, stepping outside to a broad turret where a stormy wind gusted their capes into great tents. The sky was a deep shade of charcoal. There was definitely a storm coming. The door on the far side couldn't be opened so while the boys waited, some of them started a competition to see who could lean furthest against the wind without falling over. Fulmars hung above them, unimpressed with their leaning-in-the-wind abilities.

'The Dreamers live there.'

At the far end of the castle, beyond a gully in the roofs where a windmill turned, past rickety towers held upright by singing metal cables, and near a flagpole against which a cable struck a repeated *ting-ting-ting*, was the edge of the scaffolding. It covered that whole end of the castle over the harbour, like a girdle. On top of that end of the castle was a lawn, and on it stood a swan. The swan wore a gold collar shaped like a crown, which was tethered to the lawn by a golden chain. It didn't look very happy.

'And the Regent's office is there too? And Queen Fadranga's apartments?'

'The Regent's office, yes,' said Myles, leaning close so Toby could hear him. 'But it's not Queen Fadranga. She died years ago. An evil, violent woman. She was mother of both Regent Malladain and the last king. She's grandmother to the present queen.'

'But that's strange,' yelled Toby.

'Why?'

'Stop that!' called the tall man to the boys in their leaning competition. He had got the turret door open. They descended a spiral staircase to a wooden hall. Toby knew exactly what the hall was. The smell was the unmistakable smell of school dinners.

They went through the servery and took what appeared to be bowls of mush and found a seat at long benches. All the surfaces in the canteen had a sheen of grease: the tables, the benches, the cutlery, even the mush in their bowls. Yet everyone ate as if they were ravenous. The mush tasted of hot sick. Toby gagged, eyes watering. Myles finished his own bowl and Toby's. The boys were even mopping their bowls with slices of bread. Myles disappeared into the kitchen, and while he was gone Toby thought about Queen Fadranga. Old Mrs Bleverhasset in the royal apartments had mistaken Tamurlaine for Queen Fadranga. But Queen Fadranga was many years dead. There was something in this mistaken identity that was strange. Toby didn't think it was simply that old Mrs Bleverhasset was mentally ill; that didn't make her stupid. She had seen something in Tamurlaine that made her think Tam was Queen Fadranga. But what? Myles returned holding a folded napkin which he opened, revealing kippers and cold meats.

After breakfast they returned to the bedrooms. There was just time for Toby to share the cold meat and kippers with Alfred, refill the earthenware jar and flask with water for the day ahead, put his dry clothes in the rucksack and finally Alfred, before the handbell tolled.

'That's it,' said Myles. 'We're off to Dreaming School to dream you home.'

'Thanks, Myles,' grinned Toby.

'The Beebox awaits.'

CHAPTER 19

Dreaming School

The Beebox was nothing to do with bees. The name came from the noise made by the boys' and girls' voices blending and echoing under the flat roof, which sounded like the buzzing of bees. The name might also have come from the box-like feel of the place, similar to an airport departure lounge, a warehouse, or a sports centre – except the roof of the Beebox was much lower. There were many floors below the Beebox, which Toby had glimpsed when they first approached the top-floor entrance of the school across a windy turret, but what those floors might contain, Toby did not know.

Wooden railings divided the Beebox, separating the Dreaming School's classes. The school went from infants to eighteen-year-olds, only the best of whom would graduate as fully fledged Dreamers. Until they left, they were known as cygnets. There were maybe a thousand cygnets in the open-plan Beebox. One class of smaller children was raucous, cheering in a circle around three of their number who stood fast asleep, heads lolling while they dreamed. In front of the three children, three brown clouds appeared. The clouds swelled then popped like balloons into brown dust and a smell of farts. Their classmates roared with laughter and made enjoyable sounds of disgust.

'They start them off dreaming Stinkies,' explained Myles.

The Beebox was very cold that morning as a strong breeze was blowing through it, which meant that the cygnets were allowed to keep their capes on. The draft came from a hole in the wall where carpenters and glaziers from Works and Buildings were fitting a new window frame and glass. Myles threw a meaningful glance at Toby, who widened his eyes as if to say *Really?* and Myles nodded – that was where the Regent had defenestrated Gasper.

'Here, Toby, look at this.'

They stopped to watch a class of older cygnets. One girl was called to the middle of the circle of desks where she bowed her head and fell asleep. For a moment, nothing happened, then a metre in front of her the air darkened the way it does at dusk. But only a patch of air darkened.

Everywhere else remained morning-bright. Toby began to see something in this patch, barely there, a dimness, a shade. It thickened, gained substance, and Toby began to make out a shape, bulky, quivering ... panting? The shape had a long tongue and was wheezing. It had a scrunched-up face of furry folds. A bulldog. But hanging in the air. Then appeared some short, triangular wings. This flying creature strained forward, flapping its wings, unable to move from where the girl held it through the power of her dream. The creature's tail wagged madly round and round, like a propeller. The girl swayed dizzily, woke, and the flying bulldog shot straight for the hole in the wall and out into the stormy sky.

'Hey, you pair!' called their teacher. 'Get a move on.'

'The oldest kids are over there,' said Myles, hurrying to catch up. He nodded to the far end of the Beebox.

'And those two girls?'

'Yep. We'll be able to speak to them at break.'

They passed a gang of skulking, unhappy older teenagers attempting to dream some boyfriends and girlfriends for themselves, a metallurgy class where the children were dreaming the various parts of a hideously shaped weapon, which was exciting some of the cygnets and upsetting others so much that they were crying, then a botany class where exhausted eleven-year-olds were trying to dream the correct delicacy of flower petals, before they went through a gate in a railing to join about a hundred other boys and girls who were also arriving and filling row after row of desks. Around them, low shelves extended into the middle distance with books.

'History first. Yuk.'

A trolley came round from which the children took big books, booming and thudding them onto their desks. They found pages and began reading. Out loud. Toby took the first volume that came to hand. Myles shot a desperate, bored glance at him and began reading aloud too.

The book that Toby had taken mainly consisted of charts naming departments and sub-departments and under-departments in the Administration of the Order of the Swan, and lists of boring jobs and the names of the boring people who had held them for the last 400 years. There were a few more interesting bits – a brief description of neighbouring kingdoms, including the wild north lands – but mostly, it was boring.

'Are history lessons this bad where you're from?' whispered Myles.

'No,' whispered Toby back. 'Why are we reading this stuff out loud?'

'Who knows? I think it's to make us believe how great the Order of the Swan is. Nearly everyone in Dreaming School believes it by the time they're eighteen. It's only a few who don't. Nearly all our house don't. Because of Gasper.'

'It's madness.'

'Botany and zoology are all right. And geography. Dreaming rainstorms and snowstorms is great. But you have to learn the details first. The ingredients of whatever the thing is that you dream. It takes hours. All those atoms and electrons, all those cells. Amino acids and minerals. Biological processes. So many. From morning to night. Too much pressure. Don't pass exams and you're out.'

'It sounds hard.'

'It is. But you have to learn everything otherwise what you dream isn't really there. It's defective.'

A member of the Watch in a dove-grey cape with yellow flashes on the shoulders came through the gate into their area and spoke to the teacher.

'Class, may I have your attention,' announced the teacher. 'We have a special visitor – the Regent.'

A disgruntled murmur spread. There was one incoherent shout. Toby and Myles exchanged a glance.

'He's here to visit the archive,' continued the teacher. 'But he wants to speak to you first. About our dear departed cygnet, Gasper. He wants to pay tribute, and share your pain.'

'But he's the one who killed him!' someone shouted.

'Who said that?'

There was silence.

'I'd hold your tongue if you don't want to meet Gasper's fate.'

Myles looked at the great window being fitted into place, and Toby knew he was thinking about poor Gasper.

'There he is,' someone said and hundreds of kids stopped what they were doing and turned.

Through the iron entrance doors – his long leather coat flapping behind him, his black hair with grey at the temples swept back from a high, white forehead, his thin mouth cruel and his clear eyes dead (deader than the dead eyes of the deadest corpse in the rottenest coffin in the wormiest corner of the castle graveyard) – appeared the killer. The man who had stabbed Kerten in the stomach, who had held the knife against Toby's throat. He was walking towards their class.

'It's him,' whispered Toby, tugging on Myles's cape.

'Who?'

'The man who killed Kerten.'

'Where?'

'There,' said Toby, nodding at the man striding towards them.

'But that,' said Myles, 'is Regent Malladain.'

And Toby finally understood: the killer was not working for the Regent of Balthasar. The killer *was* the Regent of Balthasar. Regent Malladain.

CHAPTER 20

Fadranga

Toby dropped to the floor. He was rapid on hands and knees, motoring along the row of desks past people's feet. He zipped across the open space to the first book aisle, shifting as fast as a baby who has just learned to crawl, away from the killer, Regent Malladain. Toby kept on going, going so fast his palms bent backwards and hurt his wrists, blurring past leather-bound volumes with shiny lettering. Stairs ahead! Toby was only too glad to disappear down them.

*

Beneath the Beebox it was dark. Tall bookshelves blocked natural light. Toby lurked in the shadows. If the Regent saw him, he would kill him, Toby was sure. Toby was a witness to the murder of a Dreamer, which seemed to be the greatest crime in Balthasar. And the Regent wanted that crime *un*-witnessed, i.e. un-Tobyed. With a knife.

It was quiet down here, safe. The place felt like it was dreaming deeply about the past. It felt like a giant old person slumbering in an armchair dreaming of all that had happened.

Alfred was stirring again, punching the rucksack with paws, bashing his head, miaowing angrily. Toby told him to shut up. Alfred argued. Grumbling, Toby let him out and warned him to be as silent as the mist. Alfred darted off into the bookshelves.

'Alfred!' he called hoarsely. 'Come back!'

Blue stones lit up automatically, illuminating the bookshelves. Two people were descending from the Beebox. Alfred appeared at Toby's feet then scampered off along an aisle and Toby followed. The cat led him to a flight of stairs. Toby took several steps at a time. There was another flight down so he kept going, floor after floor, until they reached a basement. The only light was in the distance, from caged blue stones at the end of a corridor. The people were still coming. Toby and Alfred sped towards the light. It felt like they were deep underground. They passed closed doors until, ahead, one was open. The people were still coming. Toby stepped into the room.

On the right stood four tall bookshelves, perpendicular

to the wall, and on the left was an open space with a large reading table, four chairs, and against the wall a big safe. They walked along one row of books, right to the back, to the deepest shadow. Toby could hear his own breathing, fast, shallow. The footsteps came closer. Two people entered the room. Toby hardly breathed. Alfred lay flat on the floor.

The people moved without speaking. Knees clicked. A dial fizzed then slowly ticked. A metal door-handle clanked. A rustle was followed by a sound of papers washed along the surface of the table and a woman's voice said, 'Here you are, sir.' When she spoke, her lips and the inside of her mouth smacked loudly, as if her mouth was very dry.

'And this document is always kept under lock and key?' said a stern voice, the question searching out weakness.

'Yes, sir.'

There was a sound of a chair being pulled out then the stern voice said, 'Do you want something else?'

The woman was so nervous Toby could hear the sound of her lubricating her mouth with saliva. 'I – I could wait for you upstairs, sir?'

'Why don't you do that?'

She left. Her heels clacked away into silence. The man appeared at the end of the aisle. An alarm screamed in Toby's mind. Blood sped round Toby's arteries. It was

Regent Malladain. He stood in profile. To see Toby, all he had to do was swivel his head ninety degrees. He flicked out the tail of his long leather coat and sat at the table.

Toby tried not to move. He tried not to blink. He could hear his heart pumping in his chest, his blood roaring round his skull. He could hear his clothes crinkle with each breath. He was certain Regent Malladain would be able to detect the very heat from his body. Smell him. Toby wished with all his might that Alfred would not move.

The killer slipped a hand into the inside pocket of his coat and withdrew an object Toby couldn't see. There was a creak and Regent Malladain slipped on a pair of glasses. His hair was waxed and there were comb-marks in it. He seemed very keen on his appearance and his haircut was trying to accentuate the thinness and whiteness of his face. He was so white he looked like he never saw daylight. His thin lips were bloodless, almost as if he wore lipstick. In fact, Toby thought, the man was going for a bit of a goth look, what with the long leather coat. Except this man's gothy interest in death was not romantic but murderous. His hands, now lifting the sheets of paper, were hands that would close around a throat and draw a knife across it. Hands that liked blood. His whole existence seemed concentrated upon destruction. But not at that moment. Right at that moment he was concentrated upon those few sheets of paper.

Regent Malladain read for several minutes. The only sounds were the occasional swish of a page being turned, and a heel beating on the floor. Toby wanted to shift position, just a little, because of an ache, but he couldn't.

The killer put down the sheets of paper and took off his glasses. He stared into space for perhaps a minute. Then he stood and left the room.

The Regent's footsteps dwindled then vanished into the deep quiet of the building. Toby did not move. Nor Alfred. Gradually, it felt as if the room relaxed, as if the air itself could breathe again. The building knew that the Regent had gone.

When Toby stepped from the bookshelves, he saw the document which Malladain had been reading. Toby listened but the basement stayed silent. He glanced at the papers to see what had so interested the man, and once he saw the title and author, he had to read it all:

HOW FADRANGA BECAME QUEEN OF BALTHASAR

by Mervyn Sump, Head Archivist
The Library Below the Beebox, Balthasar

Fadranga was seventeenth in line to the throne. Her side of the family had fallen on hard times and though she worked in the castle, she was a washer-upper and spent her days fetching pails of water and scrubbing pots and pans. This gave her enormously strong shoulders and a deep sense of resentment. In the cellar bedroom that she shared with a large, red-faced cook who drank too much, Fadranga wrote down a list of the sixteen heirs ahead of her and then she asked for a change of job.

She became a serving girl. Her task was to carry the tureens and salvers and serving bowls from the kitchens to the royal dining room, and she managed it easily due to her strong shoulders. Sometimes she delayed to watch the white-gloved servants place the plates and glasses before the members of the royal family. She would let her eyes slide over the princes and princesses, the dukes and duchesses, seeing in them not people, but obstacles. Because she wanted to be queen. And they were in her way.

The first murder happened like this. She found a family of four who were all heirs, and one day injected a partridge with poison and delivered it to them for lunch. She stayed to watch. The family – a woman, a man, and two boys – ate. They banged down like bowling pins, a froth of blood from each mouth staining the white tablecloth.

Two more died of poison before all the kitchen staff were interviewed by the Watch. The Giver of the Keys interviewed Fadranga himself. In the head cook's whitewashed office he asked her questions. 'What time did you take up the dishes? Who prepared the food? Did anyone else have access to the food other than you? I understand you are now eleventh in line to the throne of Balthasar, is that right?'

Fadranga was scared, but she made her eyes go big and her face go long, and lied. She almost believed herself when she told her lies, speaking in her quiet, fearful voice. Then she went back to her tiny cellar room and lifted the brick in the floor under which she kept the small bottle of poison, and hid it somewhere else.

Fadranga was at work scrubbing pots when she heard the screams. The Giver of the Keys appeared, holding the bottle of poison, and behind him shuffled men of the Watch, pulling the red-faced cook through the kitchen. Fadranga's room-mate struggled against them. The great kitchen fell silent, and all anyone could hear was the cook's laboured breath and the scraping soles of the Watch's boots on the flagstones. Then the cook was pulled outside and no one ever saw her again.

After that, Fadranga was sent to work in the laundry. For years she bounced great bags of sheets and pillowcases down servants' stairs, scrubbed linen, fed washing through the wringer and hung it up on lines to dry on the windy turrets. And all the time she thought of her plan.

Then, one day, she was assigned the job of laundry for the Bleverhasset family, and after a few weeks discovered with surprise that the mother and child were on her list of heirs. The child, Urthax, was a toddler who had only recently learned to walk and banged through the family's apartment, yelling with excitement. The apartment was at the top of a tower, and the roof had been turned into a garden where the family would spend their days when the weather was fine. It was a sun-trap, so they could sit out there wrapped under fur coats and blankets in the deepest winter and still take the sun. But that day was a hot summer's day. Young Mrs Bleverhasset and little Urthax were playing, and Fadranga had been stripping the beds, stuffing four great bags with sheets, when Mrs Bleverhasset called her from the roof. 'Fadranga! Oh Fadranga! Can you come here a minute?' So Fadranga climbed the spiral staircase and popped her head through the trapdoor. 'I have to fetch some medicine for this little gannet, can you watch her for a quarter of an hour?'

Urthax screamed and ran circles round the garden. Although it was a hot day, it was cool on the tower, high up in the breeze. There was not a cloud in the sky, but it was hazy towards the horizon, and the sea glittered. Fadranga lifted the little girl and stood her on the battlements. Then she said, 'Shall we play a game?' Urthax nodded, and Fadranga said, 'Let us race around the tower.' The little girl's eyes widened. Fadranga set off. The little girl squealed and followed, running along the top of the wall, right on the edge. So they ran until there was a small cry, suddenly cut off, and Fadranga stood alone.

She had not even intended to kill the child, she told herself. It had just happened. When the Watch arrived she wailed and sobbed, she sobbed and wailed, berating herself for letting the child out of her sight for a few moments, and the men of the Watch listened as, later, did the Giver of the Keys.

There was no evidence, only suspicion. After nearly a month, she was released.

The mother, Fadranga heard later, went mad. And the law of Balthasar is that the mad cannot inherit. Fadranga remembered young Mrs Bleverhasset's face as she climbed into the tower's sunlight, and how her expression had changed as she slowly understood what had happened to her child.

Over the years, more heirs died. This was

300

not always the result of Fadranga's plan. It was sometimes the result of time. One heir died of old age. Another of a bronchial infection. A third died in childbirth and this woman's addition to the list of heirs, her baby, was stillborn. A fourth died in a war campaign in the snowy, northern lands. And then there were only five.

By this time, Fadranga was no longer a teenage girl, she was a woman, assured in what she wanted to do. She was also coming to the attention of men who wanted her hand in marriage, not because she was attractive (she was plain, but her bearing, her confidence, and that gleam in her eye made some men want her) but because she was now sixth in line to the throne.

She chose the suitor with the most ruthless ambition. Then she set about, each quiet, hot night of their honeymoon, whispering into his ear of the power that would come to them and to their children, if the remaining five heirs to the throne of Balthasar were to die. She suggested they invite the five heirs to dinner in their rooms. She suggested that her husband kill them with a long cruel knife. When they returned from honeymoon, they invited the other heirs to dinner, and while she was cooking the meal, using the skills she had learned from all those bitter years in the castle kitchens, she heard the warm chatter from the dining room, and laughter, and the voice of her husband. After a time, he came through. She kissed him, she gave him the long cruel knife, she told him that she would wait for him to do what he had to do. He looked deeply into her eyes and his own eyes shone with ambition and madness and murder, then he went into the dining room to slaughter the five heirs to the throne while Fadranga ran to the Watch and screamed, 'He has gone mad! He has killed them!' The duty sergeant jumped up, the men of the Watch ran with her, and they burst into the apartment to find the walls running with blood, the wooden floor sluiced with it, and Fadranga's husband covered head to toe in gore, the long, cruel knife in his hands.

Fadranga's husband was tried for murder, found guilty, and executed. Fadranga was brought before the Giver of the Keys, and interviewed. She appeared in deep shock, and found it difficult to answer his questions. But the Giver of the Keys could find no evidence against her. 'He must have lost all reason,' said Fadranga, staring at the desk between them. The Giver of the Keys observed her in silence. They could hear the gulls crying in the wind. 'You have gained the throne,' he said, finally. Fadranga only shook her head. 'I have lost a husband'. The Giver of the Keys waited for her to

302

say or do something incriminating, but she said and did nothing to give herself away.

When the reigning king died, Fadranga assumed the crown. At her coronation, the Giver of the Keys thought that perhaps for a moment she caught his eye as she walked down the aisle, but he could not be sure. He went home that night through the dark streets of the city with a feeling of fear running up his back, and every shadow seemed to hold an assassin with a long, cruel knife. As for Fadranga, her husband had not only given her the throne as a wedding gift, he had also given her a future, because within a few weeks, Fadranga realised she was pregnant, and nine months after her wedding night, she gave birth to twins – the future King Sigobert and the future Regent Malladain.

Toby put down the document with a feeling of terror. What old Mrs Bleverhasset had said about Fadranga was true – she had killed Urthax. Myles said Fadranga was dead. Toby was glad about that. A queen like Fadranga wouldn't spare a thought for his life if she was still ruler. Fadranga had given birth to two sons, the older brother Sigobert, and Malladain. Sigobert must have died and it was Sigobert's daughter who was queen. Which would make Regent Malladain the queen's uncle. And he was in charge because the queen wasn't able to rule. Perhaps she was sick. Or mad. Or perhaps Malladain had done something to her. Whatever the reason, it was a nasty, dangerous family.

But something in the story troubled him, something he couldn't put his finger on, a feeling, a dim impression that wouldn't quite come clear ...

On the table beside the papers was a leather pouch. Toby picked it up. Inside was a pair of reading glasses. At the exact moment that Toby realised they belonged to Regent Malladain, footsteps sounded along the corridor. It had to be Malladain, coming back for his spectacles. Hurrying to get back to his hiding place, Toby knocked the chair. Its legs banged on the floor. The steps in the corridor stopped. Then they started again, quicker than before. Toby whirled. There was nowhere to hide.

The books! Toby took the biggest. It was so heavy he had trouble lifting it off the shelf. It was broader than his body. He put it on the table, put a chair behind the open door, heaved the book up again and, because of its weight, had difficulty stepping onto the chair. Alfred saw what Toby was planning and leapt onto the table. A figure appeared in the doorway and hesitated, seeing Alfred on the table. Toby raised the book. The gold lettering on the spine shone and for the brief moment that he had to wait for Regent Malladain to come into the room, those gold letters seemed to imprint themselves on Toby's brain, then Regent Malladain's black hair and leather coat were in front of him. Toby slammed *The Mervyn Sump Bumper Book of Royal Murders with Bonus Genealogical Tables and Illustrations by Lady Philomena Snow* down on Regent Malladain's skull.

The Regent crumpled. The last part of him to fall was his face, which smacked the floor, his bony forehead making the exact sound of a cricket ball being struck by a bat in the sweet spot. Toby stepped down from the chair. 'Nice work, Alfred,' he said.

They dashed along the corridor, pelted up the stairs, passed the female archivist in her blue cape, who was astonished to see them, and ran up into the Beebox. Myles, who had been looking out for Toby, saw him and gave the thumbs up. Toby nodded and walked towards the gate in the railings. He had nearly reached it when the voice of the female archivist called, 'Stop him!'

For some seconds, nobody did anything. They were all looking towards the archivist, not Toby. They did not know what had happened or who she was talking about. Then the woman saw Toby and started running after him. Myles put out a leg and tripped her. Toby strode through the gate and kept going, fast.

He had nearly made it to the entrance doors when the female archivist shouted, 'Him!'

'The boy!' called someone else. 'That boy there! Stop him!'

Toby was glad of how well Ranger Widgeon had

mended the soles of his school shoes. As he sprinted, their leather gripped the wooden floor so tightly it seemed to give him additional speed. The children in the classes watched in surprise as Toby raced past. He slammed into the iron doors, snatched a metal ring, rotated it, heard the deep click of the latch, and hauled.

They were coming after him now.

The door was heavy and he strained to open it. Behind him, boots were thundering on the wooden floor. The door widened a fraction, Toby pulled some more, then he slid outside. There was a furious wind. He didn't run away. Instead he hauled on the iron door to shut it. It didn't move. He leaned backwards, straining again. The door moved a fraction. Then, slightly faster, it began to close and at the last moment Alfred slipped out and the door shut with a deep boom. The wind blew. Toby tore off Gasper's cape, threaded it through the two large rings of the two door handles, pulled the cape tight and tied the ends together with a strong knot.

The doors were more like gates than ordinary doors. They were decorated with figures that emerged from the iron surface as if trying to escape, writhing figures of children or dream-creatures – who knows what they were? But these gate-like doors could not be opened no matter how hard the adults on the inside tried. Toby's knot was too good and the material of Gasper's cape too strong.

CHAPTER 21

The Key

Toby found his way to the Central Hall, that busy, echoing, rumbling space where the wheel on which McGinty had been working was still out of order and inside which Toby hid.

Once Toby closed the hatch it was nearly dark, light filtering through gaps between the boards of the vast wooden drum. Running in a ring around the inside of the drum were iron rungs, and Toby climbed down them to the bottom.

He did not know what to do. He either had to go to the Dreamers who lived at the end of the castle somewhere behind the scaffolding and beneath that roof garden where the swan was kept chained, or to the two girls at Dreaming School, the ones whom Myles knew. Either the

Dreamers or the two cygnets would dream him home. But the Dreamers were under lock and key and also beside the Regent's office. So it made more sense to get back to the Dreaming School, find Myles and then go to those two girls. Yet that was dangerous too because the Regent and the Watch would be watching for him there now. The Beebox itself was out of the question. There were too many people. So he would have to go after dark to Myles's room.

He waited inside the wheel as the morning passed. Alfred miaowed with hunger. Toby's stomach rumbled sympathetically. Around lunchtime, he climbed up and opened a hatch. A clap of wings so startled him he nearly fell off his rung while an equally surprised pigeon flew up to the dome, where it joined its pals, cooing and *oohing* as they shuffled along to make room. There was a dark yellow, almost gelatinous light, the light that comes before a storm. The galleries were quiet. Then Toby spied a freckled boy of about thirteen wearing the grey cape of a cygnet. Myles appeared to be wandering aimlessly around a lower gallery but stopped every so often at the balustrade and looked about. He acted like he was sightseeing. Or searching for someone. Toby couldn't get Myles's attention without opening the hatch fully and waving, and there was no way he was going to do that. He watched Myles for perhaps half an hour, willing him to ride to a nearer floor so Toby could catch his eye. Eventually Myles did. 'Psst!' Toby hissed when the boy passed. Myles spotted him, checked no one was looking then walked onto the platform, ducked through the hatch, and they climbed down to the bottom of the wheel.

'Are you all right?' Myles asked in a whisper.

'Yeah,' said Toby. 'You?'

'Yeah.'

'Did you get in trouble?' Toby wanted to know.

Myles nodded. He picked up Alfred and stroked him. 'I saw the Regent.'

'I hit him on the head with a book.'

'I knew you got him, Toby! He kept touching the top of his head and making a face. It's a pity you didn't kill him. I thought he was going to defenestrate me.'

'Seriously? What happened?'

'The teachers caught me,' said Myles in a quiet voice, not looking at Toby but at Alfred, mechanically stroking his fur. 'They took me to a room. The Regent questioned me. I said I didn't know anything about anything. But he must have questioned the others in my house because he knew you'd been there and that I'd helped you. And that lady archivist said I tripped her.'

'That was a good trip.'

'Too right,' said Myles, meeting Toby's eye for a moment. His gaze dropped to the floor. 'The Regent let me go.'

'That's good,' said Toby.

'Yes and no,' said Myles. 'I think he's up to something.'

'What?'

'I don't know. But I know he wants to catch you. That's what he was interested in.'

'Because I'm a witness to that murder he did.'

'Yeah,' said Myles. 'I can't believe he killed a Dreamer.'

'Do you think,' said Toby, with a thudding heart, 'he's got the Watch following you? You find me then they swoop?'

Both boys looked at the hatch above, anticipating it being thrown open and the armed Watch abseiling down. The hatch remained closed.

'Listen,' said Toby. 'Can you get me to those two girls you told me about? The ones who can dream me home?'

Myles blew out a long breath and shook his head. 'That's just it,' he said. 'I can't.'

Toby was shocked. He wanted to demand Myles take him, but instead, he nodded.

'They're not there any more,' explained Myles. 'He's moved them from their house to stay with the Dreamers. Any of the cygnets who are powerful enough to dream you home, he's moved them to the far end of the castle.'

They were quiet. Alfred wanted to get down. Myles released him and the cat dropped lightly to the floor. Toby noticed that Alfred had lost a great deal of weight in the last few days – however many days it was that had passed since he arrived in Balthasar. Toby was losing count, it felt like one long continuous day, or nightmare.

So, Toby realised with a sigh, he was going to have to go there, to the end of the castle, the heart of the Regent's domain – his office, the Queen's apartments, and the Dreamers.

'Can you give me directions, Myles?'

'I'll take you.'

'No. Give me directions. You're in enough trouble.'

Myles remained silent. Toby rummaged in his bag for a pencil and paper.

'He told his mates something,' said Myles suddenly. 'I don't know why, but he told them in front of me, right before he let me go. He told me where he keeps the keys to the Dreamers' quarters.'

'That's brilliant,' said Toby. 'Where?'

'He keeps them in the drawer in his office. And he's not going to be in his office from about seven o'clock tonight. He told his mates he was going to the big feast.'

'What feast?'

'The Feast of Queen Edwige. It's to celebrate the Great Dreaming of Balthasar, when Queen Edwige dreamt the city here. It's an annual event. Everyone will be there, all the people in Balthasar who think they're important.'

'Then that's perfect. I'll get the key while he's out.'

'The thing is,' said Myles, 'I think it might be a trap.'

Neither boy spoke. There was a rumble. Not the rumble of wheel machinery, but deeper. The rumble of thunder.

Speaking quietly and slowly, as if he was thinking out loud, Myles went on: 'When he spoke with his mates, he did it right in front of me. Why? And why did he let me go? I think he wanted me to find you. I think he wanted me to tell you where the key is. He's trying to lure you to his office.'

The thunder rumbled again, then the light increased as if clouds had passed.

'You're right,' said Toby. 'It might be a trap.' Gently moving rain-shadows fell through the thin gaps in the boards of the wheel. 'But what other choice do I have? I have to go to the Dreamers.'

Toby handed Myles the pencil and exercise book, the paper stiff and warped from its dousing in the harbour water. By mobile-phone torch light, Myles drew a map to the end of the castle.

'Good luck,' Myles whispered as he prepared to go, shaking Toby's hand. 'It's a shame I'm not a better dreamer.'

'It's all right, Myles, you've helped me a lot. And one day you'll be able to dream people home as much as you like.'

'I wish I had the power to dream about a zillion bees that would sting that man to death.'

*

The corridor was dark. The gas lamps remained unlit and the blue stones, placed at long intervals, gave barely enough light to see by. Toby and Alfred met no one. It was as if the Regent had given everyone the night off at this end of the castle where, no doubt, that poor swan stood miserably chained in the rain. Toby unzipped the top of his rucksack, which once more sat snug against his chest, and he and Alfred exchanged a glance as if to say, *Let's do this thing.*

Toby put his ear to the panelled door. No sound but rain beating on a window. Toby's heart knocked at his ribs. It knocked so strongly it leapt through his tongue and clicked his teeth together.

He tried the handle. The wood gave a mighty crack like a branch snapping, and the door opened.

The sound of the storm was enormous. Rain smeared the window in waves. Night had fallen and the scaffolding around the casement deepened the darkness and gave, along with the pale bellying ceiling, a sense of being inside something – a beast's underground lair. There was a big desk by the window. Over to the side Toby thought he could make out a fireplace and two high-backed armchairs with big projecting wings.

Leaving the door ajar for the faint corridor light, Toby started for the desk. Alfred slipped away into darkness.

The whole room seemed affronted by their entrance, the floorboards cracking, the casement rattling, a few pages under a glass paperweight on the desk fluttering. A pile of documents and some darker objects he could not properly see were also there. The door slammed. Toby jumped.

Now it was even darker, the lair closing in. Toby's ears picked up a high-pitched whine – some noise in his own skull. It faded.

Myles said the key was in the desk. He went round it. The drawer was locked. He needed something to open it.

The light from the window illuminated quills and pencils, and a knife. He knew it was the long, sharp blade that the Regent had held against his throat. His guts shrivelled but he lifted the thing. He wouldn't think about what it did.

He slid the blade into the gap between drawer and desk and levered. The drawer didn't budge. He strained. Still nothing. He held the haft tight and gave it a powerful jab against the desk edge and the drawer coughed open. Toby pulled it wide and, by the light from the window, saw what was inside.

Nothing. Nothing but the smell of damp wood. Except, like a kind of mockery, when he felt to the back, a cold oval of metal. Toby held it up. It was a clasp, and it bore the symbol of the swan.

Toby gripped it so hard it hurt his palm. He dropped it

in the drawer and shoved the drawer shut and the pile of papers slid over and several sheets cascaded to the floor.

He faced the window. The storm was growing. Below, far below on the rocks, waves boomed and sent up spray several storeys high. The wind was so strong it was making the building shudder. He wondered about going out there and climbing along the scaffolding to get into the Dreamers' quarters. But the metal poles were shaking and creaking dangerously.

'Is this what you're searching for?' said a voice.

Toby spun.

The room was a blot of darkness. For a moment he stood frozen then he grabbed the knife from the desk.

A great cracking noise, as if the entire sky had split open, filled the room and in the simultaneous flash of lightning Toby saw that in one of the red chairs by the fireplace sat a man, his leg crossed at the knee, his head tipped back, a thin smile on his cruel mouth. Regent Malladain. And in his hand he held a long, black key.

CHAPTER
22

A Taste of Medicine

'Light a lamp, would you?' the Regent purred.

Toby could see nothing but the Regent's after-image, imprinted by the flash of lightning.

'Do I have to do everything in this place?' the Regent sighed, standing up.

Toby stepped back and hit the corner of the window recess. It felt better having the wall behind him, the window to his right now, a faint light falling from it onto the desk, but beyond the desk lay darkness, and now he was close to the window, all he could hear was the storm. The Regent made no noise and could be anywhere. Toby gripped the knife more tightly, the leather strapping damp in his palm and the brass end digging into the heel of his hand. He swung the blade warningly.

A match was lit. Malladain was by the fireplace, the match flame casting shadows up his face, distorting eye sockets and bony nose, deepening creases, making him grotesque. 'I thought it was you,' the Regent said, lifting a glass shade from a lamp. He touched the flame to the wick, replaced the shade, and tossed the match into the fireplace. Taking up the key once more, he turned to Toby and said, 'This is what you want, is it?'

Toby did not respond.

'Do you know who I am?'

Toby did not speak.

The Regent walked towards him.

'Stay where you are!' Toby cried, pressing harder against the wall, pointing the knife.

The Regent continued towards him.

'Don't!' Toby called, hoping there was no fear in his voice. He felt fear.

The Regent stopped on the other side of the desk. His glance fell to the knife in Toby's hand. Then he placed the key on the corner of the desk closest to himself. To pick it up, Toby would have to lean right across.

The Regent dropped to a crouch.

'Stand up!' Toby said, his voice emerging as a whisper. He wished it was stronger, he wished he didn't have fear in it.

There was a rustle and scrape and the Regent stood, papers in his hands.

'I am only collecting what you disturbed,' he said, putting the papers on the desk. 'I detest mess.' He gave the word 'mess' a special emphasis, as if 'mess' was something that should be wiped off the face of the planet. Toby wondered if 'mess' included him. 'Do you know who I am?' the Regent said again.

'The killer of Kerten.'

Lightning flashed. Thunder banged. They stood opposite each other, man and boy.

The Regent's mouth opened a fraction, and he smiled. 'How old are you?'

'Old enough to cut you.'

'Do you want this?'

The long bony hand picked up the key, wagged it nonchalantly, then placed it down again, this time closer to Toby.

Toby blinked, hard. He wished he hadn't blinked. It felt like everything he did told the Regent something about his fear while the Regent's face told nothing. It was a mask.

'I'd like you to take the key.'

Toby heard his pulse in his ears.

'Take the key.'

Toby's head began to pound.

'Go on, I'd like to see you take it.'

Toby needed that key. He stepped closer. The Regent watched. Toby took another step. The Regent did not move. Now Toby was in touching distance. He had only to reach out with his left hand to take the key.

'Why do you want me to take it?' said Toby.

'So you'll go on your merry way. Take the key and get yourself dreamed home. Once you've gone, my problem's solved – no witness to my crime.'

With his eyes trained on the Regent's face, Toby lowered his left hand. It was a blur beneath him but he didn't want to glance away from the Regent. He should have touched the desk by now but it was further away than he expected and he had to twist his body slightly to extend his reach. He touched the surface of the desk with his fingertips. He tapped forwards.

Then he glanced down.

The desk honked over the floorboards and its corner struck Toby in the thigh and pain burst through his leg and he staggered backwards. The Regent was coming round for him but Toby was fast, moving sideways, going to the other end of the desk. But if Toby was faster than the Regent, the Regent was more cunning. He'd anticipated Toby's move; his stride forwards was only a feint and he was already stepping across to prevent Toby's escape. Toby's charge for the door was converted into backward thrust as the Regent blocked his path and grabbed his throat, cutting off his windpipe as he walked forward, propelling the boy into the wall at speed. Pain erupted over Toby's back. He was off the floor, clamped to the wall by that hand. He was like an animal in an iron trap. He couldn't breathe. He kicked but the kicks were on the Regent's legs and weak. Toby had dropped the knife when the desk hit him and he could only scrabble with his fingers. He couldn't prise the man's hand off and couldn't reach the man's face. He couldn't even see the face any longer; his vision was darkening from the lack of air supply. He thumped the Regent's forearm but he might as well have been thumping the metal arm of a crane. He couldn't breathe. Waves boomed. Scaffolding rattled. Toby began to pass out. He could just see a faint mask, looking not at him but out the window.

Was the Regent considering defenestration?

'A barbarous nuisance,' said the Regent mildly and Toby wasn't sure if he was talking about him or the storm.

The Regent began to disappear. Toby was losing consciousness. Darkness was coming up. A white flash of fur, a man's high-pitched yelp, and Toby was dropped. He staggered. Then he ran. Hands hurled him across the room. He hit the wing of an armchair. Agony sprang around his body as he slid into the seat. There was something wrong with his throat. He couldn't swallow properly. He was shaking uncontrollably. The Regent kicked Alfred and Toby tried to shout but his throat wouldn't let him. The Regent picked up the knife, then took the key from the desk and put it in his pocket. He advanced on Toby. Toby was unable to move but the Regent, astonishingly, did not attack. He sat in the other chair, nursing a cut on his cheek where Alfred had scratched him.

In that cabin-like office with the low, bellying ceiling, Toby trembled. He looked for Alfred. The cat was hiding somewhere.

Gradually, the Regent's rapid breath slowed while Toby grew aware of little details in the room – the noise of the burning wick, the wind whistling in the chimney, the draft rising from between the floorboards and up his trouser legs. Something dripped from the ceiling. It landed on the Regent's forehead. The Regent wiped it off. Any moment now, he'd rise from his chair, come over to Toby, and stab him.

Another drip fell on the Regent's forehead and again the Regent wiped it off but this time he wiped his fingers on his chair afterwards. In the last moments of his life, Toby had the irrelevant, unhelpful thought: *I bet his mum would have something to say about him wiping his fingers on the furniture like that.*

The Regent's dead eyes twinkled. This was it. The tendons in the man's right wrist stood out as his grip tightened on the knife, and he stood. He paused, giving a quick irritated frown at the ceiling – another drop had landed on his forehead. He wiped it off and examined the tips of his fingers. Then, strangely, he tasted his fingers. A puzzled expression crossed his face. He checked the ceiling and Toby couldn't help it – he glanced up too.

There was a stain in the middle of the plaster and from this a new drip began to form. It lengthened and lengthened until there was a thin strand between the ceiling and the Regent's upturned face. This long drip kept coming, almost pouring. It was as thick as syrup. Then, as Toby watched, the ceiling fell open and down slid what looked like a church organ. It was made of golden wooden pipes, but gooey ones, and the thing came slopping and squelching, dripping and grunting, before it slid free of the roof space altogether and felled Regent Malladain.

The Regent was twisting around inside the church organ, trying to stand. The object was making a droning hum so noisy it was audible above the storm. Then Toby realised what it was – not a church organ but a honeycomb. The Regent rose from its broken cylinders. Then he began to sway and jig. Because with the honeycomb had come all its manufacturers. About a zillion bees. Dreamed bees. Extremely angry dreamed bees, furious about the destruction of their home. They were stinging Malladain, and the more he waved, trying to fight them off, the more angry they became and the more frequently they pierced his skin with their barbs.

Toby was transfixed. The bees swarmed. They formed a dark cloud. They made what looked like a furry coat

for the Regent. It fit him perfectly. It was made of bees.
Attached to it was a diving helmet, also made of bees. Toby
edged towards the door. Alfred, bruised, crept after him.
Men of the Watch had entered. They had been waiting
to catch Toby but hardly noticed him now. Because bees
attacked them. The insects seemed uninterested in Toby
and Alfred. The pair stepped over nets and weapons and
handcuffs which the men of the Watch had dropped, their
hands now full with swiping and swatting and waving.
The room became a box of buzzing, howls and screams.

CHAPTER 23

The Feast of Queen Edwige

At the top of a flight of steps, a big wooden door opened outwards. Toby pushed. It felt like someone was pushing from the other side, then the door shifted an inch and something ripped it back and smashed it against the outer wall. The wind roared, rising to a scream when it met the cables holding up the castle's towers. The scream was accompanied by a loose cable hitting a flagpole and ringing crazily. It sounded like the percussionist in an orchestra of hooligans.

Toby picked up Alfred and when they moved beyond the protection of the building the rain struck them like flung gravel. Toby might have turned back except the wind lifted him off the ground. It carried him through the air. The battlements approached and beyond them was a gulf of nothing. He yelled then struck the top of the wall, nearly throwing Alfred over it, and slapped one palm against the stone to keep them both from going headlong to their deaths. The scaffolding far below was twisted, come away from its fixings, leaning far out, threatening to fall. Rocks snarled below that. Surf gnashed. His stomach somersaulted. He slithered off the parapet to safety. For a while they lay on the grass of what was a roof garden, the rain whipping them. The chained swan was nearby, huddled beneath the wall, its white feathers ruffled, its head buried in its wing, unable to fly away because of the chain. Toby crawled to the iron ring that secured the chain but could not undo it. He and Alfred slithered across the roof garden to the far door.

Lightning flashed. The door wouldn't open. The wind was pushing it shut. Toby fought the wind and managed to pull the door wide enough for them to slip through before it boomed behind them. Ears ringing, soaked, he watched as Alfred zipped down the spiral stairs.

'Alfred!' called Toby, clattering after the cat.

The stairs opened onto a small gallery above a banquet hall. There was no sign of Alfred. There was movement below. A table ran the length of the hall, its white tablecloths covered by silver and crystal, candelabra and flowers. Two servants were going up either side, placing a menu at each place. Stained-glass windows, as tall as those in a cathedral, ran along one wall, their pictures

325

showing the heroic deeds of old kings and queens of Balthasar, as if they knew no current king or queen could ever do anything as heroic. The stony rain threw itself at the stained glass, perhaps because it disliked the snootiness of the windows, or because it felt excluded from the banquet – or maybe it just wanted to smash its way in and chuck Toby off the top of the castle. The stained glass, even its stone mullions and stone frames, flinched at each blast. Oh, those poor, snooty windows! Between each window a flagpole saluted the table with a damp-stained flag showing a white swan on a green field. The swans fluttered weakly in the draft. There were more swans on the high wooden vault, painted ones, no longer white because the vault leaked and the swans had moulted, regrowing feathers of black mould. There were several buckets dotted around, and silver basins on the table, to catch drips from the leaky roof. At the far end of the hall, a servant uncorked bottles with a regular pop. Above him hung a second gallery, where a singer was rehearsing a last song, his voice floating out sadly over a small audience of musicians who listened mercilessly with crossed arms and hands pressed to mouths.

Toby's gallery had a low curtain on a brass rail, pulled half across, and peeping round the edge of this, her back to Toby, watching the activity below, was Tamurlaine.

'Tam!' She turned and without thinking he went to hug her. 'What happened? Are you all right?'

She looked a mess, her ragged dress more ragged, her bare feet filthy, but she seemed unhurt.

'Did you catch that Dreamer – the blond one, the flying boy?' Her stare was so cold and pure, it scared Toby. She seemed to be staring through him. 'What's wrong, Tam?'

It was difficult to meet her gaze. He glanced away, searching for Alfred. There were rolls of carpet, a dismantled drum kit. He found Alfred hiding between the wall and the back of a drum. He wouldn't come out. Tamurlaine returned to her position behind the curtain. There was something wrong, definitely. Something had happened to her.

'Tam!' hissed Toby. He had to call her name several times before she came over and sat beside him on the rolls of carpet, hunched over her knees, arms wrapped round herself. 'Are you all right? You seem a bit weird, like something's happened.'

She laughed a humourless laugh.

'Tell me!'

'I'm responsible.'

'For what?'

'This.' She twirled her forefinger as if to indicate the entire hall and went back to hugging her knees.

'What, this hall?'

'The whole castle, the city, Balthasar.'

'How?'

'Even you, Toby. It's my fault you're here. If I hadn't come to your house. If you hadn't followed me through the hole.'

'I followed Alfred, not you. And you're helping me to get home.'

'I'm not doing a very good job of that.'

'Well, that's the Regent's fault, not yours.'

At mention of his name, her face darkened.

'We just met him, by the way,' Toby added, massaging his throat.

'Are you all right?' said Tamurlaine, worried for him now, searching his eyes. She had grey eyes, Toby noticed for the first time. He smiled at her. It was nice to see her again.

'Well, my throat hurts,' he said. 'And my back. But I think I'm all right.'

'I'll kill him,' she hissed, her eyes wild again.

'Tam.' He had to repeat her name several times and shake her by the shoulder to regain her attention. 'What's going on? Tell me.'

'I remembered who I am. I remembered everything.'

She didn't say any more.

'Who are you, then?'

She got up and went to the curtain and peeked around it. Toby sighed and shook his head. She wasn't going to tell him. He decided to get changed. He was soaked from the roof garden. He took his own, dry clothes from his rucksack and changed out of his borrowed things. Tamurlaine returned from the curtain and sat beside him.

'There were four of us,' she said.

Toby waited.

'Me, Kerten, Ollie Reckless and Burston,' she said.

'Burston Shimpling?'

'Yes. Burston Shimpling. He kept hanging round with us, desperate to be part of our gang. He's so persistent, in the end we let him. He was in the year below. We were at school together, you see – Dreaming School. Me, Kerten and Ollie were the best in our year at everything, but we were especially good at dreaming. Burston liked to think he was good but he wasn't. He was average. But we three were brilliant. Oh, we could dream the pants off anyone. The whole school. We loved the adulation. The respect. The teachers told us we were going to be the greatest Dreamers Balthasar has ever known.'

Tamurlaine sighed, as if she was thinking about that time.

'I think I fell in love with that adulation. I think I believed it. I think we all loved the glory. Certainly Ollie Reckless did. He's handsome, don't you think?'

'I don't know. Is he?'

'Yes. Anyway. He loved it, being handsome, people loving him. I think I … I think I loved him a bit myself. It was hard not to. His vanity was annoying but I sort of believed in the confidence he had.' She shut her eyes and shook her head. 'We were such idiots.'

'I know what that's like. I'm always being an idiot and doing things wrong. It's annoying.'

'Ollie loved the glory and the celebrity. That's what drove him. And dreaming came easily to him. He didn't have to think about it. Kerten, though, he loved the dreaming. He had an affinity for it. His dreaming had a different feel to Ollie's.'

'What's your dreaming like?'

'Me? I was a bit of a huffer and puffer, but when it goes right, the effort leaves you and you're free. There's a joy in it, it sort of lifts you up. It's like nothing else.'

'It sounds like when I sail my yacht sometimes at the boating pond.'

'Maybe it is. Anyway, then something changed.'

'What?'

'It was before Malladain was Regent but he was still powerful. He was high up in the government and oversaw the Dreamers. He wasn't in charge of Dreaming School, there was a headmaster, but he basically controlled it. And he intensified the work the Dreamers had to do and also the classes at Dreaming School. It became like a factory for dreams. The Dreamers started failing earlier than they used to do – they were used up and finished within a year or two of graduation. And some of the cygnets lost their powers even before they graduated to become Dreamers. They had breakdowns. Or quit.

'But that wasn't the only thing. At the same time as this, some of the problems that Balthasar had been having got worse. There were more wildfires, floods, storms, even earthquakes. Our harvests failed. Disease ripped through livestock. Fishing grounds emptied. Some people said it was because of the dreaming.'

'How?'

'People didn't know. But the two happened at the same time so the king set up a commission to investigate the cause of all the problems. And they found the holes.'

'Between your world and mine?'

'Between this world and lots of other worlds. Some people said the dreaming was causing the holes, and in turn the holes were causing natural disasters. Malladain said that was nonsense, the holes had no link to dreaming. Plus there was nothing that could be proved.'

'But what's that got to do with you?'

'Kerten read everything about dreaming and the holes,' continued Tamurlaine, talking now as if she was explaining it to herself. 'He read the commission report, he spoke with the commission investigators, he joined a society in the city that was convinced the natural disasters were caused by dreaming. He concluded that dreaming had to be stopped. At least, the way we were doing it had to be stopped.'

Alfred appeared, slinking from behind the drum kit. He came up to Tamurlaine and waited to be picked up. Tamurlaine lifted him and stroked his long white fur absently, and Alfred, glumly musing on human behaviour, settled.

'My father died when I was fifteen,' said Tamurlaine.

'Oh,' said Toby, not sure what to say.

'I never knew my mother. She died in childbirth. But my father's death changed everything.'

'I can imagine.'

'No, you don't understand. You see, my father was the ruler of Balthasar.'

'The king?'

'Yes. King Sigobert.'

'Wait a minute. That means that you – You're the ...'

'Yes, I'm the queen, Queen Tamurlaine, ruler of Balthasar.'

'Wow,' said Toby, not sure what to say. 'That's so good,' he said in the end. 'You can do what you want, then.'

'No. I can't. When my father died, I was too young to take the throne so a regent was appointed – my uncle, Nicodemus Malladain.'

'So Malladain's your uncle? Imagine having that guy for an uncle.'

'It's even worse than you can imagine.'

'I bet it is. That means that Fadranga is your ... grandmother, right?'

'Yes.'

'So that explains why Mrs Bleverhasset mistook you for Fadranga. You must look a bit like your grandmother.'

'Do you know what it's like being trapped in this family, Toby? A family of murderers.'

'No.'

'It's horrible. Knowing death is in your blood. Listen. Here's what happened. I was in tutelage when my father died. I was fifteen and I wouldn't come into my majority until I was sixteen. I never wanted to be ruler, anyway. I never wanted to have power. And I never wanted to have all the silly money that goes with it.'

'But you need money to eat. You can't live without money, can you?'

She shot him an irritated glance. 'Will you let me tell you what happened?'

Toby nodded and she went on.

'The Regent wanted power for himself and he had a year to get it. Because as soon as I turned sixteen there would be a ceremony and his power would end and I would assume control. And he was worried about Kerten. He thought I'd been influenced by Kerten, that I wanted to change how things worked with dreaming. That I was going to stop dreaming, or curtail it, at least.'

'And had you been influenced by Kerten? Were you against dreaming?'

'Well, I wasn't sure how dreaming related to all the

problems. And before I could come to a conclusion, Malladain put a plan into action.'

'Uh-oh.'

'He decided to marry me off.'

'Can he do that?'

'It's not like your world here, Toby. Once you're sixteen, you can get married. And the marriages in the royal family – for women, anyway – are usually arranged. So he planned to marry me off before I could take power. Because once I took power I could say no.'

'That's disgusting.'

'Suitors arrived, invited by the Regent. He only invited young men he could control, who'd do what he said. They came from distant kingdoms, all eager for money, power. That's what people want, isn't it?'

'I don't know if that's true.'

'All right, all right. Anyway, whoever married me would have more power than me because that's what happens – the king has the power, not the queen. They'd be made for life and our child would be future king or queen.'

'That's disgusting. The whole thing.'

'The suitors were disgusting too. Dis-gust-ing. So, everything became bad. School was awful. I couldn't dream anything into being any more. Kerten and Ollie weren't there any more either. They'd been made Dreamers. They were the youngest cygnets at Dreaming

School to become Dreamers. I was good enough to join them but I wasn't allowed to because I was going to be married off. I couldn't sleep. I couldn't eat. I felt sick all the time. When I wasn't crying, I was being ill. I couldn't hold a conversation or hear what anyone was saying to me. The only thing I could think was how to escape. How to escape.'

'He couldn't actually force you to marry, could he?'

'Yes. They could actually hold the marriage without me being present.'

'I'm not surprised you felt sick.'

'That's what he was going to do. Have the wedding as soon as I turned sixteen, before the ceremony when I would assume power. Before I could take power in my own right. Then he selected a suitor. That's when I realised his plan was becoming real. I no longer felt upset, I felt nothing. Inside me was nothing. I didn't care any more. I didn't go to school. Didn't get out of bed. I couldn't even make the effort to wash myself. I sat in a daze. Everything in the world – the castle, the city, the palm trees on the promenade, the sea itself, lost its colour, its life. The world was dead. And me – myself, my own body – was dead too. My body was another *thing*, dead like the rest of the world.'

Toby touched her icy hand. 'I'm sorry, Tam.'

'The only person who noticed something wrong with me was Kerten. He used to visit me. He used to tell me his ideas about dreaming. About the holes. But sometimes we'd say nothing. Just sit together. And he used to take me for walks. We'd go for long walks through the city. He showed me places I'd never seen before. Beautiful places. Strange places. But Malladain didn't like him coming to see me. He thought Kerten was a bad influence. And he saw him as a threat to his own power. Which he was, I suppose. Kerten was a Dreamer but he was refusing to dream. Because of the damage he thought dreaming was doing to the world. So Malladain had him arrested. He said Kerten's views were sacrilegious. At the trial, the judges found him guilty, and he was locked up while they decided the punishment.'

Toby nodded. He didn't know what to say.

'And you know what I did?' said Tamurlaine.

'No.'

'I don't know how, when I could hardly get out of bed, but I fought back. I got Burston to help me. I went down to the cells and ordered the guard to unlock Kerten's cell. And I took Kerten out. Burston had a carriage waiting. He drove it out of the castle with Kerten and me hidden in the back. We would have escaped except Burston – such a stupid thing to do – had boasted to Ollie Reckless beforehand how he was going to help us. And Ollie, glory-hunter that he is, told the Regent.'

'What an idiot.'

'The Watch were waiting for us at the city gates.'

'Oh no. What happened?'

'Kerten escaped but I was caught. I was brought before the Regent. He confined me to my apartments and I was not permitted to leave until I was married on my sixteenth birthday, to the suitor he'd chosen. I was taken to the royal apartments by an armed guard. An armed guard. Can you imagine, Toby? The Queen of Balthasar, under lock and key. Anyway, there I fell asleep, and I haven't woken since.'

'I don't understand,' said Toby. 'You're here now. How can you be asleep in the royal apartments?'

'I'm not really Tamurlaine, you see.'

'But you said you were. You just said you're Queen Tamurlaine. I don't understand.'

'I'm Tamurlaine's shadow. Her dream self.'

'You seem pretty real to me,' said Toby.

'Thanks,' said Tamurlaine.

Toby thought about her story. 'So are you still asleep, then?' Toby asked. 'The other you, I mean?'

'I must be. Otherwise I wouldn't exist, I think. The real me is still in the Queen's apartments. I don't know how the real me fell into that sleep. I don't know if it's a sleep of illness or despair, or if the Regent drugged me. But whatever caused it, I left my body and became the shadow.'

There was a strange look on her face now, a sort of demented enjoyment in what she was about to say.

'When I became the shadow, I had no memory of who I was. I didn't know I was Tamurlaine. All I knew was hatred. That was all I had. And I hated everyone. I mean, I really hated them. I've done terrible things, Toby. I've attacked people. I've punched them and kicked them and tripped them down stairs, and spoiled their dinners and whispered poisonous thoughts in their ears. It didn't matter if they were good people or not. I've whispered nasty things to children about their parents. And told lies to parents about their children. I've caused rows and betrayals and estrangements and feuds. I've slipped inside the dreams of girlfriends and made them certain their boyfriends are about to leave them, and slipped inside the dreams of boyfriends and made them believe their girlfriends were being unfaithful. I've started duels. I've cut holes in the nets of poor fishermen. I've given people nightmares and laughed at their terror. I've made the person with the deepest faith have doubt. I've mocked the weakest beggar. I've entered the minds of scientists and corrupted their equations and the brains of poets and ruined their rhythms. I've added pointless items to shopping lists and removed important details from exam questions. I bit the ear off a man once. I bit off his *ear*. I didn't care, Toby. I loved it. I *loved* it. Only it made no difference. I wasn't happy. I couldn't destroy what I really wanted to destroy.'

'The Regent?'

'No – me.'

'I don't understand. Why would you want to destroy yourself? It was the Regent who tried to marry you off.'

'I hated, hated, hated. I hated myself.'

'You're a good person, Tam.'

'I'm not, though, am I? I'm from a long line of murderers. And that's what I am, too.'

'No, you're not.'

'Malladain's just the most recent. Before him was Fadranga and before her the rest of that murderous crew. I'm the latest in a long line of evil.' She buried her face in Alfred's fur. She sat up. 'Do you ever hate, Toby?'

Toby said nothing for a long while, then said, 'I hate myself sometimes.'

'What do you hate about yourself?'

'I don't know. My life, I suppose.' Toby sighed. 'Everyone hates me. Even my dad. There must be something in me that makes him dislike me so much.'

'Your dad doesn't dislike you, he's just selfish.'

Toby felt himself getting angry. 'No he's not. You don't know what you're talking about.'

'But I do, don't I? I've hung about your house long enough to see him in action. Come on, you've got to admit it.'

Toby thought about it. He frowned hard. 'Maybe you're right,' he said eventually. Suddenly emotion whirled inside him. He felt like crying. He had to fight back the tears. Then they passed, like a wave, and his mind was clear. He took a deep breath. 'So you think it's not me, it's Dad?'

'Definitely.'

There was another quiet. They could hear the distant babble of guests just beyond the banquet hall in a reception room, waiting to come in.

'Tell me the end of your story,' said Toby.

'One night they tricked me into entering the castle. They nearly caught me. The Regent, the Watch, and Ollie Reckless. I flew away. Ollie flew after me. I escaped when I fell through a hole. I found myself in your world.'

'So that's when you came to Arnold Street?'

'Yes. I was lost. I was already lost because I didn't have any memory of who I was but now I was worse than lost, I wasn't in my own world. I had a vague sense of Balthasar, that was all. That was why I stopped outside your house. I heard you mention Balthasar.'

'I must have been talking about my dad's novel,' said Toby. 'How does Dad know about Balthasar?'

'I don't know. Maybe he came here once. Or someone who has been here told him about it.' Tamurlaine continued: 'When I came back to this world a few months later, down Angel Lane, when you followed Alfred, that's when I saw Kerten again. I think he was in the mountains because he'd come looking for me. He must have heard there was a hole. And I think maybe the Regent was

340

following Kerten to kill him, or maybe he thought Kerten knew where I was. Maybe the Regent thought he could catch me through Kerten.'

She stood and went to the gallery balustrade.

'Any minute now they'll be coming in.'

'What are you going to do?'

'The great and the good of Balthasar.'

'What are you going to do?' Toby asked again. He suspected the answer to his question. She was still consumed by hatred. That was why she was here. She was going to do something terrible. And for some reason, her revenge wasn't like Myles wanting to take revenge on the Regent for the death of Gasper; there was something different about Tamurlaine's desire for revenge. He wasn't sure what. Maybe it was because when Myles wanted to take revenge, he didn't really understand the consequences. With Tamurlaine, Toby knew she'd actually carry out what she threatened. She would really damage people. Then, in a sudden flash of understanding, like when he solved a maths problem at school, he saw the logic of whatever she was about to do. She hated herself and she wanted to destroy herself. And she knew that hurting another person was wrong so if she attacked another person, she would also be destroying the part of herself that believed in good things. She wasn't just going to take vengeance – she was also trying to destroy the best part of herself.

'You mustn't, Tam. You mustn't,' he said, rushing to her.

She looked deeply into his eyes, her expression softened, and two vertical creases appeared at the corners of her mouth. 'You're kind, Toby Porter. You're not like your father at all.'

'But you've remembered who you are now. That means you can change things. You can go and find yourself and go back to yourself and wake up and go to the Regent and chuck him out. You're the queen. You're Queen Tamurlaine. You're probably sixteen now. You can do what you want.'

With a cruel smile, she turned her focus back to the hall.

'Please don't,' said Toby. 'If you do, you'll be just like the rest of your family. It'll be no good for you. You shouldn't do it.'

Tamurlaine faced him. 'I'm the granddaughter of a murderer. The niece of a murderer. Killing runs in my family like the colour of our hair. I'm just continuing the family business, and I'm going to murder Regent Malladain.'

CHAPTER 24

King Sigobert

'Don't, Tam, please. You're not like your uncle or your grandmother and you don't have to kill anyone. That's a mistake to think that. You don't have to be like them. You have a choice.'

'I'm going to kill Nicodemus Malladain, Regent of Balthasar, and you can't stop me, Toby Porter.'

'Everything can be fixed. Everything. You can go back to yourself and wake up and be Queen of Balthasar and lock him up and rule on your own and do what you want.'

'You can't fix everything, Toby.'

'I can. I can fix you being separated from yourself.'

'How?'

'We can take you to the Queen's apartments and you'll go back to yourself. There's a key in the Regent's office. Trust me. I got you here didn't I?'

'You did, yes. Like I got you here to the castle.'

'Then we helped each other.'

'Only so far. Because the world – this world, your world – isn't fixable. And it isn't make-believe either. It's real. People's lives here are real, and they depend on what I do next. And all those souls out there – Jinky and Burston and Mervyn and the rest, are my responsibility. And what I have to do is remove that parasite Malladain from the face of the planet.'

In the banquet hall, a white-gloved servant was going up the long table, lighting candles. Through the open doors at the far end people waited in the reception room. The tenor had finished his rehearsal and the musicians were playing. The rain crackled on the windows and the roof groaned under the wind. Two figures walked out from beneath Toby's and Tamurlaine's gallery. One was a man with long greasy hair, which he kept scratching, the other a teenager in a threadbare black suit. Each carried a sheaf of papers and they were stopping at each place to insert a single sheet into the guest's menu.

'Mervyn Sump,' said Tamurlaine, giving the word 'Sump' an emphasis which suggested something nasty, say, a stagnant pond. And when she added 'Burston

344

Shimpling' it was pretty clear she didn't have a much higher opinion of Burston.

'Tamurlaine,' said Toby, turning to her. 'Can you get the Dreamers to dream me home? If you're Queen?'

She whirled on him. She thought a few seconds. 'Yes, once I've killed Malladain.'

Toby shook his head. 'I can't be involved in that. It's wrong. I'll go to the Dreamers now. By myself.' And so saying, he turned and leaned over the gallery rail. 'Oi, Burston!' whispered Toby, loudly.

Burston looked about but couldn't see who had spoken.

'Oi, Burston!'

Again Burston searched for the whisperer, saw no one, and went on.

'Oi, Burston Shimpling!' Toby shouted.

Burston looked round. So did Mervyn, the servants, and the musicians in the other gallery.

'Shh,' said Tamurlaine. 'You'll spoil everything.'

Burston spotted him, finished his menu-work, and hurried towards the gallery stairs, Mervyn Sump limping behind, as if in great pain.

'So you made it into the castle, then, Toby?' said Burston, panting onto the gallery, arms full of papers.

'Yes, but not to the Dreamers. What are you doing here?'

'We're here to bring down the Regent.'

345

Toby shot him a look of surprise.

'What's the matter,' said Burston, 'don't you believe me?'

'No, of course I believe you.'

'You know me, Toby, I laugh in the face of danger.'

'No, you don't, Burston,' said Mervyn, appearing from the stairs behind him. His face was so bruised and swollen he was almost unrecognisable. He should really have been in bed. Or a hospital.

'Sump,' said Tamurlaine.

Mervyn and Burston saw Tamurlaine at the same time. They were shocked. Mervyn recovered himself first. 'Your Majesty,' he said, bowing. A look of agony crossed his face when he bent his back.

'Tam-Tam-Tamurlaine, I mean, Queen Tamurlaine, your Majesty,' said Burston. He curtseyed nervously, then bowed, then lifted an imaginary hat.

'So, Sump,' said Tamurlaine, 'I hear you betrayed my friend Toby Porter first opportunity you got.' She gave Mervyn's name her special emphasis, as if she might catch a nasty disease by saying it.

'I'm sorry, your Majesty. If it's any consolation, they did this to me.' He pointed at his bruised face.

'No consolation whatsoever.'

'I'm here to make amends,' said Mervyn.

'*We're* here,' Burston corrected the archivist. 'I've stepped into the lion's den for you, your Majesty.'

Mervyn added, 'Only because I threatened to turn you over to the Watch for helping a fugitive.'

'Stop bickering,' snapped Tamurlaine. 'Why are you here? What are you doing?'

Burston said, 'Mervyn came to the Bureau first thing, face swollen like a pumpkin, and made me spend the entire day on our printing press putting this together.' Burston tapped the loose papers in his arms.

'What is it?'

'It's an account of Regent Malladain's crimes,' said Mervyn. 'With witness statements. Toby's statement about the murder of Kerten. Everyone down there will read it in about five minutes' time. There's no way Malladain can survive this news.'

'See, Tam,' said Toby. 'You don't have to do anything to him. He's finished. The Regent's finished.'

'The city's on the verge of turning against him,' said Mervyn. 'This will tip the balance.'

Tamurlaine gazed down into the hall. The guests were beginning to come in. Toby watched her. He wasn't going to wait to see what she'd decide – this was his opportunity to go home.

'So, Burston,' said Toby, 'can you persuade the Dreamers to let me into their apartment and dream me home? You were at Dreaming School with them. They'll help you.'

'Oh, I'd like to Toby, I really would, but I'm going back to the Bureau. Things to do, you know.'

Burston was already sidling away.

'You're not scared, are you?' said Toby.

'Not at all. Not. At. All.'

'So you'll help me, then?'

'Help him, Burston,' said Tamurlaine. 'Or else.'

'I've a much better idea,' said Burston. 'There's a Dreamer coming to the feast. I saw his name on the guest list. He'll be here in a minute. He's a friend from Dreaming School. I'll ask him. I'm sure he'll help you.'

'Really?'

'Arrange it, Burston,' added Tamurlaine. 'I'm warning you.'

Burston gulped, and Toby knew he'd fetch the Dreamer.

'Alfred, we're going home.'

Tamurlaine, distracted, watched the guests. Toby saw she was still thinking about her plan. 'You don't have to do anything, you know,' he said, then went on in an undertone so the other two wouldn't hear, 'you don't have to kill the Regent. He's finished.'

'Maybe,' said Tamurlaine. 'I have to think about it.'

Burston put his papers on the rolls of carpet and went off to find the Dreamer and Toby sat beside the documents, elated. He was going to be dreamt home.

Even Alfred seemed to have picked up on his positive mood, and came over, arched his back, and rubbed his head on Toby's thigh, as if to say, *Well done, Toby.*

'That's all right, Alfred,' said Toby, and laughed.

The ink on the sheets glistened in the light, still faintly wet, and Toby took one to read what Mervyn Sump had written. He read the paragraph that included his statement. Below that was another story, with a much bigger headline, and Toby was shocked:

HOW REGENT MALLADAIN
MURDERED KING SIGOBERT
AND I KNOW BECAUSE I WAS THERE
by
Mervyn Sump, Head Archivist (retired)[1]

There was once a pair of twins, born within minutes of each other. The first to appear was Sigobert. He eased his way out of his mother like a graceful swimmer in the local pool, and smiled. Isn't the world wonderful! his smile seemed to say. The second twin was Nicodemus Malladain and he came out miffed. He was due to emerge first

---

[1] I didn't really retire. I was sacked because I know too much. See my heartbreaking memoir, *Digging in the Balthasar Archives: a Papery Sort of Life* (Balthasar, 1546).

but got tangled in his brother's umbilical cord and arrived blue-faced from nearly being strangled. He also had a black eye from being accidentally kicked by Sigobert on the way out. Nicodemus Malladain didn't much like what he saw when he looked around. So this is the world, is it? his frown seemed to say. His brother was being placed in the arms of their mother. She was gazing at her first born, Sigobert, a child destined to be king; Nicodemus Malladain, who was meant to appear first and one day be king but had come out second, thought how unfair life was – right from the start.

As they grew up, it didn't matter what Nicodemus Malladain did, his older brother was the favoured one. Sigobert got to choose what they had for dinner, which puppy they'd take home when they went to the kennels to choose a pet, which storybook their mother would read to them at bedtime. Sigobert got the biggest bedroom, the best birthday presents, and brand-new clothes; Nicodemus Malladain, even though he was a prince, had to wear hand-me-downs. When they started school, it was the same. Sig (as his friends called him) was popular while Nic (as his friends didn't call him, because he didn't have any) was unpopular. This miffed Nicodemus Malladain, because he was far better at all the lessons than Sig.

But the lessons gave him some pleasure. It wasn't that he enjoyed them (he didn't) but he received better marks than his brother. Sig hardly ever received a good mark from his teachers because he didn't do his school work. He wasn't interested in school work. He didn't have to be. He was going to be king.

When they left school, it was the same. They both fell in love with a beautiful girl named Kate, and of course Kate fell in love with Sigobert, not Malladain. It wasn't fair that she loved Sig and not him! He wanted to kiss her. He wanted her to call him Nic, which no one ever called him. People always called him Nicodemus, or Nicodemus Malladain, or Malladain, or even Mal. Which BTW means 'bad' in one of the languages on the other side.

So Sig and Kate got engaged, then married, then Kate fell pregnant. This miffed Malladain even more, because a child meant an heir, which meant any hope of Malladain becoming king one day would be gone forever. Then a lucky thing happened. Well, lucky if you were Nicodemus Malladain. Not if you were Sigobert or Kate. There were complications during the birth and Kate died while in labour. Nicodemus was overjoyed when he heard this news because that meant that he might, one day, be king, if he outlived his brother. Then his hopes were dashed – the doctor had managed to save the baby.

The baby's name was Tamurlaine. And Sigobert and baby Tamurlaine loved each other dearly.

A few years later Queen Fadranga, Sigobert's and Malladain's mother, died. So after the funeral Sigobert was crowned. You wouldn't believe how much this miffed Malladain. All his hopes gone forever.

King Sigobert was just as relaxed about his royal job as he had been about his school work – he hardly did anything. It was left to Malladain to do the work. And, brainy and ruthless as he was, Nicodemus Malladain was good at it. He soon had the government moving like an efficient machine and all King Sigobert's enemies had been ruthlessly removed. With a knife.

But Malladain was still miffed. In fact, he grew more miffed as time went on. He couldn't stop being miffed, thinking how it wasn't fair. It wasn't fair that Sig, who did nothing, had all the power, the nicest clothes, the people's adulation and the love of Tamurlaine, while he, Nicodemus Malladain, had nothing. When it was him doing all the work. While Sig went swanning round like a ... well, like a swan.

Things went on like this for a long time. Tamurlaine grew older. The king aged. Then King Sigobert fell ill with an ailment of the stomach. It lasted several years, and the doctors could find no cure. Eventually, the king was confined to bed. All the doctors who examined him agreed that the king was going to die. During the final months of his life, King Sigobert was attended by the royal doctor, by Nicodemus Malladain, and by Tamurlaine. And also, unusually, by the kingdom's archivist, Mervyn Sump.[2] This last person attended because Sigobert wanted to know about his kingdom's history. He told the archivist he was trying to find from the past what he must put in place for the future. His daughter, Tamurlaine, was only fifteen and not old enough to rule on her own. So King Sigobert had the archivist read to him from the royal histories every day, to see what the old kings and queens had done in similar circumstances.

And he found in the histories the answer to his problem.

King Sigobert ordered that after he was dead, for the year of Tamurlaine's minority reign, until she was sixteen, Nicodemus Malladain would rule on her behalf – Malladain would be Regent. And

[2] Me.

Sig made his brother promise that he would rule fairly and protect Tamurlaine from danger.

What Sigobert did not know was that he was being poisoned. By Malladain. Each evening when the doctor arrived to give his patient medicine, Malladain added a teaspoon of poison. The archivist witnessed this by accident one evening, in the little kitchen off the king's bedchamber. The archivist could hardly believe what he saw. So, to make sure he hadn't made a mistake, the next evening he hid in the kitchen cupboard and watched as Malladain prepared the medicine again, and again Malladain added poison. The archivist hid every night and witnessed the same thing. Yet the archivist did nothing. Because he was a coward.

King Sigobert died.

Nicodemus Malladain became Regent. Now he possessed what he had always wanted. He had taken the place of his twin brother. He had his brother's fancy clothes, his brother's apartment, he even had his brother's daughter in his charge. And most important to Malladain, he had power over the kingdom and all its people.

Yet he was still miffed. It was because he did not have the adulation of the people. They knew he got rid of opponents with a knife. And he did not have Tamurlaine's trust. She felt something was wrong even if she could not name it. Worst of all, because everyone was terrified of him, nobody gave him what he craved most of all – love.

And no one ever called him Nic.

Toby put down the sheet of paper. Tamurlaine stood watching the hall, awaiting the arrival of Regent Malladain. Toby knew that even if he could persuade her from taking revenge on the Regent for the murder of her friend Kerten, she could never be persuaded from taking revenge for the murder of her father. Toby didn't care about the Regent – Toby hated Malladain himself – but he cared about Tamurlaine, and he knew her soul would be destroyed if she committed murder.

CHAPTER
25

Arnold Street

The storm had decided that enough was enough and that it was going to get into the castle if that was the last thing it did. So it began picking tiles off the roof and smashing them like plates, barging accidentally-on-purpose into the battlements, stamping on the unfixed scaffolding so it fell into the sea, toppling chimneys just for the sound the bricks made when they tumbled together onto the pavement below, headbutting windows, ramming doors, and snapping the towers' cables so they streamed about in the wind like long beautiful scarves – until they touched something, when they became lethal steel whips that tore open stone – and the untethered towers started to sway. Finally, the storm tore off the confused, spinning weathervane and flung it like a magician's knife across a courtyard *thunk!* into a wall where it quivered.

The feast was getting underway in the banquet hall, the guests flowing in, finding their places, sitting down and studying menus or standing around talking, while white-gloved servants brought in trays and salvers and dishes, and delicious aromas rose.

Scratching his scalp, Mervyn Sump watched as more guests picked up the menus into which he had inserted his account of the Regent's crimes. And Tamurlaine watched for the Regent himself.

'Alfred,' murmured Toby, gathering the cat into his arms but worrying about Tamurlaine, 'it won't be long now.'

A beaming Burston Shimpling appeared at the top of the stairs, propping up a barely conscious Dreamer.

The colour drained from Toby's face. 'Ollie Reckless? He's your Dreamer?'

Tamurlaine spun.

'I know he's in a bit of a state,' said Burston, 'but there's a few dreams in him yet. Once he's had his eyedrops he'll be raring to go. Won't you, Ollie?'

In response Ollie Reckless lolled his head to one side, opened his mouth and drooled. Tamurlaine advanced on the Dreamer.

Toby stepped between them. 'He can dream me home.'

Tamurlaine regarded Toby for several seconds then lunged. Toby put his arms out to protect Ollie Reckless from her but she was only leaning to hug Toby. She wrapped her arms round him and squeezed him tight. Her body was chilly. 'Good luck, Toby Porter, my friend.' Abruptly she released him and walked to the turret staircase and slipped out of sight. Toby stared after her. So that was her goodbye. She didn't even wait for him to respond. He didn't know what to do for the best now. He nearly went after her to force her to give up on her plan for revenge.

'Evening, Ollie,' said Burston, finishing the application of gel to the Dreamer's eyes and screwing the top back on the tub. He dropped the tub in his old school friend's pocket.

Ollie smacked his lips and wiped the back of his hand across his mouth. 'What am I doing here?' he said, looking about, super-alert.

'Well, my friend Toby – this is Toby – wants to go home.'

'So?'

'Well, we hoped you'd dream him home.'

'Official dreams only. I don't do anything off the books.'

'Go on, buddy. Do a favour for an old pal.'

'No. What's going on down there?'

'It's the Feast of Queen Edwige. You're a guest.'

Ollie started to leave. Toby had only a moment to decide. Stop Tamurlaine killing, or get himself and Alfred home?

'Wait!' he called.

At the head of the stairs, Ollie Reckless turned. 'Yes?'

'No, it's fine,' said Toby, glaring at the vain boy. 'You go on. I knew you didn't really have the power to dream me home.'

'It's not that I don't have the power, it's that I don't want to.'

'Sure,' said Toby sarcastically.

'I could dream you home like that,' said Ollie Reckless, snapping his fingers, 'if I wanted to.'

Toby snorted.

Ollie Reckless took a step towards him. 'I'd be careful what I say, if I were you. I'm friends with the Regent. I could get you thrown off a tower.'

'Mate, don't worry, your secret's safe with me,' said Toby. 'We both know you couldn't dream a mouse back to its hole. Few weeks' time and you'll be standing around in that garden at the back of the Bureau of Broken Dreams with all the other ruined Dreamers. You're finished, mate.'

Ollie Reckless stepped so close to Toby their noses almost touched. Alfred sat up straight in Toby's arms, ready to protect his boy.

'Go on,' whispered Toby, 'I dare you.'

The Dreamer's pupils were almost as big as his irises. His breath smelled of sleep. Suddenly he stepped back and said, 'Think of home.'

For a moment, Toby wasn't sure what Ollie Reckless meant, then he understood – he was actually going to dream him home. But where to think of – the new flat with his mum? Then he knew. Arnold Street. It had to be Arnold Street.

He nodded. He was ready.

Ollie Reckless immediately fell asleep. But it was a controlled sleep. He stayed perfectly upright and perfectly still, his face deeply relaxed. Toby tried to picture Arnold Street in his mind but it was difficult. He could hear the storm outside, the voices in the hall, and the tenor singing and the musicians playing. He wondered if he could feel something in his brain, a sort of prickle. But he wasn't sure. He concentrated on the sensation, and still he wasn't sure. He tried to think of Arnold Street again. Should he see it from outside, the front door with its misted glass, the bush in the tiny front garden behind the pavement wall, and the grille in the ground that covered the gloomy space outside the basement bathroom? The image kept fading.

There was a patch of light on the stone wall behind Ollie Reckless. It had been there some time but it seemed to have grown stronger while Toby was trying to think of

360

home. It wasn't a reflection from the candles or lamps in the banquet hall, it was more like sunlight. Then Toby noticed the floor had turned a ruby colour, although it seemed to be growing paler, and over to his right, where the curtain hung above the banquet hall, was more light, the size and shape of a door, while on his left stood what might be a bed. The gallery with its wooden floor did not disappear but rather, the patch of light ahead, the door-shaped light to his right, the ruby-coloured floor and the bed shape, were present at the same time.

A strong scent of lily of the valley hit his nostrils and he was instantly in Mrs Papadopoulos's attic room in Arnold Street. Alfred realised it too because he scrambled around in Toby's arms. Toby released him and Alfred dropped with a soft thump and scampered away. Toby could still hear the storm and the guests' voices and the tenor and musicians, but when he looked to his left there was Mrs Papadopoulos's bed. It had been stripped. Her room was empty, her possessions gone. Toby took a step across the carpet, which was deep and soft and a lilac colour, then walked to the dormer window, putting both hands up on the windowsill, feeling the hardness of wood against the heels of his hands. The sill was drifted with pollen dust from the vase of flowers Mrs Papadopoulos would often place there.

The long, narrow back garden lay below, and beyond it the block of flats, and between the garden and the flats was that emptiness where the beech tree had once stood. In spite of everything that had happened to Toby, it still felt wrong to see that absence – it was like a part of his own life was missing.

He turned and went to the door and listened. He could hear the noise of the banqueting hall as a murmur now. The house was quiet – not silent, but quiet. He went downstairs to his room. He had taken a lot of his things with him when he and Mum left for their new flat but had left a lot too. Someone had put this in plastic crates – his books, board games, and boxes of construction pieces. Even his white yacht with the blue trim. He opened a lid and lifted out the boat, enjoying the sensation of the rounded hull and the narrow, hard keel in his hands. He rubbed the canvas of the sail between his fingers, loving its texture. He put down the yacht and went to the old, familiar curtains with their blue sails, the only things of his that had stayed in place. A black four-by-four drove past in the street, beneath the September trees. In the front garden stood an estate agent's sign that read: SOLD.

Toby surveyed the room afresh. He had not fully understood – he was not coming back here. It was being packed up for them to go their separate ways. He tried the other rooms. His mum's small office had not yet been cleared – the shelves still held her books and her thesis papers – but on the next floor his parents' bedroom had been emptied. His dad's office was empty too. He opened the linen chest with the scar. Empty. The living room and dining room. Empty. In the basement kitchen, there were more plastic crates, this time filled with kitchen ware. He took the key and unlocked the French windows and went out. He breathed the London air, heard the soft roar of city traffic, the faintest music and a distant jet on the approach to Heathrow, then he went across the grass to the stump. In the weeks since the beech tree had been cut down, the stump had darkened slightly and the sawdust blown away. He sat down on the remains of the trunk.

Alfred appeared.

Toby watched him approach. Stroking the white cat, Toby thought how much Alfred liked Tamurlaine, always following her, and how fond of Alfred she was. Toby had deserted her. Regent Malladain would harm her and she would murder Regent Malladain – she would become like him. She would become like the rest of her family. Like one day he would become like his dad – selfish and thoughtless. Like he had already become by abandoning his friend.

'Alfred,' said Toby, standing up. 'I'm going to help Tamurlaine.'

He took out his mobile. He had a signal so he texted his mum that he was safe, that he'd found Alfred and brought him back to Arnold Street, and that he would come back to her as soon as he could. He had to help a friend first.

'I want to come back,' he said upstairs in the attic room, hoping he was in the same spot. He closed his eyes. He could still hear the road traffic, and smell Mrs Papadopoulos's lily-of-the-valley perfume. He hoped he could get back. Please, please, he asked. He opened his eyes.

A pair of yellow eyes watched him curiously from the lilac carpet. Alfred leapt. Toby caught him.

'Make your mind up, Toby Porter,' said a voice and there stood Burston Shimpling in Mrs Papadopoulos's attic room, holding a slumped Ollie Reckless in his arms. The light dimmed in the window behind Burston, the carpet felt hard beneath his soles, the storm blew and the music played over the guests' excited chatter and Arnold Street had gone and he was back in Balthasar.

Tamurlaine appeared. For a moment she looked at him then said, 'I thought you wanted to go home.'

'I do. You must not kill the Regent, Tam. It's bad for you.'

Tamurlaine didn't move. Mervyn muttered to himself, peering into the hall, 'Why aren't they doing anything? The man murdered King Sigobert. What more do they need?'

Tamurlaine turned. 'Sump?'

'Hmm?'

'Say that again.'

'Didn't you read my story? I thought – Your uncle – I – Your uncle Regent Malladain killed your father.'

Tamurlaine grew very still and her eyes gained a sharper, steelier quality, but other than that, she didn't react. Perhaps Toby had been wrong, perhaps she wasn't going to take revenge on the Regent.

'Is he here yet?' said Burston, dumping a slumbering Ollie Reckless onto the rolls of carpet with a thud and going over to the curtain. 'There he is! What a sight! Looks like he's washed his hair in gunk.'

Toby looked. The Regent stood at the far end of the hall. His hair was stuck with honey and his face was red and swollen from stings. Tamurlaine had gone. Toby strode for the stairs. 'Tam!' He heard footsteps. At the bottom he caught her but she wrenched herself from his grip and stepped into the hall.

A buzz of animated chatter met Toby as he entered a few paces behind her, people responding to the arrival of Regent Malladain. Lord Snow stood at the table right in front of Toby, leaning over the shoulder of a man twisting in his chair to listen. The seated man wore the long black cape and swan clasp that showed him to be a member of the Watch, but his swan was gold. He was obviously high up in the organisation. 'General,' said Lord Snow, 'I'm a great admirer of Regent Malladain but he's overplayed his hand this time. He should be put out of the game.'

'I agree,' said the general.

'Look!' someone yelled. 'It's the Queen.'

Heads turned as Tamurlaine walked up the gangway alongside the table. Someone said loudly, 'Your Majesty!' People stood to greet her, blocking her path. Tamurlaine couldn't get past. A crowd gathered. Tamurlaine, infuriated, changed, swirling into darkness. A woman screamed. Tamurlaine became a shadow-leopard and leapt onto the table, smashing crystal glasses.

'The shadow!'

'Call the Watch!' boomed Regent Malladain. 'Now!'

Lord Snow and the general exchanged a knowing glance then Lord Snow shouted, 'The Regent's a murderer!'

The general stood and met the first men of the Watch running into the hall. 'Men,' he barked, 'the Regent's a traitor to Balthasar. Your first duty is to the kingdom. Arrest the Regent!' The general marched towards the most powerful man in Balthasar, calling in a clear, military voice over the hubbub, 'Regent Malladain, I am arresting you for the murder of King Sigobert.'

There was an atmosphere of wildness, arguments breaking out, some on the side of the Regent, some on the side of Lord Snow and the general. Lightning flashed. Thunder clapped. Someone shrieked. Someone giggled. Someone lobbed a bread roll.

Unable to get through the crowd blocking the gangway, Toby put a knee onto the table and launched himself up. Tamurlaine-as-shadow-leopard was prowling over the dishes towards the Regent. Someone grabbed Toby by the shoulders to pull him back. Toby took what was nearest to hand – a long carving knife – and swung it at his assailant. Released, he scrambled along the table, knocking over a lit candelabra. When he stood, the tablecloth was alight. Mrs Bleverhasset clapped her hands in glee. Up in the musicians' gallery, the tenor and musicians reached a *crescendo*. The storm tried to outdo them with a louder piece of music, tuneless, an improvisation, the wind screaming a high note, the thunder banging drums and the rain playing the cymbals. That wild triangle-player, the flagpole cable, joined in too.

Tamurlaine in her leopard form was moving more slowly now, stalking over the tablecloth towards the Regent. Toby ran after her. He booted a chicken. It hit someone in the head. He jumped out of the way of swinging dinner knives and dessert spoons. He slashed back and forth warningly with his carving knife. The snooty windows flinched at another fist of rain. Some of the Watch were going after Tamurlaine with golden nets, some were going after the Regent, some were going after Toby. Others were fighting guests, who were fighting back, or fighting one other, using whatever came to hand, including food – cabbage, sprouts, carrots, cheeses, cubes of ice, a domed green mousse, boiled turtles, roast owl, hogs' feet, castles made of green jelly, lobsters, oysters and sausages – it all flew through the air.

The storm finally did get into the party. It punched out the snooty windows and put its fingers under the eaves and ripped off the roof and pelted everyone with raindrops as hard as stones and tore down the mouldy flags. People screamed. People ran. The Regent made for the door. Tamurlaine couldn't stop him – she had been delayed by a painful golden net from which she could not fight her way. Toby cut the net and while she disentangled herself, he slid the knife through a belt loop on his trousers so it hung at his hip like a sword. The Regent reached the door, then looked round. Not at the riot but for Tamurlaine. The Regent spotted her. Toby didn't like that look. It was as if Malladain was hatching a plan. Tamurlaine wriggled out of the broken net and still in her leopard shape she bounded towards the end of the table. Toby sprinted after her. The Regent smiled. Tamurlaine leapt at the Regent. Toby flew over the outstretched arms of the guests and grabbed her ankle. The pair crashed to the floor.

It took them a while to regain their feet, Tamurlaine now in smoky human form, and furious. Alfred trotted up to them. Tamurlaine rushed out, and Toby and Alfred went after her.

CHAPTER 26

The Broken Castle

There was no sign of Malladain. There were various staircases and corridors he might have taken but Tamurlaine didn't know which one.

'You fool, Toby. I nearly had him.'

'You have to get back to yourself.'

She paced back and forth, trying to guess which way to go.

'He's finished now,' Toby said. 'They'll arrest him. Let's find the sleeping you.'

She glanced at him as if briefly considering this, then once more paced.

'He might be going to kill the sleeping you,' said Toby. He said it without thinking, but once he had spoken, he thought it might actually be true. The Regent was next in line to the throne; if Tamurlaine was dead, the Regent would be king.

'He's going to kill the sleeping me?' said Tamurlaine.

'I don't know. Maybe. The Queen's apartments – do you know where they are?'

'This way.'

They found the door to the Queen's apartments locked. Tamurlaine dissolved into shadow, dropped to the floor and slid inside. It was the strangest thing, to watch a shadow move with its own will. Alfred crouched, half-frightened, half-curious. The latch clicked and the door opened.

A flock of white birds flew at Toby. Wings struck his face, his shoulders. Something sharp cut his lip – not birds, sheets of paper. They rapped and cartwheeled past him as he entered. Beyond an iron spiral staircase lay a dark room, the only light coming from a tall, partly curtained window, one pane broken where the curtain was sucked to the glass. Toby stumbled over a felled lampshade. The walls trembled with the force of the storm. The curtain was sucked back into the room and flowed in the wind and a vase smashed and Toby felt rain on his face.

The shadow was looping the room then she flew up the spiral staircase. Toby and Alfred followed. The iron steps were slippery beneath Toby's soles, and he had to hold the rail firmly. Alfred ran ahead. At the top, darkness seemed to edge back from Toby as if to give him space.

It was the Queen's bedroom. An unglazed window stood in the far corner, all the panes smashed and the storm funnelling in. The floor, as he walked across it, was wet. Tamurlaine stood beside the bed, once more in her human form, Alfred next to her.

Under bedclothes lay a girl, her face identical to Tamurlaine's except that the sleeping girl was paler. Her skin was as white as a sheet. She lay on her side, one hand cupped loosely on the pillow. Toby had been wrong; the Regent had not come to kill her. The girl was fast asleep.

Now that Tamurlaine saw herself, Toby didn't know what would happen, whether she would return to herself or not. And if she did, if the sleeping Tamurlaine would wake. And then, if the sleeping Tamurlaine woke, if she would still exact her revenge.

Tamurlaine lay down beside her sleeping self, once more became shadow, changing into something resembling a fox cub, almost circled in the sleeper's arm.

The shadow burrowed in closer to the girl's body, curling herself in the hollow between chin and chest, the way Alfred sometimes did when he slept with Toby. After what seemed an age, she drifted out along the sleeper's arm to the cupped hand, and there she formed a shape that fitted within that hand. After a time she moved back towards the girl, slipped around her head and down her hair then across her cheek and, as the sleeper took a deep breath and rolled onto her back, vanished into her mouth.

Toby stood immobile.

The shadow did not reappear. The sleeping girl did not stir. The storm did not lessen. Rain fell into the cold room. And all the castle seemed now was a cold, badly lit building full of brutal people. And all Tamurlaine seemed was a girl who had the bad luck to have been born in such a place as Balthasar, and into such a nasty family.

The girl's eyes flickered. Then they opened. She stared upwards. For the longest time she did not move. Toby held his breath. She rolled her head to the side, her attention taken by her curled hand. How long had she been asleep, wondered Toby? A year? Her fingers twitched. She let out a breath that might have been a laugh or a sigh.

Toby stepped closer and Tamurlaine noticed him. She tried to speak but nothing came out. Toby crouched beside the bed. She tried to speak again but Toby couldn't make out what she was saying. Then, after a time, he understood she wanted him to help her sit up. He took some of the pillows, bashed them with his fists and pushed them under her back and propped her head. She was thin, even thinner than the Tamurlaine he knew. Her skin was papery. A vein fluttered at her temple.

Her eyes were fixed on him but she seemed to have lost the use of the muscles in her face so he could not see any expression. Her vocal cords would not work and she was whispering something and he had to lean close to make out what it was.

'Hugo Right,' is what it sounded like.

'What?'

She said it again, and he thought this time it sounded like, 'You go right.'

He turned to his right. There was nothing there.

She was saying it again and now he realised she was trying to say, 'You got it right.'

Toby met her eyes. Deep in them, the devilishness of Tamurlaine. She smiled. At least, he thought it was a smile. It was more of a twitch. Her eyelids drooped, she lost focus, then something clouded her features and she found his eyes again.

'The Regent,' she breathed.

'Let's go,' said Toby. 'Somewhere safer.'

Her muscles had wasted and he had to put his arm round her to help her out of bed. Her whole weight was held by him and she was so thin he could feel her ribs – she was all bone. She was fighting to stay awake, her head nodded, then she slipped and he had to clutch her so she didn't slide to the floor. Once she was on her feet again, she took a step towards the spiral stairs.

Someone was banging up them. In the darkness, a figure paused then moved towards Tamurlaine. Toby had no chance although when he thought about it afterwards, he told himself he should have been quicker. But in that moment all he saw was the white, mask-like face of the Regent. And the knife.

Toby twisted across Tamurlaine to protect her but the Regent knocked him aside, bringing up the knife. Regent Malladain was moving fast. Too fast, and the man slipped on the wet floor, both arms lifting instinctively, and the knife which had been aimed for Tamurlaine's heart missed its target. But it stabbed her under the armpit, the blade going up diagonally through her flesh towards her collarbone.

Tamurlaine swooned. Toby held her up. Trying to adjust her meagre weight in his arms so she didn't fall onto the knife and injure herself more badly, he lowered himself to the wet floor. Tamurlaine lay on top of him, unconscious. Toby was terrified to touch the leather haft stuck in her side.

The Regent stood. He leaned towards the knife.

His hand never reached it. The carving knife swished from the belt loop and chopped down hard on the man's wrist. Malladain cried out. The silver blade returned black.

'Get back!' Toby barked.

The Regent moved round swiftly and kicked from a new angle, across Tamurlaine, so Toby couldn't risk the knife in case he cut Tam. The Regent's boot connected and Toby's forearm exploded in agony, his fingers opened, and the knife skidded away. The Regent slid into darkness.

Scrambling up, Toby crouched in front of Tamurlaine. He could only vaguely see the iron rails at the head of the spiral staircase and a few shapes of furniture. No Regent. He could hear nothing but the storm and rain falling through the broken window, pattering on the floor.

Malladain's white face hurtled towards him. A void opened like a mouth above Toby, and it seemed the castle itself was opening, Toby heard himself utter the word *No* then something groaned deeply and even above the noise of the storm, there was a splitting sound, and he saw the knife drawing a great arc towards his body but the floor was tilting and Toby was sailing backwards and Tamurlaine was sailing with him and the Regent past him and the sky was falling, or at least the ceiling was, then everything stopped, tilted.

The storm was louder. It had got into the room, or the room had got outside, and the wind was screaming and the rain was falling on them. Toby lay with Tamurlaine on a section of the floor that that had somehow sheared off from the castle. Across a chasm was the rest of the building. The floor on which they lay listed at a steep angle. They were at the top of the slope, perched on its edge. Peeking over it, Toby saw the ocean directly below. It was not only the castle that had broken, the headland had also. The tip of the headland had completely come away from the rest of its peninsula. They were balanced on a pinnacle of rock. This tower of rock and broken building leaned precariously; at any moment it might topple into the sea. The roof had gone so their small area of bedroom floor was now exposed to the storm.

From the body of the castle lights shone. People came up the spiral staircase carrying lamps – Lord Snow and the general who led the Watch, and men of the Watch, but others too – guests from the banquet, and Burston Shimpling and Mervyn Sump.

'Help!' Toby shouted. 'Tamurlaine's injured. Help!'

The general yelled instructions. Several men ran downstairs while others tore down curtains and began to make a rope to throw across to Toby. The sea boomed against the rocks.

The wet floor was as steeply pitched as a roof, and Toby and Tamurlaine were at the top. At the bottom of the slope stood what remained of the outer wall of the bedroom, no longer intact but knee-high, and against it sprawled Regent Malladain. He was dazed but when he saw Toby and Tamurlaine he staggered to his feet. Getting traction was difficult, but he began to climb towards them.

'Quick!' Toby shouted. 'The rope!'

The Regent lost his grip and slid back to the low wall. He tried again, and failed, then tried again. With each new attempt he climbed nearer. Tamurlaine's eyes were shut but she was still breathing. Blood stained the side of her nightdress. The men of the Watch made the rope.

'Quick!'

The Regent was nearly upon them.

'Get away!' Toby shouted. 'Get away!'

The Regent grasped at them.

Toby kicked but the Regent grabbed his ankle and tugged. Toby went shooting down the angled floor into the low wall where he was slung across the top and clutched the brick to stop himself from going over. White waves smashed below. He looked up the slope. The Regent had his hands on Tamurlaine. He was going to roll her off the edge down into the sea.

'No!' screamed Toby.

A white shape flashed from Tamurlaine's nightdress. Extended claws sank deep into the Regent's eye and small sharp teeth bit the Regent's cheek. Alfred tore his head from side to side and came away with a chunk of Regent flesh, which he spat out. Toby heard the man's scream as he fell. Not over the edge but back down the slanted floor. Alfred came with him. The Regent crashed into the low wall beside Toby. Tamurlaine stirred. The Regent rolled over. He had been hit on the head, stung by bees, chopped with a carving knife, bitten and half-blinded by a cat, but he still wanted to destroy. Destroy. Destroy.

His hand came up and gripped Toby's throat. Behind the Regent, at the top of the slope, Tamurlaine opened her eyes. Alfred jumped on the Regent's back, scratching.

The Regent forced Toby up and backwards so Toby was hanging over the wall. Below him the waves churned.

All the Regent had to do was release Toby's throat and lean down and flip Toby's legs up and over the wall and gravity would do the rest. From the main section of the castle, the rope made of curtains was thrown. They were yelling for Tamurlaine to take it, to put its loop over her. Toby shouted, 'Take the rope, Tam!' The Regent looked over his shoulder to see what was happening. Slowly, weakly, Tamurlaine put her legs through the loop and hoisted it to her waist and began to tighten it. The Regent was in two minds – kill Toby now or prevent Tamurlaine from swinging across to safety. He decided and turned to Toby and smiled. For a moment Toby thought the man was going to let him live. Then the Regent's dead eyes twinkled and he let go of Toby's throat and bent down to grab Toby's ankles. Toby saw Tamurlaine's face change as she realised what was about to happen to Toby. There was a flash of connection between them. Tamurlaine closed her eyes and fell asleep. There was a bang and flash and Toby was hurled backwards over the wall, not down but through the storm, at high velocity. The blast was stronger than the air-blast at the city gates, stronger than the blast which broke the fabled gates of Alkazabad, stronger than any blast any Dreamer ever dreamt. Toby flew head over heels away from the castle and as the flash faded he saw – in glimpses through driving rain – a somersaulting white cat, a pinnacle of rock topple into the waves, a tall thin man tumble seawards, his arms flailing, the tails of his long leather coat flapping uselessly, and Tamurlaine swing on her curtain-rope towards safety; lastly, briefly, Toby saw a swan beat its huge wings through the storm, a broken chain trailing behind it, making for the open sea.

Toby hit something hard.

When he opened his eyes he found himself on a spinning surface that he thought was the deck of a ship. He was dazzled. The source of the light was so powerful it hurt his eyes. It hung above him. The sea grew calm. The dazzling light, when he turned his face away, became the sun, and the deck became flat ground. He sat up, blinking. He was on a road. The sky was blue and clear. A train went by in the cutting. Traffic passed at the end of the road. Something was rasping against his cheek. He raised a hand to brush it away and his fingers touched the softest fur and he found Alfred clinging to his clothes, licking his face. His mobile phone beeped.

Carefully putting Alfred down, Toby remained seated, taking in his surroundings. He was on Angel Lane.

At the far end of the lane was the main road, cars going by. In the other direction, where the trench had been, lay a thick strip of new tarmac, like a scar. Beyond the tarmac stood the fence, and beyond that lay the slope of the railway cutting, the overhead wires of the train line and the cutting's far embankment.

Toby banged his palm hard on the hard ground to

make sure. The road was real. He checked himself for injuries, and pressed them to make sure they were real too. He had multiple painful bruises and scratches. His shoes were damaged but the well-stitched leather soles intact. He was wringing wet from the storm. Alfred, also bruised and soaking wet, his white fur patchy, waited at Toby's side.

'All right, Alfred?'

Alfred miaowed.

Toby looked to that black scar of tarmac where the trench had been. Beyond it, somewhere between the slope and the overhead train lines, in that vacant September air, lay Balthasar. Tamurlaine was there. His friend. She was safe. Alfred was here. They were safe. Alfred looked up at him with his sour, world-weary expression. Toby grinned at him, feeling as if a great weight had lifted. He got to his feet.

'Come on, Alfred,' he said. 'Let's go home.'

Acknowledgements

Lots of people helped me write this novel. A crew of wonderful writers read extracts and suggested improvements: Alex Ivey, Armando Celayo, Birgit Larsson, Ellie Wasserberg, Gordon Collins and Tom Benn; Tom also came up with the title. Generously, Cherise Saywell, Alex Ivey and Charles Walker read the whole first draft and set me right. Charles also read the final version as it progressed, and supported me through each stage of writing it. Vicky Rangeley-Wilson shouted encouragement from the sidelines and read the final manuscript at extraordinary speed and with insight and meticulous care, suggesting improvements; the errors that remain are mine but Alfred's curiosity and bravery are thanks to Vicky. A grant from The Society of Authors and the Authors' Foundation gave me time to complete the re-write. During the re-write, I was inspired by having Holly Ovenden's wonderful cover art in my mind's eye. Without the faith that Mikka Haugaard showed, *Shadow Town* would never have reached this final form. That it's become an actual book and been brought into the world is entirely thanks to Mikka. Lastly, this novel was written during lockdown, and many people got me through the hardest parts with their love and generosity, but in particular Cherise Saywell, Shirley De Marco, Vicky Rangeley-Wilson, Ellie Wasserberg, Heidi Williamson, Jon MacLaren and Dad.

Thank you to all of these for helping me keep the dream alive.

About the Author

Richard Lambert was born in London. He has had many different jobs including teaching medieval history. For the last ten years he has lived in Norfolk where he works for the NHS and writes stories and poems. One of his stories was shortlisted for the Sunday Times Short Story Award and another won the Fish Short Story Prize, and his poems have been in the Times Literary Supplement, The Spectator, and The Forward Prize Anthology. His second poetry collection, The Nameless Places, was published in 2017 and many of the poems in it are a response to the landscape around the River Waveney, on the Suffolk-Norfolk border. The collection was shortlisted for the East Anglian Book Awards. His debut, The Wolf Road, was a Book of the Year 2020 in the Times, Sunday Times, Guardian and FT.

15-03-22

PILLGWENLLY